THOUGH I WALK THROUGH THE VALLEY

by

DAVID ABIS

Sweet Spot Publishing

Though I Walk Through The Valley

Sweet Spot Publishing

Paperback Edition

Copyright 2015 David Abis

Cover image courtesy of Jurassic & Canstockphoto.com.
Cover by Joleene Naylor.

ISBN 978-0-9907739-5-5
eBook ISBN 978-0-9907739-4-8

Prologue

She'd never seen so much blood in one place. Just how does one small hole in a person make such a mess anyway? That's all 19-year-old Jaime Jo Tremper could think to wonder as she cradled her daddy's head in her lap. One shot to the head and he was gone. The only thing left of the preacher's once larger than life presence was his still warm body lying in an ever-expanding sea of crimson. Mesmerized by all the blood, she couldn't seem to focus her thoughts, such as why, or more importantly, what now? She had none of that. All she could think of was the redness of it. And just as if it were a traffic signal controlling an intersection along the road that was Jaime Jo Tremper's life, she'd come to a complete stop. Everything. All movement. All thought. She just cradled his head in her lap and stopped, waiting for the signal to change, waiting for a new set of instructions.

"Let's go," chimed a deep and ominous voice, like a clap of thunder, all business.

She could just make out his muddy military-issue boots from the corner of her eye. She turned to look over at the source of the command, and shivered at the coldness of it.

"I said let's go," barked the voice again, this time adding an impatient edge.

She slowly lifted her head to look up at the man giving the orders. He was a big man. Not heavy big. But muscular big. A human weapon, honed for battle, one side of his face grotesquely scarred in some previous confrontation. He loomed over her threateningly from the shadows of the dimly lit church, his unwashed smell assaulting her nose, his camouflaged fatigues stained with blood. When he lowered his rifle, she thought to reach out for the gun resting in her dead father's hand.

"Don't," he commanded, before her thought ever reached her hand. "Leave it right where it is." He yanked her to her feet by the arm, a sharp ache deep in the marrow reminding her that the bone was broken.

"But—" she protested weakly, lightheaded from the pain.

"Just get in the damn car!"

"What are you planning to do?"

"Put some distance between me and your daddy's body, that's what." The soldier shoved her roughly through the front door of the church and out into the driveway. She hurt all over from the repeated beatings. She could still taste blood oozing from her swollen lip.

"Where are you taking me?" she pleaded.

"Anyplace but here."

The sound of the church door slamming behind them announced the closing of one life and the opening of another. Jaime Jo took one last look back at the familiar headstones, including her momma's, jutting up from the old churchyard, before she let Tommy Harris cram her through the passenger door of his Camaro.

Tommy, on the other hand, never looked back. Instead, he thought briefly of setting the whole church ablaze right along with the girl's dead father inside it. That'd serve him right. But there wasn't any time for that now. Let him burn in hell. All he thought about now was crossing that state line. First things first.

As the Camaro peeled out of the driveway, neither one of them noticed the old couple almost motionless in their rockers on the front porch nearby. Jeb and Alice Kwartler lived across the street from the church and the preacher's place for over 50 years. They'd seen and heard a lot of things from that porch over the years. And they'd seen and heard what happened just minutes before, too. It wasn't the first confrontation they'd witnessed coming from across the street. But they assumed this would be the last of it. Jeb and Alice continued their rocking long after the dust from the Camaro settled.

People are apt to think nothing ever happens in a small town. But Jeb and Alice knew better. They'd seen and heard plenty. It's just that small towns tend not to air their dirty laundry. Oh, everyone knows what goes on, all right. You can't stop people from talking. And half the talk might even be true. But that's the town's business and no one else's.

On the other hand, one couldn't just bury his head in the sand forever. Some things just had to get addressed.

"Breeze is pickin' up, Alice," Jeb remarked.

"Sure enough," she agreed, looking up from her embroidering.

"Reckon we better call Sheriff Buckner 'for any unpleasant odors start blowin' our way. I hate to let things get out of hand, ya know," he added, sniffing the air.

"Always thinkin' ahead, you are, Jeb. You want me to make the call?"

"No dear. Why don't you just set and enjoy what's left of this beautiful morning while I go ring up the sheriff." Jeb Kwartler pried himself up from the rocker, unsure whether the creaking sounds came from the chair or his old bones. "Want me to fetch you another cup of that fine coffee of yours while I'm up?"

"No thanks, Sweetie. I think I'm good 'n' awake now. Nothing like a shooting across the street in the morning to get the old ticker aflutter."

She watched her other half head inside to take care of business. Then Alice Kwartler sat rocking on her front porch thinking about the preacher and his family and all their trials and tribulations.

But mostly she thought about what a glorious morning it was, the sun shining, a crisp breeze stirrin' up the autumn leaves, and the whippoorwills chirping. She hated to see such a beautiful morning go to waste cause o' some ol' shooting. She hoped that sheriff would take his damn sweet time.

Chapter 1 – One Month Earlier

Billy Sawchuck's mother never knew very much about his relationship with Jaime Jo Tremper and Tommy Harris, other than the three had gone to high school together. In fact, Billy'd grown up with Jaime Jo and Tommy, being the same age as Tommy, Jaime Jo two years younger. But then again, Billy's mother didn't know much of anything about his life at all. And that's how Billy preferred it. Like most parents and their high school-aged children, they led separate lives, only occasionally intersecting about meals.

Closets were much bigger in 1972. So much so, that certain people tended to live their whole lives in them and never come out. Billy'd been in love with Tommy Harris for the longest time, but anyone with eyes could tell Tommy wasn't that way, and Billy knew it was doomed to remain a one-sided affair. Tommy was always tolerant of Billy, the harmless, meticulously groomed kid who always seemed to be hanging around. And Billy appreciated that, just being around Tommy. There was just something about bad boys that Billy couldn't resist. So when Tommy fell in love with Jaime Jo Tremper during high school, Billy decided he couldn't fight Mother Nature, and the twosome became a threesome. He grew to love Jaime Jo too, not the same way, but maybe in a better, more honest way. Jaime Jo needed a friend, and that was something Billy was good at.

Billy worked at his mother's beauty salon and bridal shop all through high school. And ever since graduating three years earlier, he'd developed no greater aspirations. Besides, he liked working there. He liked being around the ladies, the makeup, the hairdos, and especially the bridal gowns. He loved it all. The high school taunts questioning his choice of clothes, his voice, his walk— his masculinity— no longer bothered him, not ever since he realized what gay was. And that was no easy task, growing up in a small town in the sixties. He still wasn't sure he had it all figured out. But whatever gay was, he was it.

Billy was doing one of his favorite things at the shop that Sunday morning, organizing the bridal gowns. Not that there were that many, or that many brides in need, but every young woman and girl, and even some long over the hill, seemed to like coming in to mess them up, touching them and dreaming.

Other than Charlotte's place, there wasn't much could be considered feminine about Pleasant Valley, North Carolina, a town so small and forgotten it practically didn't exist at all. Life was hard, the men harder, and the women, well someone had to keep the men in line. Not to say the women were manly. They weren't. They didn't have to be. The women had their own way of running things, not by brute force but by a certain matriarchal pack mentality laced with helpings of guilt and gossip. And that center of power, or headquarters, naturally swirled about that testosterone-free zone down on Main Street called Charlotte's Beauty Salon & Bridal Shoppe.

Charlotte Sawchuck had no aspirations of power herself. She found it hard enough just to keep a man, let alone control one. And the prospects in Pleasant Valley were far and few enough between as it was without driving them away. But she was an excellent listener, and with the natural lack of Y-chromosomes on the premises, killed off by a lethal combination of permanent applicator and hair spray, Charlotte's place was the perfect spot for the ladies of Pleasant Valley to run things.

They were holding court that Saturday afternoon, getting themselves primped before Sunday church. Billy, not wanting to cramp the ladies' style, could overhear the proceedings from back in the bridal area. Frankly, the ladies never seemed to notice he wasn't just another one of the girls anyway.

"Tommy Harris is coming home," stated Dot Elliot, without looking up from a six-month-old copy of the Ladies Home Journal, awaiting her manicure. She savored the momentary silence that followed. That meant she'd brought some particularly savory bit of news, when the other ladies were caught off-guard like that, not even a cough in reply.

Charlotte hadn't even realized she'd stopped working on Sally Wright, mid-roller, something she never did. After all, there were only so many hours in a day to get through so many heads. When she went to resume rolling, Sally put up her hand to hold off the distraction.

"You shittin' me?" she asked suspiciously.

June Parker tipped the noisy dryer back from her head when she sensed something momentous had been said. "What? I couldn't hear. What'd I miss?"

"Tommy Harris is coming home. That's all," repeated Dot, smiling inwardly at her established prowess as head gossip.

After another silent pause, Sally took the first bite. "Alive? Or in a box?"

"Sally!" shouted Charlotte at Sally's insensitivity.

"Oh, he's alive all right," stated Dot, finally lowering the magazine. "Take more than two years in Vietnam to kill that worthless troublemaker. Just like a damn cockroach. You can use up a whole can o' Raid and smash it with the heel of your shoe, but the damn thing keeps crawlin' back."

"Jeeze," remarked June. "I guess no one ever thought he'd be coming back."

"June!" shouted Charlotte again.

"Well you hear about all those poor boys dyin' over there. And Tommy Harris bein' sent and all, instead of going to jail, everyone just assumed the problem was solved. And here he's comin' home after all. Just no one ever considered it, I don't think."

"Does Preacher Tremper know yet?" asked Sally.

"I'm sure Sheriff Buckner will let him know," answered Dot. "Sheriff's the one mentioned it to my husband."

"That poor man. What's the preacher going to do?" asked June. "He'll have to lock that daughter of his, Jaime Jo, up in the house, for her own protection."

"You never know," replied Sally. "Maybe the military done the boy some good. A little discipline never hurt where boys are concerned."

"You don't fix what that boy got," argued Dot, distractedly flipping the pages of her magazine.

"Come now, Dot," offered Charlotte. "They were just kids. Things happen."

"Don't you kid yourself, Miss Free Spirit," said Dot. "You know damn well we're not talking about no Romeo and Juliet, two sweet young love birds. You saw what he done to that girl. Now the poor thing's afraid of her own shadow. That girl's ruined for life, not to mention the baby and all."

The chatter stopped briefly all around as they each rehashed their own recollections of those events.

"Well, word is, Tommy's a little ruined himself," Dot resumed. "The war's changed him, taken its toll."

"How do you mean?" asked June.

Dot looked about at the ladies, milking the attention for all it was worth, then, lowering her voice for added effect, "They say he ain't right."

"What's that supposed to mean?" asked Charlotte.

Dot didn't hesitate. "He just ain't right, that's all. They say it's got something to do with the trauma of war, the rough conditions, people dyin' all around. They say sometimes the boys just ain't tough enough and it gets to them. They just kind of fall apart."

"Well maybe he's gotten his just deserts," offered June. "After what he did to that poor girl, seems kind of fair-like that he'd suffer from the results of a little violence himself."

"June!" moaned Charlotte at the less than ladylike remark.

"It's just such a shame," answered June. "Jaime Jo seems to be doing OK with that little baby of hers. Must be almost two years old by now, isn't she?"

"Cute as a button," answered Sally. "So, what now? That baby finally going to meet her daddy?"

"Oh, I don't think so," answered Dot with some authority. "Even before they packed him off to the war, that was part of the deal. Preacher insisted he's to stay away from both Jaime Jo and the baby. He's to have no contact with either of them."

"Well, we'll see," said Sally. "That boy was all over that girl like she was a bitch in heat."

"Sally!" gasped June.

"Well, he was," countered Sally, blushing at her own choice of words. "All's I'm sayin' is the sheriff's gonna' have his hands full keepin' that boy off that girl."

"Poor thing," Charlotte remarked. "Haven't seen a bruise on her since that boy was run out of town. She and the baby seem to be doing so well. I just hope she's grown stronger over time, done some growin' up. She's a momma now. She's got to take care of herself, make better decisions. I wonder how she's going to handle the news. I bet the poor thing doesn't even know yet."

So preoccupied were they with the news, none of the ladies even noticed the sound of the screen door at the back of the shop slamming. Neither did they notice Billy Sawchuck driving off to see his friend, Jaime Jo Tremper. He wanted to be the one to tell her. And if she'd already heard, he wanted to be there anyway. She was going to need a friend. And that was something Billy Sawchuck was good at.

Chapter 2

Billy Sawchuck had no idea how he was going to break the news to Jaime Jo. But that didn't stop him from driving Tinkerbell, as he'd named his little yellow Gremlin, as fast as she'd go. Not that that was so fast. But she was doing the best she could. As soon as he heard the ladies spill the beans, he knew he had to drop everything and run to Jaime Jo. Let the chips fall where they may. She just had to know.

It was only a few blocks over to Frank's Diner at the other end of town, but Billy was too excited to walk, and his long layered hairdo might get messed up running. Billie was the first in conservative Pleasant Valley to adopt the latest look for men. Besides, once he'd arrived at Frank's, it gave him a chance to sit in the car and pull his thoughts together. After all, he hadn't had to think about the names Jaime Jo Tremper and Tommy Harris at the same time for a couple of years now.

He didn't know how she'd take it. He wasn't sure how he was taking it himself. Initially, he felt profoundly relieved. Tommy'd made it. He'd beaten the odds. His ticket to Nam was round trip after all. He was coming home. Sure, he wasn't coming home to Billy. That would be too much to ask. He belonged to Jaime Jo, the cute little bitch that stole his man, as he would tease her. It wasn't really like that, he admitted. Tommy was as straight as a two-by-four. Billy figured out early on that he couldn't compete with the ladies for someone like Tommy Harris. So, just as well, if anyone were going to have him, it might as well be a sweetie like Jaime Jo. Billy couldn't have left him in better hands. Still, he'd be kidding himself to ignore the twinge of jealousy he always felt in their presence.

Maybe he was only a romantic at heart, but Billy Sawchuck just knew the town had it all wrong about Tommy and Jaime Jo. The whole thing just never made any sense. Even after he'd seen the evidence himself, he'd always had a hard time accepting the idea that Tommy Harris would ever hurt that girl. Sure, on the surface, he was a certified club-toting Neanderthal. But Billie always saw beyond that. He wasn't born that way. Tommy Harris was merely a product of his environment. A little rough around the edges, the boy wasn't even welcome on the wrong side of the tracks. But Billy Sawchuck believed in the transformative power of love. Tommy was body and soul in love with that girl. And it was the real thing, the kind of love Billy suspected he would never know, not in Pleasant Valley anyway.

And yet, none of that mattered now. He knew in his heart the trouble would start all over again as soon as Tommy came home. They'd never stay apart like they were supposed to. They were made for each other, like flowers in spring, strawberries and chocolate, high heels and lipstick. Oh, there'd be trouble all right.

Poor Tinkerbell stumbled into the diner parking lot, sputtering and gasping. She was never built for that kind of excitement.

Jaime Jo was working her usual Saturday shift at the diner when Billy burst through the front door. Noticing the turn of heads upon his abrupt entry, he immediately tried to stay cool.

Jaime Jo looked up from behind the counter and threw him a smile that said, give me a minute, and I'll sneak away to chat. Billy spied little Scarlet, caged up in her playpen over in the corner. Frank was nice enough to let Jaime Jo bring her to work. She'd been doing so since the baby was born, so everyone, including the customers, knew the little imp, and had pretty much adopted her as their own.

Billy just had to go over to say hi when the little girl threw him a kiss just the way he'd trained her to. A girl's never too young to learn how to flirt. He noticed how big she was getting. Soon she'd be climbing out of that pen of hers to experience the world. Her mother hadn't fared so well in that particular endeavor.

"Hey, Pumpkin," said Billy, picking up the baby and accepting the little stuffed cow she shoved at him. He was constantly taking needle and thread to the poor warn-out thing, patching it up for her. "You're almost all grown up. Pretty soon Uncle Billy's going to have to show you how to catch a man. Well, not that Uncle Billy's been doing so great in that department himself."

When Jaime Jo came out from behind the counter, Billy had to smile at the sight of her. Two years had made a world of difference. No longer the traumatized little victim afraid of her own shadow, she'd changed, seemed to come into her own. Gone were the ill-fitting clothes and unkempt hair of someone who'd given up on life. Gone were the anxious twitches, nail biting, and nervous stutter. Two years ago, well, the girl was a complete mess. Yet out of the wreckage had grown a beautiful young woman, at peace with herself, competent, if not confident. After all, she was a momma now.

Billy gave Scarlet back her cow and returned her to the playpen, not without a certain amount of protest from the child, as Jaime Jo emerged from behind the counter with a jerk of her head toward the back door, calling the meeting to order in their usual spot.

Billy shouted to the kitchen in back. "Hey, Frank. You're working this poor girl to death. I'm taking her on a break. Doesn't the union have some kind of rules about this?" he joked.

Frank wasn't one to turn down a challenge, his shiny bald head poking out from above a sink full of dirty dishes. "Union? Doesn't it take more than one employee to form a union? I could use some more help around here. When are you going to stop playing dress up at the beauty shop and come get your hands dirty?"

"You kidding me? I wouldn't be caught dead in one of your tacky uniforms," Billy shouted back, playfully picking up the hem of Jaime Jo's orange miniskirt, revealing her matching panties. Jaime Jo smacked his hand away. "Besides," he added, "you know damn well I don't have the legs for it."

Billy shoved a giggling Jaime Jo out the back door, leaving Frank shaking his head and blushing more than a little. There just wasn't any shame in that boy, he thought. Word to the wise, he ought to be a little more discreet about his... uh... condition. Fine to joke now, around the hometown that knows all your idiosyncrasies. Won't be so safe when he grows up and moves out into the big world where most aren't as accepting of those with such unnatural tendencies. But Frank knew the boy wouldn't heed such advice. Damned kids all think they're immortal. Besides, there was a sink full of dishes needed washing.

Out back in the parking lot, Jaime Jo had to smile at Billy's little Tinkerbell, so ugly she was cute. He used to loan that thing to her a couple of years ago when she'd sneak out of her house to be with Tommy. She couldn't help but reminisce about the places little Tinkerbell'd taken her, both good and bad. But those days were behind her now... thankfully. Tommy was gone. It was just she and the baby now... and Billy. She'd always have her Billy.

"We don't get out much anymore, Billy," she said, fixing her hair as they took their usual seats on Tinkerbell's rear bumper. It never ceased to annoy her how Billy's hair always looked better than hers.

"Not with that little brat of yours stealing all your attention," he joked. "You know how the world has to revolve around *me*, princess that I am. I feel like an older sibling, pushed aside when the new baby comes along. You know I don't share well."

Jaime Jo kissed him on the cheek. "Aww. Poor baby. Mommy's been neglectful."

Billy's smile was brief. Enough kidding around. There was a reason behind this visit. Billy found it difficult to look her in the eye.

"I've got news."

Jaime Jo sensed the serious tone in his voice, but tried to ignore it. "News? In Pleasant Valley? Shoot, nothin' ever happens 'round here."

Billy exhaled and shut his eyes. "Well, this is news."

"Good or bad," she countered, trying to make a game of it.

"Don't know," he answered, finally making eye contact.

That's when it hit her. Something was happening. Something big. "You're leaving me, aren't you? I knew it. It was just a matter of time 'till you outgrew this shit-hole of a town and ventured out to find others of your own kind." She threw her arms around his neck. "You just can't. You're all I have."

Others of my own kind, chuckled Billy to himself, remembering their little joke. Billy was always telling her how he felt like an alien from another planet, but he'd heard there was life out there somewhere, others like himself. And yet, he still wasn't ready to venture out to find it. He hadn't gathered the requisite courage yet.

"No, honey. I'm not going anywhere," he assured her. "Not just yet."

Jaime Jo unwrapped herself from his neck and stared at him. "What then?"

Billy knew it was like pulling off a Band-Aid, the quicker the better. He had to just spit it out. So he took a deep breath and said it.

"Tommy's coming home."

Initially he thought she hadn't heard him. Her expression frozen, she hadn't seemed to comprehend. He thought he might have to repeat himself, until something finally seemed to register on her face. It was just for a second, only a glimpse, and he almost missed it. But it was undeniable, brief though it was, what Billy knew he saw in his friend's face. Sheer childlike joy. Heavenly bliss. But then, almost before he could make it out, it was gone, as if it had never been. And just as suddenly, she was doubled over, moaning as if she'd been kicked in the gut, hugging herself, and rocking back and forth like some catatonic imbecile. Before Billy could even reach out to catch her, she'd fallen to her knees and begun vomiting.

He didn't exactly know what to do at first, but being no stranger to feminine emotions, he did what any real girlfriend would do. He dropped to her side, one comforting arm around her waist, the other holding her ponytail out of the puke.

Only after her heaves turned dry and the convulsing ceased did Jaime Jo wipe her mouth with her apron and stumble on shaky legs back to the car bumper. She continued rocking back and forth with her hands over her head. She couldn't hear Billy's concerned pleas. All she heard was the noise in her head. Damn him! Damn Tommy Harris! She thought she was done with all that. The nightmares had finally stopped. She had Scarlet, and life went on. She was surviving. And she didn't miss the beatings.

Tommy Harris had been the love of her life and she'd never forget it. But that already seemed a lifetime ago, long dead and gone, never to return, for her own sake, and the baby's.

Then, in defiance of her anger and distress, in spite of it, a small shaft of sunlight broke through the storm clouds in her mind. She knew what that light would bring, but was powerless to snuff it out. Just as she'd been powerless to walk away from him those two years ago.

Soon that small sliver of light began to grow, and before she knew it, all signs of the storm were gone, like it never happened. And there he was, her Tommy, emerging from the sunlight.

It was the first time she'd seen him, four years earlier. She was 15, he 17. Everyone from school had gone to the county fair. Even her father, the preacher, normally strict about those things... well, about everything... had let her go. A group of girls were all trying to drag her onto that ridiculously high double-decker Ferris wheel spinning way up in the sky.

But she was scared. Jaime Jo Tremper seemed to be scared of everything since her mother'd passed, as if her spirit had been buried in that pine box right alongside her momma, that unbreakable bond between a mother and her little girl apparently still intact, but in a perverted and unhealthy way, six feet under ground. No more mother-daughter time. No more comforting hugs and kisses. It left a void in her very soul, a void her father just couldn't, or wouldn't, fill. She'd naturally shifted to her daddy for those little hugs and kisses— not too much to ask— but it just wasn't the same. Not even close. When she tried putting her arms around her daddy, it was a one-sided thing. He was clearly uncomfortable with it, stiff and unwelcoming, and never hugged her back, as if it was somehow wrong, unnatural. Her preacher father, it seemed, loved God more than his little girl. She soon stopped expecting his love and transformed from a fearless outgoing girl to a sad little thing with a hole in her heart, an empty vessel afraid of her own shadow.

The other girls didn't know just how deep it went. But clearly, shy Jaime Jo'd been shortchanged in the guts department. So like sharks smelling blood in the water, they'd begun to circle just to see just how far they could push her. Jaime Jo, however, told them there was no way she was going up on that thing. She was way too scared, and she meant it...

... until that green-eyed boy with the devil tattoo appeared out of nowhere. Jaime Jo was intrigued by his rebel façade. She'd only known boys from church. And she'd seen the older football players the other girls swooned over. But Tommy was different. He stood out like a weed, strong, yet out of place. He had a wicked look about him, tight T-shirt, messed up hair, a cigarette dangling from his lips, the last thing you'd expect to see with the preacher's daughter. Yet the preacher's daughter thought he was gorgeous.

He was trying to bribe one of the toothless carnival workers to buy him some beer when he overheard the battle between Jaime Jo and her girlfriends. Anyone within a hundred yards couldn't ignore the girlish squeals. And Tommy, being the prince in shining armor most 17-year-old boys believe themselves to be, had no choice but to intervene. He was honor bound to save the beautiful damsel in distress and slay her dragon.

He and Jaime Jo were two years apart. He'd never even noticed her when she was younger, but he sure noticed her now. It seems at some point, out of nowhere, a girl suddenly changes, sprinkled by fairy dust, and just like that, like magic, Tommy couldn't take his eyes off her. He unconsciously sensed a bit of the outcast in her, like himself, a poor fit with the clique of girls who surrounded her. He found her shyness endearing, her innocence disarming. Of course her blue angel eyes and kicking ass didn't hurt either. How had such an enchanting creature escaped him? He made his move.

"It's not so bad."

When the giggling girls heard a deep voice, they turned and froze, hands covering their mouths. They parted when they saw the boy staring at Jaime Jo. The other girls found Tommy unsettling, kind of scary, not the kind of boy their parents would approve of. Jaime Jo Tremper and Tommy Harris would never be no Barbie and

Ken. And yet, Jaime Jo Tremper, the good girl, the preacher's daughter, well she'd never seen anything so beautiful as Tommy Harris in her life.

Jaime Jo immediately forgot what it was she and her friends had been arguing about when she saw the boy looking at her. Most people never even noticed quiet Jaime Jo. And she knew it. People seemed to look right through her. Even in church. She'd sit through her father's fire and brimstone sermons about evil, dreaming young girl fantasies of true love. She'd wish she had someone to share her thoughts with, trying to remember what her mom looked like. But no one was there for her. No one. So she tried sharing her feelings with God. Maybe He would understand. She prayed to God for a lot of things, but mostly just that she wouldn't be invisible anymore. Yet it never seemed to do any good. Even God didn't seem to notice her.

Now here was this boy, staring right at her. At her, not through her. And Jaime Jo was staring right back, caught in the headlights. The heat of those headlights must have been white hot, because they lit a flame inside Jaime Jo Tremper that day that no amount of common sense, guilt, fear, threats, pain, or God Himself would extinguish.

She hadn't exactly heard what he'd said, distracted by his eyes, but knew she had to break the silence or she'd explode.

"Were you talking to us?" she stammered, her friends seeming to fade into the crowd.

"To you. I was talking to you. I said, it's not so bad," repeated Tommy, stepping closer with his bad-boy swagger.

Eye level with his chest, Jaime Jo found herself unable to concentrate on his words. "I'm sorry. What's not so bad?"

"The Ferris wheel. You were afraid of going on the Ferris wheel."

Jaime tried to remember what was happening before Tommy showed up. "Oh, yeah," she said, tearing her eyes away from Tommy to glance at the carnival ride. "I hate those things. My friends were trying to force me to go on it. But there's no way. I'd rather die."

"What if I went on with you?" asked Tommy.

"OK."

"OK? I thought you'd rather die?"

"What?" Jaime Jo just couldn't think straight.

So before she knew what was happening, as afternoon turned to evening, she found herself on the double Ferris wheel, under the protective custody of Tommy Harris, at the top of the world, looking out over the entire fair and beyond. She didn't think it could get any better, when the fireworks show began, completing the conspiracy. Or maybe the fireworks were all in her head.

Without the sun, the night air cooled considerably and Jaime Jo shivered from a fresh case of sunburn. Sitting next to Tommy, she was too distracted to remember she was deathly afraid of Ferris wheels. And even more, when Tommy noticed her shiver and took the liberty of putting his arm around her, she felt that all was right with the world, and she'd never have anything to fear ever again.

So where did everything go so wrong? When did that feeling with Tommy go away? When did she become afraid again... of everything? Why?

And then they sent him away. It was the only way. They had to. She couldn't have survived much more. So she healed. First physically, then... well... she never really healed mentally. Like a bodily wound, it appeared from the outside that her mental ones had slowly scarred over, forming a hardened shell. But while those scars protected her from further damage, they also entrapped emotions beneath, like a festering abscess, leaving one colorless day to merge into another. Wake up, get the baby ready, then trudge off to work at Frank's. Jaime didn't really mind the monotony. There was something calming about having a regular routine. At least it didn't involve the emergency room or broken bones. And that had to count for something.

But things would change now. Tommy was coming back. She sat in Frank's parking lot rocking herself on the bumper of Billy Sawchuck's car, wondering if things would ever be easy again. Jaime Jo Tremper wasn't sure she had the strength to stand up, let alone deal with the return of Tommy Harris. She couldn't. She wouldn't.

"He can't," she informed Billy.

"Can't what?" asked Billy, happy to see she'd returned to this world.

"Come back. Tommy. He can't come back."

"Well, he is. That's what they said. I wouldn't lie to you."

"He can't," she insisted. "He has to be stopped. Someone's got to tell him. He can't come back here."

"But—" began Billy.

"I don't care. He just can't. *I* can't. I can't do it again, Billy."

"How can you talk that way, honey," gently smoothing her hair. "You love him. And I know he loves you."

Jaime dropped her face into her hands in despair. "You think I don't know that? That's just it. That's exactly the problem. He'll come for me. I know he will. And I won't have the strength to turn him away. Then it'll start all over again."

Billy wouldn't let it go. "But that was then. You were just kids. You're all grown up now. It doesn't have to be that way."

Jaime Jo had no response.

"Besides," Billy continued, "they say he's changed."

Jaime sniffed, and wiped the tears from her eyes. "What do you mean?" she asked, looking up at Billy.

"I don't know. It's just what everyone is saying is all. That he's changed. The war and everything. They say it's had an effect on him and he's changed."

Jaime Jo wasn't sure she liked the sound of that. She didn't want him changed. There was nothing wrong with Tommy Harris. Never was. Not a damn thing.

Chapter 3

As the sheriff drove past Charlotte Sawchuck's place early Sunday morning, his mind wandered, recalling the night before. He'd spent a fortune taking Charlotte out for some veal parmesan. But good old Charlotte more than made up for it when they got back to her place.

Damn that woman was hot. The sheriff never noticed her clothes were always too tight, her blouses too low-cut, her makeup too thick, and her perfume too strong. No, Jo Bob Buckner thought Charlotte Sawchuck was just right. A damn sight more than just right. Hell, he thought she was a movie star. A movie star right there in Pleasant Valley. He was doin' a movie star. And she couldn't get enough of him. It don't get no better than that.

It took all the self-control he could muster to keep from stopping right there at Charlotte's shop and running two steps at a time back up to her room for seconds. There was just something so attractive about a thing so feminine as Charlotte. And feminine in Pleasant Valley was something rare to be appreciated, like a prized coonhound. So Jo Bob did his best to appreciate her as often as he could. Shit, even that goofy kid of hers was more feminine than most of the women in this town. Poor kid. But Jo Bob figured it was only natural, a teenage boy growing up in a house with a mom as smoking hot as Charlotte Sawchuck. He'd have to be gay or else go crazy. The sheriff didn't remember anyone's mother looking like Charlotte

Sawchuck when he was a kid. They'd have all gone blind from beating off all day. Yeah, just as well her kid didn't have that problem to worry about.

Thinking of Billy Sawchuck cooled off the sheriff enough to make it safely past Charlotte's place and continue on to fulfill his duty as sheriff. Sheriff Buckner took his job seriously. He knew he wasn't the brightest firefly in the jar, but the job didn't take much in the brains department. Keeping a bunch of rednecks in line was about all he was cut out for. And even that, he didn't always get right. He didn't always get his man, as they say. Or even if he did, it wasn't always the right man. But that was OK by Jo Bob Buckner's way of thinking. He did the best he could, which was a damn-site better than most, and at the end of the day, everything had a way of balancing out.

He'd already begun the task of planning for Tommy Harris's homecoming. He'd have to talk to all the key players on a need-to-know basis. He'd start with Jimmy Harris, the boy's father. And he knew just where to find good old Jimmy at seven a.m. on a Sunday morning. In fact, that was the best time to see him. Jimmy always seemed most himself when he was shit-faced. And at seven a.m., that's what he was bound to be.

It wasn't always that way. Sure, Jimmy would throw back some beers back in high school and beyond, just like everyone else. Many a night Jimmy and Jo Bob, before his sheriffing began, would raise some hell after one of their high school football games, win or lose, sometimes even before the game. Everything was simpler back in those days, at least for Jimmy, before things changed.

The sheriff hadn't really changed all that much. He went right from playing fullback to playing sheriff. Still chasing the ladies. Before Charlotte, it was someone else. And after Charlotte, it would be someone else again.

But that's not how it worked out for Jimmy Harris. Jimmy fell in love. It was a hopeless situation. The poor guy was stuck on Tommy's mom before he even graduated high school, married off as soon as he obtained his electrician's union card.

But love can be a two-edged sword. Wonderful when all is right. Tragedy when things go badly. Things went badly. Mary Harris passed in childbirth having Tommy. Tommy never knew his mom. But Jimmy did. Jimmy lost the love of his life. It's not often people find true love. But when they lose it, things sure enough go to hell. Jo Bob thought about that "better to have loved and lost" expression and knew for sure it was a crock of shit.

Jimmy could have made it after Mary's death, and in a way he had. Tommy always had a roof over his head and food on the table. And his father's love, there was plenty of that. But Jimmy missed his Mary something awful, and never recovered. He drank away his union membership and ended up working nightshift as a security guard over at the train yard. The pay and benefits were nothing near the union job, but on the other hand, being a nighttime security guard didn't much interfere with his drinking.

So Jo Bob knew just where to find Jimmy Harris at seven a.m.. The seven p.m. to three a.m. shift at the train yard over, the three a.m. to eight a.m. shift at Chezzy's Lounge was in full swing. Jo Bob had watched his pal Jimmy's life ruined by love, vowing such a thing would never happen to him. And now you could say the same thing had happened with Jimmy's kid, Tommy. Life ruined over a woman, that preacher's girl. Well no one could call it a love story, exactly, but it was, nevertheless, yet another man's life ruined on account of a woman. Maybe it was a genetic thing, thought Jo Bob. Like femininity in the Sawchuck family. Only in the Harris family, it was men ruined by women. Well, whatever it was, it was a damn shame.

The sheriff pulled up in front of Chezzy's a little after seven. The place looked closed, sitting quietly in the morning dew. Not much more than a trailer with a wooden addition, at the fork in the road at the end of town, the neon sign was turned off, as were all the lights and any other signs of life. And yet there were five or six cars parked out front. The sheriff knew the drill. Bars could only stay open legally until four. In fact, most others closed up by three because by then most of the women had gone home and that's when the fights start breaking out. That's when the regulars would show up at Chezzy's. Even back when Jo Bob was a kid, everyone knew that after four, the front lights had to go out and you couldn't have any money on the bar. Of course, that didn't mean you couldn't stick around to finish your drink. And the drinks didn't stop flowing until eight or so, so long as the front lights were out and the money was off the bar.

Even then, most of the younger crowd evaporated out the back door when the sheriff walked in. Chezzy didn't really mind, as the younger crowd had already spent their wads elsewhere and were there only to nurse warm beers, rather than go home, until they got kicked out at eight.

That left the place pretty much to Jo Bob and Jimmy, and Chezzy of course. Chezzy was a big old fat slob of a man, unshaven, wild-haired, and pungent to the nose. But all that only added to the general ambiance of Chezzy's, right along with the 25-cent pickled eggs behind the bar. He'd been there forever, knew everyone in town since they were kids, and never changed a thing. There was something comforting in consistency. The same Pabst Blue Ribbon clock on the wall, the same carved-up bar and stools, the same peanut dispenser, though the price had gone up to a dime. Even the jukebox seemed as though the music never changed. That's probably why the regulars went to Chezzy's. Change hadn't been kind to most of them, and they were hoping to avoid it.

"Hey, Jo Bob," said Jimmy in greeting, without turning around. Drinking in a bar after four a.m., you don't want nobody sneakin' up on you from behind, so Jimmy'd automatically glanced at the mirror behind the bar when he heard the front door creak behind him.

"Jimmy," acknowledged Jo Bob, settling on the next stool.

Chezzy had Jo Bob's Miller draft ready before he'd made it to the bar.

"Figured I'd be running into you pretty soon," Jimmy said, sipping from a shot glass of Jack Daniels.

"Really? Why's that?" asked Jo Bob.

"Come on, Sheriff. No need to play dumb with me. I know you too long for that."

"Got that right. And you know me too long to be calling me Sheriff."

"Well, you're here on official business, ain't ya?" stated Jimmy, turning to look Jo Bob in the eye.

Jo Bob, caught red-handed, took a swig of beer, and looked away. "What'd you expect, Jimmy?"

"Didn't say I expected nothin' else. I just like to keep my business and pleasure separate."

"Fair enough, buddy. Fair enough," replied Jo Bob before chugging the rest of his beer.

Jimmy threw back the rest of his shot, never comfortable discussing business.

"Well, call it what you want, friendly advice or an official warning," began Jo Bob. "Everyone knows your boy's coming home. And you know I'm happy he's coming home in one piece. But things have been quiet around here since he's been gone. You know I don't give a shit about Preacher. He'll always be that fucking weirdo from high school, spying on everyone at the drive-in with a pair of binoculars. Shit. Remember that time he hid in the girls' locker room and got locked in over night. They found him in the morning asleep in the dirty laundry bin. No, that pervert could go to hell for all I care. But his kid's a decent girl. And she's finally healed up nicely. Been a good momma to that little baby of hers. And I'm just hoping your boy don't stir things up again. I'm hoping, you got any pull with him, you'll help keep the peace, Jimmy. Better you than me."

Jimmy turned to face Jo Bob again. "Is that a threat?"

Jo Bob felt truly hurt by Jimmy's remark. And when Jimmy turned to reach for the fresh shot of Jack Chezzy'd laid in front of him, Jo Bob reached out for Jimmy's wrist, pinning his shot-laden hand to the bar.

Jimmy jerked back toward Jo Bob, ready for a confrontation. "What the—"

Jo Bob leaned in cheek-to-cheek with Jimmy and quietly murmured in his ear. "Now you listen to me, asshole. We may have grown up and drifted apart over the years since school. That's what guys do. But, pathetic as it sounds, you're still the best friend I got. You know I'd kill for that boy of yours. But if Tommy's planning to come back here and pick up where he left off, you know I can't allow it. You know it. Put yourself in my position, Jimmy."

Jimmy jerked his arm out of Jo Bob's grip, spilling the shot of Jack down the front of his shirt. Jo Bob felt bad about that. He didn't mean to embarrass the man.

Fury turned to defeat, Jimmy looked sadly to Jo Bob, searching for answers. "You think I did the right thing, letting you send him away?"

Jo Bob felt his friend's pain. "What choice was there, buddy?" he lied, knowing he'd never let anyone send any kid of *his* to die in Vietnam. Now if the kid wanted to go and die a hero shooting gooks halfway across the world, so be it. But *send* him? Against his will? Never. That just wouldn't be right. No, Jo Bob would never have allowed it. But that was Jo Bob Buckner. And this was Jimmy Harris. Not the Jimmy Harris that kicked ass on the football field back in school. No, that Jimmy was long gone. This was just a pickled shadow of the former man. Weak and pathetic. And it was a damn shame.

Jo Bob stood up to leave. "Hey, Chez. I spilled Jimmy's drink. Set him up again, on me." Throwing a ten on the bar, Jo Bob headed for the door.

"Hey, no money on the bar," growled Chezzy.

"Oh, go call a cop," joked Jo Bob as the front door slammed behind him.

Jimmy briefly thought of refusing the drink out of pride. But pride was a luxury Jimmy Harris could no longer afford. A shot of Jack was a shot of Jack, after all. It didn't care who paid the tab. So why should Jimmy? He accepted the drink from Chezzy, like a small boy accepting a hug from his momma after takin' a lickin' from his dad out in the woodshed. And he followed that drink with another.

Some friend, he thought, Jo Bob's words eating at him. And after I saved his ass all those years ago. He may be sheriff now, but if not for me, he'd be serving 25 to life for gettin' that girl killed. He was blind drunk that night he wrapped his father's truck around that tree after the tri-county playoff game. I don't think the girl felt a thing. But I was the one who didn't have any money for beer, so I was the one who put Jo Bob and the dead girl in the back seat, slipping behind the wheel myself before the cops showed up. It was just an honest accident. Shit happens. We both felt terrible about the girl. But she was dead, after all, and no amount of prison time for Jo Bob could change that. Jo Bob knew what I'd done. He wasn't that drunk. Yet, we never even spoke about it. That's what pals were for. And now this is how he treats me. Threatening my kid. Shit, he owes me big time.

* * * *

Jo Bob slipped behind the wheel of his sheriff's cruiser in Chezzy's parking lot. The horizon was aglow with the start of a new day. Many a day he and Jimmy'd walk out of Chezzy's at seven or eight in the morning, like moles blinded by the light of day. Funny how Jimmy turned out to be the drinker while he, Jo Bob, had settled down to just a couple of beers now and then. Who'd have thought that's how it'd turn out after that nightmare all those years ago. He never forgot that night, never forgave himself for what he did to that poor girl. And he never forgot what his pal Jimmy did for him. He owed Jimmy, all right. He owed him big time.

As Jo Bob pulled out of Chezzy's and headed down Main Street, he wondered if Charlotte was sleeping in. Well, he'd see when he drove by. If her light was still off, maybe he'd stop on over and help her make the bed. Nothin' like a little action in the morning, a little breakfast of champions. Besides, he wasn't looking forward to his next appointment anyway. Jo Bob Buckner had to get to church.

Chapter 4

He couldn't be called a regular at Reverend Tremper's First Baptist Church. In fact, Jo Bob was more like a hardly ever. That was because he didn't come there to find God. He only came to find pussy. There was just something about all those pretty young things all dressed up in their best Sunday dresses and high heels. And when the light from the stained glass window of Jesus shone right through all that sheer white material, Jo Bob knew he'd truly found God. He'd pick the finest looking one in the bunch to sit next to, inhale her perfume, and maybe get a hug at the end of services just to be neighborly. More than once, one religious experience led to another, and before Jo Bob knew it, he was looking for a way to extricate himself from an all too soon stale, purely physical— at least as far as he was concerned— relationship.

Yet he always came back when he got horny again. And Jo Bob Buckner was always getting horny. He was certainly horny that Sunday morning, still thinking of the night before with Charlotte Sawchuck, when he pulled up in front of the church. But that wasn't why he was there this time. Unfortunately, he was there on business. Sheriff's business.

He was there to talk to the preacher, Warren Tremper. And speaking with the preacher was never something Jo Bob looked forward to. It seemed he always got that same old familiar feeling every time he ran into Warren Tremper. It was something like sticking your hand down a jammed garbage disposal. You never know what you'll find, but you know it isn't going to be pleasant, and worse yet, in the back of your mind, you always say a little prayer that your hand doesn't get chewed off. Just something about the reverend gave Jo Bob the creeps.

Even back in high school, Jo Bob was never comfortable around weirdos. He just couldn't understand them. Many a time, big as he was, Jo Bob was tempted to take a swipe at them, just to shoo them away and avoid the annoyance. But Jo Bob Buckner wasn't that way. In fact, in a noble sort of way, he had no patience for bullies who would pick on the weak. And there were plenty of bullies around to keep Warren Tremper busy. There was just something about Warren that seemed to antagonize people, to bring it on himself. He just had a way of really getting under your skin. He couldn't just stay in his own weird little world. No, not Tremper. He always had to shove it in everyone else's face. Like his world was the normal one, and everyone else were the weirdos. It always took a great deal of patience for Jo Bob to keep himself from squashing Warren Tremper like some annoying gnat.

But he couldn't help feeling sorry for the little red-headed creep with the pointy nose all the guys used to call peckerhead because he looked like a woodpecker. Yet somehow, everyone, even Warren Tremper, had a place in this world, and it kind of made sense that the same teenage outcast who couldn't find pussy on a catnip farm wound up a preacher. Jo Bob just assumed that's why Warren gravitated toward the Lord. The Lord was probably the only one would have him.

So how a guy like Warren Tremper ever found a wife at all completely escaped Jo Bob. There wasn't anything wrong with Ella DeGraw. Maybe a little on the mousy side. Certainly no homecoming queen. But she had all her teeth and was sweet as could be, certainly no weirdo. Jo Bob guessed she just must have had a little something lacking in the judgment department though, because somehow she'd ended up married to Warren Tremper. But it didn't last. And now Ella was gone. Something must have been less than harmonious in Ella Tremper's marriage, as she sadly decided to take her own life prematurely some eight years ago.

Then there was the kid she left behind, Jaime Jo. The girl seemed normal enough, to a point anyway. But anything out of sort seemed perfectly understandable, a young girl losing her mother and all. Maybe she was just acting out, whatever that means, when she started dating Tommy Harris. Oh, Tommy had a good heart, all right. Jo Bob always liked Jimmy's kid. But he wasn't exactly following the straight and narrow, and certainly was no fit for the daughter of a preacher.

Now, Jo Bob was definitely no shrink, and could never wrap his head around why a boy would get physically abusive with a girl, but even after the bruises grew visible, that girl never took it upon herself to walk away. Like they say, it takes two to tango, after all. If anything, she seemed to cling all the tighter to Tommy. She loved that boy with everything she had.

Jo Bob sometimes wondered if any of that wacky slappy stuff ever went on between Warren and Ella, you know, and Jaime Jo was just following in the family tradition. Maybe it was that whole genetic thing of Jo Bob's again. With the Sawchucks, it was femininity. With the Harrises, it was letting love for a woman ruin your life, and with the Tremper women, it was loving a man for kicking the shit out of you. Maybe Jo Bob really had something with this genetics stuff. Go figure.

Despite all the pretty ladies, Jo Bob never really felt comfortable in church. His collar always seemed to shrink several sizes around his neck, and there was just something about The Holy Bible that made him itch. Oh, Jo Bob Buckner had plenty in his life to feel guilty about, but the only place it seemed to bother him was in church. So it made perfect sense to him that church was a place to be avoided at all costs.

By the time he entered the church, the sermon was well under way and Jo Bob hated that. If he had to go to church at all, he at least liked to get there in time to score a prime seat next to some over-blessed and underutilized piece of ass. Now the best he could hope for was a seat next to someone without B.O. He took his chances with the first available seat.

The preacher was wailing away about something or other to do with sin, as usual. Jo Bob spied the preacher's daughter Jaime Jo seated at the piano. She looked unusually distracted, and noticeably pale. Jo Bob wondered if she might be coming down with something.

After one last ditch scan about the pews for something pretty to help the time pass, Jo Bob decided he might as well take a nap until the preacher was all preached out.

* * * *

It seemed as though he had just closed his eyes, visions of naked angels dancing in his head, when he felt someone poking him in the arm. He looked up to see Warren Tremper glaring down at him.

"Reverend Tremper," said Jo Bob, stifling one last snore. The church had emptied but for the two of them.

"Sheriff Buckner," responded Warren, eyeing Jo Bob warily. "To what do I owe the honor of having our sheriff napping in my church? Finally decided to save what's left of that soul of yours?"

"Oh no, Reverend. Sorry. Nothing so drastic as that. I guess you could say I was here on official business," he said, pulling himself together and rising from the pew.

"Oh?" said Warren, furrowing his brow. The only business he liked to deal with in church was the Lord's business. "And what sort of, uh, business of yours would concern me?"

Jo Bob sensed the condescension in the reverend's tone, and Jo Bob was never one to back down when challenged. Maybe he could reap some pleasure out of this morning's mission after all. "Well, frankly Reverend, it concerns you."

"Me?" Warren laughed in surprise.

"You and your daughter to be exact."

Warren felt his gut twist, the smile leaving his face. "Jaime Jo?" His daughter hadn't been a problem for a couple of years now. "What about her? Has she gotten herself into some kind of trouble?

Is she OK?" He looked over to the church piano she'd been playing only a few minutes earlier.

Jo Bob sensed the preacher's concern for his daughter, and hadn't intended to torture the man. "No, no, nothing like that. She's just fine... for the time being."

Initially relieved, then suspicious, "For the time being?"

"I suppose I should just spit it out." Jo Bob looked Warren in the eye. "It's Tommy Harris. He's—"

"Dead?" Warren did his best to hide his pleasure at the revelation.

"No, he's not dead."

"Wounded then? Quadriplegic?" He just couldn't keep at least one corner of his mouth from turning upward in an eerie sort of smile.

"Now Reverend," began Jo Bob with a touch of feigned indignation, "I know you got reason to dislike the boy, but really. Don't you think you're being just a little, uh, unchristian?"

Warren brushed the question aside, not ready to concede the point. "Well, what is it then? What about him?" he asked impatiently.

"He's coming home." Jo Bob had to admit to himself, he took a certain degree of pleasure in watching Warren Tremper's jaw drop, speechless.

"Home? What do you mean, home?" Warren began to pace back and forth. "The war's not over yet. There's still plenty of them Vietnamese to kill over there. If he ain't been wounded, he ought to keep fighting." Soon Warren was shouting, spittle flying from his mouth. "The only way that boy should be coming home is in a box!"

Jo Bob tried to bring some calm to the situation. "Now Warren, the boy's been fighting over there for two years. He's done his time."

Warren wasn't having it. "I don't care how long he's been there. That wasn't the deal. He wasn't supposed to come back... ever."

"Well that may be how you figured it, Warren. It certainly turned out to be a death sentence for a lot of young men. But I guess Jimmy Harris's boy turned out to be more resilient than most."

Warren's eyes were still wild. "A cockroach is resilient. That don't mean you welcome it into your home."

"Now Warren, just listen to reason—"

"No, Sheriff, *you* listen to reason. That animal damn near killed my daughter. You wouldn't treat a disobedient dog the way he treated her. And after that, he… he raped her and left her with child, his filthy seed in my Jaime Jo."

Jo Bob began to respond, but Warren cut him off to continue his tirade. "Two short years fighting over in Vietnam and he gets to come back like some kind of hero? Where's the justice in that? Shoot, he didn't deserve the chance to die for his country. Should have been strung up from the nearest oak. That was *your* job, Sheriff."

"Now Warren, you know there weren't no rape. Jaime Jo herself said it was consensual. And the beatings? Even assuming the boy did it, weren't no evidence to convict."

Warren's voice became more shrill in disbelief. "No evidence? What are you talking about? It was there for all to see. The evidence was all over the child. And not just on her face. You saw it yourself."

"That's not what I'm saying, Warren. Your girl wouldn't press charges. She wouldn't implicate the boy. And weren't no witnesses to say one way or the other."

"Did you really expect a victim of abuse to point her finger at the animal threatening her life? He'd have killed her for sure."

"Well, nevertheless, that's all I had to work with."

The preacher dropped down onto one of the pews in defeat.

Jo Bob tried to see the upside. "Besides, we got him out of here for a couple of years. Your girl's healed up nicely, had that beautiful little baby girl."

Warren bent over in the pew, holding his head in his hands. "The bastard? You mean my bastard granddaughter? So what now? The father comes back to claim the child? He'll be the death of the both of them."

"You've got my word, Warren. I won't let that happen. That boy resumes his ways and I'll put a stop to it."

Warren slumped back in the pew, staring off at the stained glass image of Christ over the pulpit.

Jo Bob continued. "Besides, word has it he's changed."

Warren looked up at Jo Bob. "What's that supposed to mean?"

"Well I ain't no shrink or nothin', but they say the war's taken its toll on the boy. Maybe he's seen enough violence, had the fight beat right out of him."

Warren was less than optimistic, shaking his head. "Unless they made a gelding out of him and performed some kind of lobotomy over there, I ain't buyin' it. Once an animal, always an animal."

Jo Bob saw he wasn't getting anywhere. He'd come and done his job. Now it was time to get the hell out of that church. Maybe some breakfast in bed with Charlotte. "Well, just thought you ought to know," he said, turning for the door.

"What am I supposed to tell my little girl?"

Jo Bob was within reach of the door and wouldn't even turn around, as close to freedom as he was. "Tell her, if things begin goin' south again to press charges this time. Make my life a lot simpler."

The preacher stood up in defiance, shaking his fist, as he watched the sheriff exiting the church door. "Oh he'll be charged, all right. If Jaime Jo don't do it, the Lord will. One way or another, justice will be mine! That animal will be stopped, and for good this time. One way or another."

* * * *

Jo Bob was relieved to be out of church a moment later, beating a hasty retreat to his car. He had no idea how things were going to play out this time. He sure hoped Tommy Harris had indeed changed, and for the better. If for no other reason than to make Jo Bob's life easier.

He honestly felt sorry for Warren Tremper. Jo Bob didn't have any kids, at least none he knew of. But if anyone ever treated any daughter of Jo Bob's the way that boy treated poor Warren Tremper's girl, they wouldn't have had to send him halfway round the world to kill him. He'd have been killed right there in Pleasant Valley, courtesy of one Jo Bob Buckner. Uncle Sam could have saved the airfare. As Jo Bob seen it, Warren Tremper would've been within his rights to kill that boy. But Tremper didn't do it, didn't have the balls, being a preacher and all. He left it to the authorities to handle. And that would be Jo Bob. So without the girl pressing charges, Jo Bob did the best he could, packin' him off to Nam. That being said, he could certainly understand why the preacher felt short changed, as though justice had not been served.

So as Jo Bob gladly left the church in his rearview mirror, it wasn't without some remorse that he couldn't have done anything more to help the man. And yet… damn if that Warren Tremper still didn't give him the creeps. Something just wasn't right about the man. And never would be.

Chapter 5

At first it just reminded Tommy Harris of summer back home when he'd take off on his own to go hunting wild boar down in the North Carolina lowlands. Tramping through swamp all day in 90-degree heat, a million percent humidity, carrying a 50-pound pack was nothing new to him. Maybe it wouldn't be as bad as they'd said after all. But Vietnam turned out to be a whole 'nother kettle of fish, and after a few days, he'd soon forgotten what it was like to have dry feet. Vietnam just seemed to be one big swamp to Tommy Harris. If only his boots had enough time to dry out by morning so he didn't have to start the new day already wet again. He'd given up on socks long ago. They just seemed to act like sponges, holding the moisture. Tommy always felt they could beat the Viet Cong, but apparently they weren't the enemy to worry about. It was the damned fungus he knew would never surrender.

In fact, fighting Vietnamese was all there was to take your mind off the itching. So when bullets began flying past his head, seemingly out of nowhere, Tommy was almost relieved to sprawl flat on his chest in the mud. He looked for a signal from his commanding officer who was pointing him toward the mouth of a cave hidden on a nearby hill. That's where the enemy fire was coming from. And Tommy's mission was to remedy the situation.

Tommy was a sharpshooter. After basic training and before shipping out, he'd managed to qualify for Special Forces training, but his sharpshooting prowess wasn't attributable to the military. No, that particular skill was self-taught, back home, honed on all manner of game, from small squirrels and birds to large bears and deer. No, he'd never hunted a human before, but they *were* on the large side, after all. Easy targets.

Yet, long-range rifle wasn't the only method of killing in Tommy's arsenal. There's always more than one way to skin a 'possum. When he grew bored hunting large game with a rifle, he switched to bow and arrow for the challenge. It wasn't long before he was stalking with just a hunting knife. Everyone knew Tommy Harris could survive on his own in the wilderness without so much as a nail clipper. Even something as small as a pocketknife took away all the challenge. And a rifle? Well, with a rifle, it was game over. Nothing stood a chance against Tommy Harris armed with a rifle.

But he wouldn't be needing his rifle today. This mission would be up close. So while his squad continued to draw fire, Tommy was sent crawling through the tall grass on his belly toward the mouth of the cave. After what seemed like hours inching toward his goal, he found himself alongside the cave's entrance. Now came the fun part. Pulling the pin from the hand grenade with his teeth, Tommy lobbed the little football into the cave and stepped back.

The ensuing explosion brought an end to the gunfire. Yet, watching the smoke clear, he still didn't want to go in. You could never be sure what kind of booby trap might lie in wait. So when Tommy entered the smoke-filled cave, weapon drawn, he was ready for just about anything. After all, the North Vietnamese were experts in psychological warfare, going to great lengths to unhinge the American GI's.

Between the physical conditions and the killing, the sheer brutality of daily existence in Vietnam, Tommy'd suffered his share of stress. He thought he was handling it. So did most of the guys. Sure, there was the rare coward who went crying to his commanding officer about how he couldn't take it anymore, how he wanted to go home to his momma. But most of the guys just sucked it up like men and took care of business. That was Tommy's plan too. But those

Vietnamese were tricky devils. Tommy never expected to be greeted by what he found in that cave.

It was an exact replica of the church back home in Pleasant Valley. They even had it down to the stained glass window of Jesus behind the altar. And there at the pew, bathed in beams of light, dressed in a Viet Cong uniform, was Jaime Jo's father, hands spread in worship. Tommy wasn't easily shaken and didn't even flinch, not until he looked over to the cross on the wall. He momentarily lowered his guard when he saw her. It was Jaime Jo. His first impulse was to run to her and hold her in his arms, a sensation he'd almost forgotten. But then he stopped, raising his weapon again. What had her father done to her? She'd been crucified, nailed to the cross, and she was bleeding, bleeding down the cross from her womb.

Their plan was working. Tommy felt himself becoming unhinged. He swung his rifle back into position, placing the preacher in his sites, but Jaime Jo's father just stood there laughing, holding a baby in his arms. Tommy knew it was Jaime's. And when her father raised the baby up like some sort of sacrificial offering, Tommy went to take it, but it levitated just out of his reach. He didn't know what to do other than grab her father by the throat and start beating him. Tommy'd lost control entirely now and just kept beating the preacher's face into a bloody pulp. Tommy was soon covered in the preacher's blood but couldn't stop, not until he looked once more, and found the preacher's face had changed. It wasn't the preacher at all. It was Jaime Jo. It was Jaime Jo Tommy'd been beating. Upon seeing her battered face, Tommy dropped to his knees in despair, and began to cry.

That's when the lone surviving Viet Cong in the cave detonated his own hand grenade, hoping in a last ditch attempt to take Tommy Harris with him. Tommy saw a flash of light, felt intense heat off to one side, and smelled something like barbeque. That's when he knew he'd fucked up. He woke up in the sick bay on painkillers, bandages hiding what remained of the left side of his face.

* * * *

The apprehensive passengers on the bus had vacated the seats neighboring the obviously troubled sleeping soldier with the scary face. So when Tommy woke up crying on the bus headed home to Pleasant Valley, he was alone. He never remembered his dreams or daytime fits, but he'd gotten used to the fearful stares that would greet him when he came to. Such was the case with the others seated on the bus. All but two. Seated across the isle from Tommy were an old man and his grandson.

The little boy seemed more curious than frightened. "What's wrong with him?" the boy asked his grandfather, without trying to keep his words private, as children will do.

The old man glanced over at Tommy with an apologetic nod of his head. Then, turning to his grandson, "There's nothing wrong with that man, Charlie." Pointing at Tommy's uniform, "He's been to war, that's all."

"Just like you, Grandpa," remarked Charlie, proud of himself for making the connection.

"That's right, Charlie," acknowledged the old man.

"But why's he acting so strange?"

The old man looked over at Tommy, and catching his eye, "War's an awful thing, Charlie. It tends to wear on you."

Charlie nodded his head, considering the man's words and finding them satisfactory.

The old man nudged the boy in the elbow. "Why don't you go over there and thank that man? Thank him for his service."

The dutiful little boy slid from his seat and crossed the isle over to Tommy. "Thank you for your service, sir." Yet when the man turned toward him, exposing the mutilated side of his face, the boy recoiled in fear.

Tommy wasn't used to regular folks after being away in the military so long. Especially small ones. But he certainly didn't want to frighten anyone. "I'm sorry if I scared you, Charlie," he said, reflexively bringing his hand up to the side of his face

"I wasn't scared," said Charlie, collecting himself, with more than a touch of indignation.

Tommy chuckled. "I didn't think you were." Then, unable to resist, he saluted the little boy, who, grinning ear to ear, ran back to his grandfather. Tommy exchanged knowing nods with the old man before turning away.

Tommy had mixed feelings about coming home. He didn't know what it would be like anymore. He didn't know what Vietnam would be like either, and that didn't turn out so well. He'd been through some unpleasant shit growing up. It wasn't easy being trailer trash with an alcoholic for a father. But none of it compared to Nam. The sheer violence of it, constant blood and death, civilians unavoidably caught up in it all as the Viet Cong resorted to hiding among the villagers. Tommy'd seen what happened when women and children met land mines and napalm, shredded and charred bodies at every turn. No, Tommy'd never imagined anything like Vietnam. So how bad could things be in Pleasant Valley?

After a year in Nam, Tommy started to develop some... uh... quirks, and was nearly sent home early. These increasingly serious quirks kept earning him appointments with the shrink that would come through periodically, things like discharging his weapon at giant cockroaches, not just a shot or two, but emptying an entire clip until the ground under the roach was gone. Then there was the time, after a particularly deadly firefight in which Tommy'd lost some comrades in arms, where they found Tommy smearing the blood of the dead enemy on his own face as war paint, three Viet Cong scalps hanging from his bayonet.

The shrink said Tommy needed time off to relax. His superiors, however, had other ideas. As long as Tommy was killing the enemy, and not members of his own squad, he wasn't going anywhere. The shrink was overruled.

Well, he'd done his time as far as Tommy was concerned. He'd given two years to his country. Two years to Sheriff Buckner and Reverend Tremper. Two years for Jaime Jo's sake. His injury sent him stateside, back to Fort Bragg, providing him some time to mull things over. He supposed they'd have been happy to patch him up and send him back into battle, but Tommy no longer cared what they wanted. He'd made up his mind. It was time to go home, at least to see his father and settle his affairs before moving on.

Affairs, that's funny. All he owned was that beat up '68 Camaro he'd picked up cheap from the junkyard before the trouble with Jaime Jo got out of hand. Like Tommy, the car'd been in a fire, but the motor ran just fine and he'd been fixing it up, coating its beaten exterior in flat gray primer to keep the rust off, before he got banished from town. He hoped his father hadn't pawned it for drinkin' money. He'd probably just pick up the Camaro and move on. Staying in Pleasant Valley could only result in no good. Besides, home would probably be the first place they'd come looking for him. He hadn't exactly left Fort Bragg on the best of terms.

The bus pulled into a gas station in Greensboro so the passengers could use the rest rooms and get something to eat from the grocery store next door. It was the first time Tommy'd been out in public since leaving the army, at least in a city as big as Greensboro. He found his face and uniform drawing stares from the crowd.

Tommy Harris wasn't exactly sure what a hippy was, but the disheveled group of longhaired young men and their girlfriends in tie-dyed skirts who got off the bus with him didn't seem too impressed by his uniform. Finger pointing and whispers turned to open taunts.

"Hey look, it's that wack-job from the bus with the messed up face. Please don't shoot us, Mr. Soldier."

"Hide behind us, girls. They tend to aim for the women and children first."

Soon the girls started chanting, "Baby killer!"

Tommy didn't know what that was all about, but he knew there was nothing to gain by engaging them. So he turned away and headed for the restroom. He was washing the sleep off his face when they followed him in. There were four men. And two girls followed them right into the men's room. They started rolling some joints of marijuana like Tommy'd first seen in Nam, as they continued their taunts.

"Did you enjoy killing all those poor Vietnamese babies?" continued the girls where they'd left off.

"Those peaceful Vietnamese people never did anything to us. Why would you want to go over there and start a war?"

Tommy didn't begin to understand what they were talking about, but he didn't think asking about it would result in a coherent response, so he started heading for the door. One of the men stepped in front of him, blocking the door, sucking on his joint.

"Excuse me," tried Tommy.

"But hey, man, you didn't answer our question. We asked you why you'd want to go over there and start something with those Vietnamese people."

Tommy stopped and took a breath. "I didn't start anything. I was just serving my country. Now if you'll excuse me…"

Another one joined the first, blocking the door. "Yeah, right. We think you just like shooting things. Little babies. Well you don't have a gun now."

Seemed the peaceniks had something other than peace on their minds. Tommy wasn't averse to kicking an idiot's ass. But there were four of them, after all. "I'd just like to get back on the bus, if that's OK with you."

"Well, it's not OK with us. You're smelling up the bus."

"And your face is scaring the children," added another.

The girls thought that was funny and started giggling. Tommy didn't think it was all that funny and presumed the pot had something to do with it.

"Look, fellas, I'm not looking for any trouble. I just want to get back on the bus."

The larger one started poking Tommy in the chest. "That's just the problem, man. We don't want you on our bus. You want to play soldier? Well, why don't you fight someone your own size? Not women and babies."

Two of the men stood nose to nose with Tommy. He thought back to his high school scuffles against the football team, weighing the odds of taking on four dumb jocks, their cheerleaders behind them, egging them on. Tommy'd lost a few of those battles. But he'd also won a few. No matter. Too late. The first punch surprised Tommy. He tasted blood from his busted lip.

He still wasn't ready to fight back yet. He'd taken worse than that. If a busted lip was all the toll he had to pay to get back on that bus, so be it. He'd done a lifetime of fighting the past two years in Vietnam. He'd had enough.

That's when he heard the flush of a toilet and saw the old man emerge from one of the two bathroom stalls, tucking his shirttail into his pants. Everyone turned to see the unexpected guest.

"Can't a man get some privacy in the john anymore?" he said, eyeing the two girls indignantly.

The girls blurted out embarrassed giggles as they covered their mouths. The four men were annoyed by the intruder.

"Hey, man. Why were you hiding in there so long without saying anything?"

The old man went to the sink to wash his hands. "Didn't know a man had to announce himself while doing his business. And as to how long it took me, you young pups will get old yourselves one day. You probably don't even know what a prostate is."

"I'm not sure, but I think he's bein' a smart-ass, Jake," said one assailant to the other.

Then a small voice came from the other stall. "What's going on out there, grandpa?"

"Oh shit. What is there a whole party goin' on in here?" said Jake banging belligerently on the little boy's door.

"Grandpa, I'm coming out."

"You stay right where you are. Don't you come out here, Charlie," ordered the old man.

"But why? I'm done," insisted Charlie, flushing the toilet.

The old man persisted. "I said stay right where you are."

The little boy emerged from the stall, zipping up his fly.

"Shit," muttered the old man.

Jake thought things were getting interesting. "That's OK, Charlie. Want to see what real men do to baby-killing cowards?"

"What's he talking about, Grandpa?"

"Why don't you wait for me outside the bathroom, Charlie?"

The little boy smelled trouble. "I don't want to leave you, Grandpa."

"Yeah, Grandpa," said Jake. "Be good for the boy to see justice done to a war criminal."

Ignoring the unsolicited advice, the old man opened the door to the rest room and took the little boy out by the hand.

Tommy was glad the two had left. At least there wouldn't be any collateral damage.

But he wasn't glad when a blindside blow to the eye from another one of the hippies had Tommy seeing double for a few seconds. Damn that smarted. But, oh well. Tommy could handle a black eye just fine. He started to wonder just how long this was going to take. That's when another got him in a chokehold from behind.

Tommy was just beginning to think this passive resistance stuff just wasn't all it was cracked up to be when the bathroom door opened again and the old man returned, without the boy.

"Leave him be," the man ordered.

"Mind your own business, old man," Jake replied, ignoring him, as Tommy started gagging.

From the corner of his eye, Tommy saw the old man strangely walk past him into the bathroom stall. He was contemplating how this prostate problem must be a real pain in the ass when he heard a loud cracking sound and felt the choke hold limply slip from his neck. He turned to find one hippie asleep on the floor and the old man holding the broken remains of the lid to a toilet tank.

"Damned old man," muttered Jake, shoving the rickety old man so that he fell backward, landing stunned on his back.

Seeing the old man abused that way, Tommy felt the room grow hotter and strangely humid. His feet began to feel wet and started to itch.

As he ran his options through his mind, the door to the bathroom slowly edged open to reveal the little boy peaking in to search for his grandfather. Seeing his grandfather on his back, the boy swung the door open and ran to his side, concerned.

Jake was losing his patience. "Enough of this bullshit." Grabbing the boy by the arm, he yanked him away from the old man and threw him to the girls sitting on the counter by the sinks. "Hold the little pecker," he ordered. "I don't have all day for this." He then kicked his fallen comrade awake and returned to Tommy.

The dazed old man couldn't seem to get up.

Another blow to the gut knocked the wind out of Tommy, leaving him sucking air. But it was the sound of the little boy screaming for his grandfather that made him see stars. More like fireworks. No, it was a firefight, an enemy attack. Mortars struck the South Vietnamese village sending huts up in flames. Chaos ensued as villagers scattered for their lives, children screaming for their parents. Old ones, too feeble to run, fell where they were, covering their heads. The Viet Cong overwhelmed them, executing civilians as enemy collaborators with a shot between the eyes. Others were simply beheaded just to save a bullet.

Tommy's first thought was to follow orders, to retreat, outnumbered as they were. But he found he wasn't capable. He just had to do something. He had to act. He couldn't let it continue that way.

He found himself surrounded, locked in hand-to-hand combat. He struck down one after another. He was a fighting machine, all other thought driven from his mind. Right, wrong, life, death. All of it. Gone. Just the fight. That's all there was. To strike at the enemy, and vanquish it.

He didn't know if any of his comrades in arms had joined him. He seemed alone in his battle. Yet, one after another, the enemy fell, defeated, until all that remained was one, and it held a crying little boy. Tommy went to free him. He seized the boy's captor by the neck and drew his fist back to strike, but something happened. The face of the enemy began to change. Tommy hesitated. What was happening? Another Vietnamese trick, he thought. He had to finish this. He drew back to strike again, only to drop his hand once more, as the face in front of his eyes again changed from that of a Viet Cong soldier into Jamie Jo Tremper's. It was the face of an angel, the love of his life. Tommy let go of her neck and reached out to take her in his arms as the freed little boy ran to his grandfather.

She started to scream, pushing to free herself from Tommy's embrace.

"Jaime!" he called out in agony, only wanting to hold her to his chest.

"Get your hands off of me, you freak!" she shouted, and then ran out the restroom door.

Tommy felt tears flood his eyes and begin to run down his face. And soon someone was patting him on the shoulder. "It's OK, soldier. It's OK."

He turned to find the old man standing at his side on wobbly legs, supporting himself by one hand on his grandson's head.

"It's OK," the old man continued. "You won. You won. Battle's over."

It wasn't his mind playing tricks on him? There really was a battle? Tommy surveyed the room to find the four unconscious hippies scattered about the restroom floor. Oh no. What had he done?

The old man saw his concern and sought to ease his fears. "Don't worry. They're not dead. I checked them. They'll wake up, eventually, none the worse for a little lesson learned."

"I did this?" asked Tommy, incredulously.

The old man chuckled, patting Tommy on the back. "I wish I could take the credit, but you'll see. You'll get old too one day. You'd think that damn war would be going a little better than it is if all our boys can fight like you can."

"But I don't even remember—"

"Never mind that. We'd better get out of here before someone walks in and decides to feel sorry for these troublemakers. Come on, Charlie."

"You sure can fight, mister," remarked Charlie, taking Tommy's hand as his grandfather led them both out of the restroom.

The bus was about to pull out when the three of them rapped on the door. The driver let them aboard, then looking back in the mirror, thought to mention he was still six passengers short.

"Any of you all seen that group of hippies got off with us at the rest stop?"

Tommy didn't know what to say.

Then the old man spoke up with a wink to Tommy. "Oh, they decided last minute to get off here. You know how kids are these days. Impulsive things. Never can tell what they're gonna' do."

Tommy nodded a thank you to the old man, sat back in his seat, and began wondering exactly what *he* was gonna' do when he got home.

Chapter 6

Coming home to a small town is like pulling a favorite shirt from the laundry, smelling all fresh and warm from the dryer. Cities are full of buildings, gray pavement, smog and people, as if that shirt were full of stains, the color washed out and reeking of B.O. But as the bus ride home leads away from the city and out toward the countryside, the buildings slowly wash away, the color of trees and grass replaces the gray pavement that grows everywhere, and the odor of smog and hoards of people are replaced by the fresh scent of newly-cut fields and maybe a wood-burning fireplace.

That's how Tommy felt as the roads became narrower and the site of a passing car a rarity. He was coming home. But to what? What would he find when he got there? How would he be greeted?

He knew he was home when he saw the rusty old bridge heading into Pleasant Valley. That bridge was the way in and out of town, and it seemed as though most who'd managed to escape across its deteriorating expanse never came back. But unlike all those old seafaring explorers presumed to have sailed off the edge of the Earth, Tommy Harris was coming back, for better or worse.

Good old Otis Williams was right where he was supposed to be, fishin' off the side of that bridge. Otis was the crazy old homeless black man who lived under the bridge ever since anyone could remember. No one ever knew whether it was booze, drugs, syphilis, or just regular crazy that left Otis living under the bridge. But everyone knew Otis, and Otis knew everyone. He knew which of the town boys were Christian enough to share some free bait with him, and which were more likely to tease and torment him, using his cardboard hovel as an outhouse when he wasn't there to keep an eye on things. But Otis was harmless enough and never gave anyone any trouble. Otis was as much a part of Pleasant Valley as that rusted old bridge.

Tommy expected to see Otis out at the bridge, but he never thought he'd see a parade greet him at the Pleasant Valley bus depot. Yet there it was. Well, technically, it wasn't for him. It had become custom for every small town in the area to greet all their homecoming soldiers with a little parade, no matter the conditions under which they'd enlisted, be it as patriotic enlistee, dutiful draftee, or as jailbird run out of town at the point of a sheriff's gun.

Besides, Tommy wasn't the only soldier coming home on the bus that day. Zeke Purdue was on the same bus as Tommy. Only Zeke didn't have a seat in the passenger compartment. Zeke rode down below with the luggage. Zeke was in a box.

Other than the quiet heads-up call he'd given his dad, Tommy didn't think anyone even expected he was coming home. So he knew the parade wasn't for him. The welcome home signs, the balloons, the high school band, the girl scouts, the 4H club, they were all there for Zeke and Zeke's folks. Yet, apprehensive as he was to come back, Tommy did feel a certain comfort in the familiar faces of the crowd as his bus pulled into the depot.

All the old biddies from Charlotte's were there, hoping to see firsthand whether Tommy looked any worse for wear. The war'd supposedly changed him, after all. And Charlotte, she was there. She'd been sort of an adoptive mom to her Billy's friends. She was the closest thing to a mom Tommy'd ever known.

Standing right next to her, like some junkyard dog guarding its bone, was the man who'd escorted Tommy out of town two years ago. Tommy didn't really hold it against the sheriff. He used to like the man who was his father's dearest friend and always tried to give Tommy some extra line before reeling him in for one scrape with the law or another. Running Tommy out of town was just part of the job. Couldn't hold it against a man for doing his job.

There was Billy Sawchuck in the stylish sunglasses and uncomfortably tight jeans, straining to see if he could make out who was on the bus. Guess he hadn't left town yet after all. He told Tommy he'd watch over his girl Jaime Jo for him. Good old Billy. Queer as a four-leafed clover, it was good to see him. Tommy'd had his fill of macho in Nam.

No sign of Jaime Jo. Tommy didn't really expect to see her there. At least he could be thankful her father, the preacher, hadn't shown up with a shotgun or something. He was in no mood for a confrontation right off. Confrontation was something else he hoped he'd left in Nam.

Tommy saw his own father in the parking lot off to the side of the folks there for the parade. That was a pleasant surprise. Tommy wasn't sure his dad would be able to pull it off, showing up at a particular place at an appointed time. He'd fully expected to be hoofing it home. Yet there he stood, nervously smoking a cigarette, leaning against Tommy's Camaro. Looked like the car'd seen a few fender benders since his dad had taken custody of it. And his dad looked as though he'd suffered his share of wear and tear himself, thinner, paler, and noticeably twitchier from too many nights at Chezzy's. But he was there. Tommy couldn't complain.

Tommy heard the marching band start up as the bus pulled to a stop at the depot. He remained in his seat as everyone else got off the bus. Let Zeke have his moment. He watched as the little flags waved and the hankies all came out when Zeke's box was gently taken from the luggage compartment below. He watched as family and loved ones embraced. He watched as the parade passed and the crowd dissipated.

Charlotte Sawchuck and Sheriff Buckner were the only ones left on the platform after the crowd had gone. Billy couldn't wait, and had come down to stand by Tommy's bus. Tommy thought of just staying on the bus until it left town again. Why not? What was there left for him in Pleasant Valley? He didn't know. Yet maybe that's exactly what got him up out of his seat, reaching for his duffel bag, and heading for the door to bus. He wanted to find out.

Tommy had learned to unconsciously turn the left side of his face away from people, hoping to avoid those initial looks of revulsion as long as possible. But Billy noticed right away, the battle scars marring his beautiful Tommy. Yet as much as Billy missed the perfect face he'd remembered, he'd be damned if he'd let his Tommy see him cringe. Billy nearly knocked him down as Tommy took that last step off the bus onto solid ground. Tommy had to drop his bag to support the weight of Billy on his back. What a fruit, Tommy thought, smiling. Well, a hug was a hug. It felt good. He looked up to see Charlotte smiling, wiping a tear from her eye. That one was for him, not Zeke. He even got a gentleman's nod from the sheriff.

"Get off me, you faggot," Tommy joked, trying to peel Billy's arms from around his neck.

"Fuck you," was Billy's happy reply.

"You wish," quipped Tommy.

"Every time I blow out the candles," Billy whispered in his ear before Tommy was finally able to extricate himself from Billy's embrace, landing Billy on his back in the parking lot. "There's just something about a man in uniform."

Tommy threw his duffel bag at Billy and jumped up on the platform to give Charlotte a hug. After an almost imperceptible flinch when suddenly faced with his disfigurement, she didn't seem to want to let him go.

The sheriff held out his hand. "Welcome home, boy. Look at you. Looks like you put on some muscle fightin' them gooks," he said, ignoring the boy's face. "Hey, no hard feelings, I hope?"

"No, sir," answered Tommy, meaning it, when he shook the man's hand. And yet there was something unsettling in the piercing look of the sheriff's eyes that made Tommy uncomfortable, perhaps a warning, unsaid, yet at the same time, loud and clear.

"I'd better go see Dad," Tommy said, more of an excuse to duck the sheriff's stare than anything else.

Charlotte kissed him right on the damaged cheek with tears in her eyes and ruffled his hair. "Don't be a stranger now. I want you over for dinner soon. OK?"

"OK, Mom," Tommy replied with a smile. "Now, where's that bellhop?"

Billy saluted awkwardly under the weight of Tommy's duffel bag and they walked over to Tommy's dad, still glued to the Camaro.

Jimmy Harris snuffed out his cigarette on the ground and watched the soldier approaching. His son certainly had filled out. Much broader across the shoulders than when he'd left, those scars on one side replacing the baby-faced good looks. The boy was gone, all right, come back a man.

Tommy held out his hand to shake his father's when he got to the car. Jimmy almost took the hand, but he didn't. Instead, he wrapped his arms around his son's shoulders and hugged him with everything he had.

Tommy thought the man who hugged him seemed older and frailer than he'd remembered him. He smelled of smoke and whiskey. Nothing new there. But the hug was surprisingly powerful, and Tommy savored that rare delicacy.

"Good to see you, Dad."

His father didn't reply. He just gave another squeeze and a pat on the back before he pulled away. Tommy'd never seen his father cry before.

"Damned hay fever."

"Yeah, damned hay fever," agreed Billy, wiping away tears of his own.

"OK, ladies," said Tommy, concluding the awkward moment, taking his bag from Billy and tossing it in the car.

"Hey, Bill," said Jimmy, "I'll expect you at Chezzy's tonight for Tommy's homecoming shin dig." Where else would Jimmy celebrate the return of his son.

"Be there with bells on," replied Billy.

"Just leave the bells at home, Son," suggested Jimmy, shaking his head. He tossed the keys to Tommy and ducked in the passenger side.

Tommy went to open the door to his car and the handle came off in his hand.

"Oh, meant to tell you about that, Son," Jimmy said from inside. "You got to use the inside handle."

"Well, what if the window's up?" asked Tommy.

"The window don't go up," answered Jimmy.

Tommy reached inside, opened his door and got in. He fired up the motor and was glad to hear the familiar rumble. He saw his favorite Lynyrd Skynyrd album in the 8-track player, right where he'd left it, and turned the volume up, but nothing came from the speakers. He looked to his dad. "Does anything around here still work?"

Jimmy Harris took a second to ponder the question. "Well, there's the cigarette lighter... and me."

"What do you mean, you?"

"Work," replied Jimmy. "I still work, at least when I'm sober."

* * * *

The gathering at Chezzy's was just as Tommy'd expected, just him, his dad, Billy, Chezzy, and the regulars. Chezzy'd scribbled "Welcome Home Tommy" across the mirror behind the bar with a marker, and Tommy's drinks were free.

Once they'd stopped staring at his face, Chezzy and the regular crowd kept trying to pull some war stories out of Tommy, but they found his heart wasn't in it. Even one sloppy drunk young lady looking for company that night gave the man in uniform her best shot to no avail. So the crowd slowly drifted away with a pat on his back and left him with Billy and his dad.

Tommy and Jimmy were never much for dialogue, but that was OK. They were used to each other's silence. Besides, Billy did enough talking for everyone. He filled Tommy in on everything that went on since he'd left. That took all of five minutes. Yet Jaime Jo remained the elephant in the room everyone tried to ignore.

The appearance of Jo Bob Buckner didn't help the situation. "Just came to offer a little toast to our hero here after serving his country," Jo Bob said in answer to the less than welcoming glare from Jimmy. Jo Bob bought a round of drinks.

Jimmy was never one to turn away a free drink, but it didn't slide down his throat very smoothly. "We thank you for the drinks, Sheriff. You can go now."

"But I just got here. Can't I have a drink with an old friend and his son?"

"I may be old, but I'm not blind," replied Jimmy. "I know Judas when I'm looking at him."

"Now why do you need to be such an asshole?" countered Jo Bob.

Jimmy hopped down off his stool and stood face to face with the sheriff. "Who you callin' an asshole?"

Jo Bob shoved Jimmy back by puffing out his chest. "Only but one asshole *in* this place."

Billy Sawchuck could smell the testosterone dangerously rising, so he hopped off his stool and tried to wedge himself between the two rutting males. "Whoa whoa, gentlemen. Love, not war. This is a celebration. Don't make me take you two out to the woodshed."

Tommy's laugh broke the tension. "I'd like to see that. What do you think Chezzy? You think either of those two roosters'd ever be caught dead in a woodshed with our Billy taking a switch to their backsides?"

When the two men looked down at Billy coquettishly batting his eyelashes, they couldn't help but break out in laughter themselves.

"That's right," announced Billy, strutting back to the bar. "Don't get me riled. Not unless you want a taste of this," he added, flexing what should have been a bicep.

Jimmy still would have preferred Jo Bob get the hell out of there, but he decided he'd try to tolerate the man and not let him get under his skin. After all, he had some drinking to concentrate on.

So taking advantage of Jimmy's reprieve, Jo Bob decided during a game of pool to see just where Tommy's head was at these days. Tommy was just about to sink a ball when Jo Bob asked, "So when you gonna' see that girl of yours?"

Tommy didn't think the momentary hesitation before taking his shot was even noticeable. And he did sink the ball. "Whom would you be referring to, Sheriff?"

"Touché," chuckled Jo Bob. "You know, her little Scarlet's gonna' be a looker too."

"I guess I should pay my respects at some point," replied Tommy, sinking another ball.

Jo Bob studied his subject. "You seem pretty reserved about the whole thing."

"Well, sir, things change. I guess I did some growin' up over in Nam. I'm not the same boy I was back then. You pick up a little self control when lives hang in the balance."

"So you sayin' I don't need to worry about you and her?"

"I'm sayin' I've changed. A man tends to handle situations differently than a boy would." With that, he looked hard at the sheriff, eye to eye.

That look made Jo Bob vaguely uncomfortable. And it wasn't the scars that done it. He wasn't exactly sure what Tommy meant, and how exactly Tommy planned to handle what situation. But he thought maybe he was just being a little paranoid and decided to take Tommy at his word.

When Jo Bob looked down at the pool table again, he saw the boy'd cleared it during their little chat. He watched Tommy toss his pool cue on the table and head back to the bar. The boy certainly had filled out since the time Jo Bob tossed him onto that bus. A repeat of that task wouldn't be so easy this time.

Tommy didn't notice when the sheriff left. The Jack Daniels had him feeling a little too good to notice much of anything. But as bad as Tommy was, his father was worse.

"Hey, Billy, would you do me a favor and make sure my dad gets home OK?"

"Sure, but where are you going?"

"Just want to get some air before I go home," he lied.

Billy gave him a once over and said, "Don't do anything I wouldn't do."

"You mean have sex with a woman?" Tommy laughed. "Not likely. Don't know any around here anymore," he announced, as he pushed through the door of Chezzy's.

Well, there was one woman he *did* know. At least he used to. Just the one Billy was worried about. But Tommy was feeling the Jack Daniels. And when he stepped out into the sweet night air to the old familiar song of crickets, Tommy had no say in the matter. His Camaro knew the way to Jaime Jo Tremper's place by heart.

Chapter 7

Even in the dead of night, the sight of the Tremper place was as familiar as the North Star, a beacon drawing Tommy home. In days past, Tommy'd driven by that house so many times, he knew every strip of wood siding, every shingle of roofing, and certainly which window was Jaime Jo's. That's where his eyes always came to rest. Many a night, he'd driven past the place, slowing to see if he could catch a glimpse of Jaime Jo's silhouette, a hint of the precious pearl trapped within the unwelcoming prison.

Tommy pulled off the road, across from the house, killing his motor. He felt a refreshing chill from the night air, but not enough to cleanse his blood of the Jack still drowning out the sheriff's warning. He lay back against the headrest of his bucket seat, his gaze locked on her window. He sniffed for any scent of her, even though he knew she'd never been the type to wear perfume. Her daddy would never have allowed it anyway.

For a second, he thought he saw a shadow move across her window, and felt something pound in his chest. But then it was gone. Probably just the curtains moving in the breeze. He'd have known if it was her.

Did she still love him? It had been two years. Things change. His face was a mess. She had a baby now. She'd probably moved on. But back then, nothing could have come between them. Tommy tried to stop it. They both did. He knew it wasn't good for her. But they just couldn't, neither of them. They were crazy in love.

He couldn't remember how many times they'd met over at the abandoned quarry, a sort of poor man's lover's lane where all the kids went for some privacy. Tommy and Jaime Jo couldn't be seen together, or the preacher would be sure to find out. Tommy would wait for her, wait to see the headlights of Billy's ugly little car she'd borrowed emerge from the night. Then they'd both hop out of their cars and dive into the back seat of the Camaro. Sometimes only the warning light of the eastern horizon would tear them apart. She'd have to get home before her daddy found her empty bed. Then they both would somehow drag themselves through the school day, dreaming of the sleepless night before.

Yeah, they were crazy in love. And they stayed that way, even long after the beatings began. It would have killed her eventually. Tommy was actually relieved, in a way, the day the sheriff escorted him to the bus headed for boot camp. He knew he couldn't end it on his own. And neither could she. They weren't strong enough. They couldn't help themselves.

The whole town knew Tommy was beating her. She denied it, and Tommy wouldn't even talk about it. But everyone knew. Neither Jaime Jo nor Tommy could offer any plausible explanation for the bruises. People can let a thing go for quite some time before gathering the gumption to address it. And it wasn't any different concerning Jaime Jo and Tommy. But gossip can be a powerful thing in a small town. That's when they got the sheriff involved.

Tommy never had any control over the situation. And that's how he would remember it, even later in Vietnam. He'd dream that everyone in the whole town of Pleasant Valley was pointing their fingers at him, insisting he put an end to it. But he couldn't. He just couldn't. It was out of his control. Unless they could be separated. And she'd have died if they weren't.

He'd dream of those beatings he'd never consciously witnessed. All he knew was that the next day, after one of their rendezvous, Jaime Jo looked like she'd been in a brawl. It frightened Tommy to see the results of their time together, what he'd caused. So every night in Nam he'd dream of those beatings, of beating Jaime Jo, and he'd wake up hating himself for it, for all the pain he'd caused.

* * * *

Jaime Jo recognized the sound as soon as she heard it. She'd know the rumbling growl of Tommy's Camaro anywhere. She'd been asleep. But the familiar sound woke her instantly. She lay there in bed for a second, unsure of what to do, because whatever it was she did, she knew there wouldn't be any rational thought behind it. No, it would be completely irrational. It would be based on fear or love, dread or longing, but not on reason. So she threw the covers back and went to the window. Not too close. She didn't want to be seen. But close enough to see out into the night.

She saw the Camaro. Not that that was so new. She'd seen Tommy's father driving the thing around town. Even then, she'd feel her heart reflexively miss a beat or two. But she knew it wasn't Tommy. He was gone, in Vietnam. But this was different now. Tommy was back. And his Camaro was parked across the street from her house, in the middle of the night. It was him, all right. She stepped back from the window and threw herself on her bed.

She didn't know what would happen next. How long could they last, so close, yet just out of reach? She felt the pull of him, like a magnet, like gravity, like hunger. How does one ignore the laws of nature, suspend gravity, go without food? It was only a matter of time. And then what? Would it start up all over again? Would history repeat itself? How long would she be able to hide the bruises? People were already staring, right through her clothes, just waiting for the first sign of trouble.

She wished it didn't have to be this way. She wished he'd never come back, or that she'd moved away. She wished she were dead. She wished... she wished he'd come up to her room already.

* * * *

She was crying, but Tommy didn't stop. He couldn't. He wanted her so badly. He'd ripped her nightgown off, his pants down around his ankles. He had her pinned to the bed. He was so hard it ached, and all he could think of was entering her and driving home until his pent up desire erupted and they melted into one.

Just one problem. She wouldn't stop crying. So he continued striking her. She wanted him to do it. She wouldn't submit to him unless he beat her. She wanted him as much as he wanted her. Only it had to be this way, him beating her, forcing her. She insisted on it. It was the only way.

His own fist began to throb from the pounding. He wondered if he'd broken his hand. That's how much it took this time. That's when she finally gave in and accepted him. They were joined. The pain in his hand was immediately forgotten. He no longer heard her screams. He was home. Home, and headed for heaven. All his pain and troubles and memories forgotten. He was driving home. He was almost there.

He could hear his heart pounding. He saw flashing lights. The pounding grew louder. The lights turned blue. He opened his eyes to look at her.

It was Sheriff Buckner pounding his flashlight against the door of the Camaro. The blue flashing lights of the police cruiser reflected off Tommy's rearview mirror. What the hell? Tommy looked about. The sun from the eastern horizon met his eyes. It was morning. His head hurt. Where was he?

"Get out of the car, Son," the sheriff ordered.

Tommy was still fuzzy on the situation. "What? Why?"

"I said get out."

Accustomed to obeying orders from authority, Tommy automatically reached for the door handle, but winced in pain on his first attempt to open the door. Something was wrong with his left hand. He reached over with his right and opened the door.

Standing up was no easy task. Things wouldn't stand still. Tommy remembered the celebration at Chezzy's.

Sheriff Buckner was studying him. "What do you think you're doing here?"

Tommy hesitated a moment, then figured there wasn't anything wrong with the truth. "Just sleeping in my car."

"I can see that. But where were you last night?"

Tommy was confused. "You know where I was. You were there too. At Chezzy's."

"Don't fuck around with me. I meant *after* that."

Tommy didn't know where this line of questioning was leading. "I got a little shit-faced, so I pulled over here to sleep it off. You didn't want me driving around like that did you?"

The sheriff didn't answer the question. "Why here, of all places?" he asked, nodding across the street at the Tremper place.

Tommy turned toward the house and froze, suddenly realizing exactly where he was, and that it was the last place he'd wanted the sheriff to find him. "I... well... I guess it was just instinct. You know, old habit. Like I said, I was drunk."

"Old habits. That's just what I'm afraid of." The sheriff continued to stare at him through his mirrored sunglasses.

Unable to read the sheriff's eyes, Tommy couldn't help squirming under the stare. "It's not like I went inside or anything."

"No?"

"What? No. Of course not."

"What happened to your hand?"

Tommy didn't realize he was rubbing his throbbing left hand with his right. When he looked down at it, he saw the blood.

"I... uh... I don't know. I guess I hurt it somewhere."

"No kidding. Where?"

Tommy thought for a second, but nothing came to him. "I don't recall."

"That ain't exactly no paper cut. You'd think someone would remember how something like that happened."

Tommy felt the first twinge of panic. "I told you. I was wasted," he shouted.

The sheriff took out his cuffs and cuffed Tommy to the door of the Camaro. Then he took Tommy's keys and started walking across the street toward the Tremper place.

"What are you doing?" shouted Tommy.

"It's called an investigation," answered the sheriff without turning around.

"Investigation? Investigation of what?"

"Just responding to a call for breaking and entering. Possibly worse."

Tommy yanked on the cuffs. "What? Who called you?"

"Preacher called me," answered the sheriff as he knocked on the Tremper's front door with his flashlight.

Tommy's eyes shot up to Jaime Jo's window, then down at the cuffs. He was beginning to realize how trapped animals could gnaw their own paws off in order to escape.

"It's about time," said Warren Tremper, opening the door for the sheriff. "I was about to go out there and take the law into my own hands.

"Calm down, Warren. Just tell me what happened."

"What happened? He beat the shit out of her. That's what happened."

Jo Bob took the door from the preacher and slowly closed it, carefully noting to himself no signs of forced entry. "Did you call for an ambulance?"

"No. She wouldn't have it. Says she's fine," answered the preacher.

Jo Bob paused. "You say he beat the shit out of her, and she says she's fine. Well, which is it? You know I'm not big on making social calls this time of day. Haven't even had my coffee yet."

"Oh come off it, Sheriff. You know the drill. He beats the shit out of her. She denies it and protects him. Nothing new here."

Jo Bob couldn't deny history. That's exactly how it went, time and time again, until he ran Tommy Harris out of town and things calmed down.

"Well, let's go survey the damage. Where is she?"

Jo Bob followed the preacher up the narrow staircase to Jaime Jo's room. They found her sitting at a mirrored vanity applying her makeup.

"Tell him," ordered Warren Tremper.

Jaime Jo continued applying her makeup. "Tell him what?"

"You know what. Tell him what that animal did to you."

"I'm just fine. No one did anything to me."

Jo Bob was experiencing déjà vu, having repeated this scene many times a couple of years ago. "A country girl like you always wear that much makeup so early in the morning?"

"It's for work," answered Jaime Jo.

Warren Tremper thought he had her. "You don't even have no work today."

"Do too," Jaime Jo replied without missing a beat. "Told Frank I needed some extra hours." She'd become an excellent liar over the years. "So if you gentlemen will excuse me…" she said, turning to face her questioners.

Jo Bob tried to see through her makeup, but couldn't see a thing beneath all the layers of crap she'd caked on her face. In fact, he couldn't see any skin at all through her long-sleeved blouse and jeans. Well, she wasn't wearing gloves, but her hands seemed to be OK. He took a deliberate scan of the room, which didn't seem to be disturbed. No blood that he could make out. The window was intact.

He looked her in the eye. "Your daddy says that boy out there handcuffed to his car attacked you. Is there anything you want to tell me?"

Jaime Jo hesitated before answering. There was something to tell, all right. But she didn't know how. She looked over at her father and saw in his eyes what he wanted her to say. She thought of Tommy Harris handcuffed to the sheriff's car. Then she looked in her mirror, hoping the girl she saw there would speak up, would tell the truth, would say all that needed to be said, all that had remained unsaid for years.

Her thoughts were interrupted by a familiar car horn coming from the street outside her window.

The sheriff peered out the window to check on Tommy Harris who remained cuffed to his car door.

"It's that Sawchuck boy."

"Billy's my ride to work," confirmed Jaime Jo. "So, again, if you gentlemen will excuse me…"

Her father looked at the sheriff, hoping the interrogation wasn't over yet.

Jo Bob turned his palms up and shrugged his shoulders in defeat.

Jaime Jo went back to applying her makeup.

The interview was over.

Jo Bob exited the Tremper home to find Billy Sawchuck chatting it up with his prisoner, who seemed noticeably relieved when Jo Bob removed the cuffs and told him to hit the road with a familiar warning about the Tremper girl.

Both Tommy and Jo Bob, for the first time, noticed the shattered driver's side mirror on Tommy's car. They also looked down at the bloody glass on the pavement below.

Tommy Harris still held his throbbing left hand as he got in his car. He took one last look up at Jaime Jo's window before getting in his car. As he drove off with a spray of gravel, he could see the preacher through his rearview mirror sitting on his front porch cradling a baseball bat in his lap. Tommy thought the man was smiling.

Upstairs, Jaime Jo could barely stand up from the pain. She didn't know how she'd make it to Billy's car without someone to hold her up.

Chapter 8

The good old days aren't always so good. That's what Jaime Jo was thinking as she sat in the passenger's seat of Billy's car watching him secure Scarlet in the back. She'd made it from the house to the car with Billy's help. Billy was always there for Jaime Jo. He was frantic over her condition and wanted to take her straight to the hospital. Jaime Jo didn't conceal her limp from her father's watchful eyes as they crossed the porch to the car. She didn't feel she had anything to hide. Her father knew just what was going on. He'd always known the truth.

Ever since her first date with Tommy Harris, her father knew. Well, it wasn't a date. She didn't have her father's permission to go. She never even thought to ask. It was just a few kids meeting at the Dairy Queen for some ice cream after school. That was nothing new. She'd never felt obliged to tell her father before. She wasn't even sure Tommy would be there.

But he was. And that made all the difference. It wasn't just a bunch of silly girls anymore.

"Vanilla or chocolate?" he asked, sneaking up behind her. His warm breath on her ear made her shiver.

She remembered him from the county fair. The voice was deeper than she was accustomed to with her girlfriends, a little scary at first. But then she'd found herself entranced by it, the vibration of it resonating right through her.

"Vanilla," she replied.

And like a servant to his master, Tommy was off to slay the mighty vanilla soft serve for his princess.

Jaime Jo couldn't hold back a giggle when her friends elbowed her over the older boy's attentiveness. He even paid for the ice cream, no small matter, as Jaime Jo wasn't always able to scrape enough change together to do anything other than watch her friends eat without her.

She loved having Tommy there. Everyone was watching. She basked in the attention, something entirely foreign to her. Ever since her mother had passed years before, she'd been starved for attention. While her father devoted his life to God, Jaime Jo grew up in his house like nothing more than a portrait on the wall, something pleasant for guests to look at, yet, over time, completely ignored by the occupants of the home.

But now there was Tommy Harris. Not only was he infatuated with the portrait, he'd even taken it down off the wall, carried it about with him, and showed it off for all the world to see.

Waiting for her ice cream, Jaime Jo couldn't wipe the smile from her face as she sat glowing among her dateless friends like a diamond among some sorry bits of coal.

"When I told him it was for my girl, he threw in the sprinkles for free," boasted Tommy upon returning.

My girl, thought Jaime Jo. She was someone's girl.

"Thank you. But where's yours?"

"Oh, uh, I'm in training. Might try out for football or something," he replied, not wanting her to know he only had enough money for the one cone.

"You don't look fat to me," she countered dubiously, knowing someone like Tommy would never be a fit with the football team. "You can share mine."

Tommy ended up eating more than his share, just like a boy. But Jaime Jo didn't even notice. After all, the ice cream wasn't the treat that had her feeling all warm inside. It was Tommy.

She was appreciative of the fact that her friends had given her some space to be alone with Tommy. Others, however, weren't so accommodating. Boys kept showing up to tease him about his new girlfriend. Boys that never would have given her the time of day seemed suddenly upset that someone like Tommy Harris would pick up what they'd so casually discarded. Tommy coolly brushed them off like pesky gnats, that is, until one of the more brazen ones from the football team sat down next to Jaime Jo and put his arm around her shoulders, as if she was some kind of community property. Jaime Jo assumed it was just to tease Tommy and didn't think it was a big deal. But she still didn't like it. And Tommy could see it in her face.

"Take your grubby arm off her," he ordered, calmly, yet firmly.

"Why? Are you two married or something?" the boy countered.

Jaime Jo appreciated Tommy's attempt to unburden her from her unwelcome suitor, but didn't think it was worth a big argument.

Apparently Tommy didn't think it was worth any further discussion either. He took a simpler approach toward conflict resolution. His fist hit the boy's face so quickly that Jaime Jo didn't even notice until the boy's arm slipped from her shoulder and he fell backward off the bench next to her.

"What happened?" she asked, looking down at the boy on the ground who was checking his face for broken bones.

"I guess he slipped," answered Tommy with an innocent shrug of his shoulders. *He slipped all right. He slipped by putting his arm around my girl*, he thought. *He won't make that slip again.*

Jaime Jo looked him in the eye. She knew there was more to the story. But she let it slide. "I just hope you're not one of those macho Neanderthals. I think violence is a real turn off."

Tommy made a mental note of her warning. He wouldn't need to be told twice. Not where Jaime Jo was concerned. He'd just been converted to a sensitive champion of nonviolence, despite what they would later say.

Tommy walked her home. Even if he were prohibited from slaying any dragons, his mere presence would be sure to ward off all manner of threats to his fair maiden.

Jaime Jo'd lost track of the hour, so that by the time they reached her house, the sun was beginning to set. The glare of the setting sun's reflection off the window at the front of her house obscured the fact that the preacher had been sitting there for the past hour peering down the road for any sign of his child's return.

Since he'd lost his wife, the girl was all he had, other than God. He always prayed the Lord would keep watch over his little girl, but some things called for a father's attention. Now one of those things was walking down the road toward his house. And it was holding his daughter's hand.

Jaime Jo hadn't even thought about any reaction her father might have had to a boy walking her home from school after some ice cream. But Tommy had. He wanted to make a good first impression and was looking forward to meeting Mr. Tremper, or whatever the proper salutation for a preacher would be? Father Tremper? Well, whatever it was, the confidence of a teenage boy was sure it would work out just fine. After all, he'd made sure the man's daughter was safe walking home. Surely Tommy's gallantry wouldn't go unnoticed.

"Get your hands off my daughter." It wasn't an angry shout or anything. That might have been preferable. But it wasn't anything like that. It was a direct order that didn't seem to need any additional theatrics. It was cold and threatening. It was serious.

Tommy's mouth reflexively opened to say something in objection, but the totally unexpected greeting left him mute. His hand, however, knew what to do. The preacher's order went in Tommy's ear and right down his arm, leading his fingers to obediently open, dropping the girl's hand. His hand surrendered before his mind could counter the attack.

He and Jaime Jo looked at each other, watching the mutual joy of the past couple of hours drain from their faces.

Jaime Jo turned back to her father, innocently imploring, "What's wrong, Daddy?"

"Get in the house," her father ordered, not even looking at her, his eyes fixed on the boy.

"But—" started Jaime Jo, looking back at Tommy. But she was cut off as the preacher grabbed her by the wrist and tossed her through the open front door.

"Mr. Tremper—" began Tommy, stepping forward tentatively.

He stopped when he saw the preacher 's hands covering his ears.

"I don't want to hear it. What ever might come from your mouth is surely the word of the devil. I know what lives in the minds of teenage boys. And I'll not have it sullying my daughter. I'll not have it, I tell you."

By that point, Tommy had shifted from love-struck teenager hoping to impress his girl's father to indignant young man.

"All I did was hold her hand."

"And you expect me to believe that? You think I'm a fool? Holding hands is not what teenage boys are interested in. Oh, they'll hold hands before. And maybe after. It's the part in between that bothers me. And that's all that teenage boys care about. The devil lives within them. Every one of them."

"What are you talking about, before and after? All we did was hold hands. Ask her yourself."

The preacher rose to the boy's challenge, pointing a finger in his face.

"Oh, don't worry about that. I'll ask her all right. And don't think I won't get the truth out of her. She'll tell me everything. Every sick, perverted act."

Tommy found himself backing down the porch steps under the preacher's verbal onslaught. Anything Tommy said seemed only to make things worse. Before he turned to leave in confusion, he took one last look to see Jaime Jo at an upstairs window, the window to her room he would later learn. There she stood crying uncontrollably, pulling at her hair.

Distracted by Jaime Jo's distress, he could no longer make out the words of the preacher's diatribe, but he knew it was time to go, if nothing else, just to diffuse the situation. He would regret leaving her, as he would every time he let her go home, home to the frothing monster screaming at him from the front porch.

And Jaime Jo, she would regret not leaving with him. She wasn't seen at school for a week.

* * * *

Billy Sawchuck could barely keep his eyes on the road as he drove Jaime Jo to her job at the diner. He kept glancing over at the wounded bird next to him in the passenger seat. She may have been cloaked in pants, long sleeved shirt, and makeup, but Billy could see through all that. He'd seen it many times before.

True, it'd been a while, but some things you don't forget. Like when someone you love is hurting. They might smile and joke, but a true friend sees right past it all, to the stiff way they sit, afraid to move lest some deep-seated pain finds its way to the surface, to the sunken eyes trying to recede from the cruel world they've seen, to the frozen expression reflecting a heartless existence.

"Well, that didn't take long," he began, referring to the first beating since the return of Tommy Harris. "Just like old times," he added, trying to engage the numb thing in the passenger seat. He knew it was a cold thing to say, but he thought it might work like smelling salts to snap her out of it and bring her back.

Jaime Jo brought a trembling hand up to her aching cheek as a stream of tears found its way out.

Billy was encouraged by any sign of life. "You can't allow this to happen. Not again."

Jaime Jo looked at him through bloodshot eyes. "What am I supposed to do? I was asleep in my own bed, for God's sake."

Billy'd heard all her excuses before. "You're not a little girl anymore. You're an adult. You've got your own little girl now. You've got to stop him."

"But how? I don't know how." The tears resumed streaming down her face.

He tried not looking at her. Billy couldn't stand it when she cried. It always went right through him. And before he knew it, he was crying too. It was hard to see the road in front of him.

But he knew what the solution was. It was always the same. Only she was never willing to do it before. Maybe this time she'd listen.

"You have to stop it. Tell Buckner. Tell him everything."

When she didn't respond, Billy abruptly stopped the car and turned to look at her. There was a trickle of blood coming from her ear. He felt himself gag at the sight of it.

"I'm taking you to the hospital." He put the car back in gear and stomped on the gas.

"No!" she shouted, grabbing him by the arm.

He slowed the car. "Is it your ear? Didn't you hear what I'm telling you?"

She hesitated. She would have liked the excuse, but she heard him. Every word.

"You have to tell. You have to. Did you hear me?" he repeated, impatiently.

"I heard you. I heard you," she confessed.

But Jaime Jo'd heard it all before. She'd played this scene with Billy many times. She knew the lines by heart.

"I can't. He'll kill me."

Billy, too, could follow the script.

"He'll kill you if you don't."

Chapter 9

With a kiss on her forehead, Billy placed Scarlet within her playpen at Frank's Diner. He then scrambled back outside to help Jaime Jo from the car. With one arm around her waist, and another holding her arm about his shoulders, Billy half-carried his wounded comrade inside.

Frank looked up from the register and observed the scene suspiciously as Billy lowered her into one of the dining booths.

"What's all this about?"

Billy looked at Jaime Jo, who started to speak until he interrupted her.

"Female trouble," he offered, giving her a private wink. "You know how they get a certain time of the month."

Frank wasn't sure he was buying it, but he certainly wasn't about to discuss it either.

"Well, how are you gonna' work in that condition?"

Jaime Jo started to get up with a wince. "Oh, I'm OK. Just let me get dressed and—"

But Billy cut her off. "Nonsense," he said, gently urging her back into the booth. Then, grabbing an apron, "Looks like I'm your new waitress, Frank. You always did want to see me in that uniform."

"Waitress?" Frank whined skeptically.

"Where's my miniskirt?" teased Billy, moving behind the counter. "Or would the customers prefer me in hot pants?"

Filling in for Jaime Joe at Frank's Diner was just as bad as Billy Sawchuck thought it would be. No, it was worse. He was feeling a little dizzy from the pesticide. He'd just used up a whole can of the stuff trying to kill a cockroach that confronted him when he'd gone to get some pie for a customer. Frank handed him the can of Raid when he heard Billy scream for help.

Billy couldn't believe Jaime Jo did this every day. Gathering dirty dishes, cleaning crumbs and ketchup off countertops. No normal person should have to stoop so low. That's why you hired laborers to do such lowly work. Between the filthy cleaning rags and the soapy dishwater, his hands were a disaster. The whole thing was a nightmare. He didn't know which he wanted to do first, shower or have a manicure. Either way, Jaime Jo owed him big time.

Perhaps hoping to forget the deplorable situation in which he found himself, Billy's mind wandered back to the first time he'd noticed Jaime Jo Tremper back in high school.

It wasn't actually Jamie Jo that caught Billy's attention. Billy had his eye on Tommy, his first crush, but the object of Billy's attentions never knew it. Tommy Harris was beautiful, but he would never see Billy's attraction as anything more than a lonely outcast in need of a friend, a peculiarly entertaining kid full of goodness, without a bad bone in his scrawny body. Billy wanted Tommy to look at him the way he looked at that little slut named Jaime Jo. What did she have that Billy didn't? Well, OK, so she had tits and a cunt. But that isn't all there is to life. Well, OK, maybe to a 17-year-old straight boy it is. Damn. Just Billy's luck that his soul mate had to be straight. Just another of God's cruel jokes.

The funny thing was, when Billy took his frustrations out on the little slut, spilling his soda all over her in the cafeteria— accidently, of course— or clumsily knocking her books out of her arms in the hallway, the girl took it all the wrong way. Absent any functioning "gaydar", Jaime Jo took his attentions the wrong way. She actually thought Billy liked her, in that awkward way that adolescent boys tend to show their affections. So Billy didn't know what to say when she took him aside one day to gently let him down, calmly explaining to him how she knew he had a thing for her, but that she was in love with another.

When he was left at a loss for words, she must have assumed he was devastated. And when Billy realized this, he couldn't help but break out in laughter. Jaime Jo didn't get it at first, but when Billy explained the situation, the sweet girl felt truly sorry, as if she'd stolen a friend's boyfriend. Billy appreciated her concern, instantly taking a liking to her, and took her to his mom's place where they shared a whole pint of chocolate ice cream and a manicure. They'd been best friends ever since.

Billy sometimes felt the friendship he began with Jaime Jo played a role in the trouble that followed.

Despite the fact that Jaime Jo had succeeded in winning over Tommy Harris, she didn't seem particularly happy about it. Even when she was with Tommy at school, she only seemed to mope about like an undead zombie from some cheap horror flick.

Billy began to wonder if that's what love was supposed to look like. Jaime Jo certainly seemed to be in love with Tommy Harris. They seemed to be inseparable at school, retreating into a world of there own, two lost souls marooned together on a desert island. Yet there were no signs of happiness, no joy. They seemed more like co-survivors of some grievous event, merely finding consolation in each other's arms.

"What's up with you two?" Billy asked, giving Jaime Jo an opportunity to open up.

"What do you mean?"

"What do I mean? You always look like you're on your way to a funeral, maybe even your own, and you ask me what do I mean?"

"Oh, it's just me and Tommy, I guess," she offered.

"What? The honeymoon already over?"

"Over?" she asked with surprise. "It hasn't even started. How could it? The only time I have with Tommy is here at school."

"Really? I thought you'd be all over that sweet thing by now. Cause if you're not, I'm ready to make my move," he joked.

Billy was glad to see even the smallest smile cross Jaime Jo's lips. It had been so long since he'd seen her smile.

"Well, that's part of the problem," she began. "Daddy doesn't like Tommy. He won't even let him come over, and I'm not allowed to go out with him. Tommy's strictly off limits."

"Why is that?"

"Honestly? I think it's just because he's a boy," she answered.

"Well that can't be it. Your father doesn't mind me and I'm a... oh, I see." Then something else occurred to Billy, leaving him almost offended. "Hey, wait a second. Your father knows about me? That I'm... you know?"

Jaime Jo looked at him like he was an idiot. "Well, it's not like we discuss it or anything, but I'm sure he knows. Everyone knows. You don't exactly hide it or anything."

Everyone knows? Billy found the idea frightening, yet, at the same time, somehow liberating. Then, just like that, Billy came up with an idea that would change everything. "Well, if your father feels I'm so safe, why don't you go out with Tommy and just say you're hanging out with me. I'll cover for you."

Jaime Jo jumped into her friend's arms in ecstasy over the precious gift he'd given her. She'd officially become the happiest girl in the world... for the moment, anyway. She just never imagined where it would lead. She never thought of the consequences.

She and Tommy spent more and more time together, at imaginary after school clubs, nonexistent evening sporting events, and even make-believe dinners at Billy's house. Billy always served as her alibi. But he was never there. It was Tommy. It was always Tommy. And Jaime Jo was in heaven.

At least in the beginning. Then things started to change. It was slow. It was subtle. But anyone who really knew Jaime Jo couldn't ignore the changes she was undergoing. Her Billy was the first to notice.

He saw right through Jaime Jo's gradual dependency on makeup not too long after she'd started dating Tommy. That was the first giveaway. After all, Billy was more interested in cosmetics than Jaime Jo was. She wasn't the makeup type, even to impress a boy.

Besides, he couldn't imagine how she was getting past her father wearing all that face paint.

But that was just the start of it. Jaime Jo'd always had a posse of girlfriends. As the makeup got heavier, the friends seemed to fall to the wayside. That was mostly Jaime Jo's doing. She grew weary of constantly having to come up with excuses for the growing number of unexplained mysteries that seemed to surround her.

Why the long sleeve shirts and pants in place of the sleeveless sundresses? Why the variety of ailments that kept her from Phys. Ed. Class? Why the persistent hangdog look, the inattention to personal grooming? For as she wore more and more makeup, she seemed to wash her hair less and less, completely forgetting what a comb or brush was for. Her easy teenage smile had gone, replaced with the bone weary expressionless face of a refugee.

Billy couldn't take it any more. So one day at school, he cornered the pathetic looking girl and asked her all about it. "What's wrong with you?"

Jaime Jo wouldn't look him in the face. "Nothing's wrong with me."

"What do you mean, nothing? You look like you've been dragged ten miles behind a pickup truck."

"Thanks for the compliment," she replied, holding her head in her hands, "but everything's just fine."

Billy wasn't ready to give up. "It's me, Jaime Jo. It's Billy. What's going on with you?"

"I said everything's fine." She turned to walk away from the inquisition.

Billy grabbed her by the arm and Jaime Jo screamed, wincing in pain. He dropped her arm and she cradled it in her other with an involuntary moan.

Billy grew frightened, thinking he'd somehow hurt his friend.

"I'm sorry," he offered. "What happened? I didn't mean to hurt you."

Jaime Jo was rubbing her arm, attempting a smile to cover for her unexpected reaction to Billy's touch. "It's nothing. Don't worry about it."

But Billy *was* worried about it. He reached for her hand this time, gently, and before she could pull it away, he yanked her sleeve up, exposing her arm.

Jaime Jo tried to cover it up again, but couldn't pull it away due to the pain shooting down her arm. She covered her eyes with her other arm as if that would keep Billy from seeing her.

"What's this?" asked Billy, mouth agape, staring at Jaime Jo's arm. Her wrist was red and raw as if it had been restrained in some fashion. The rest of her arm was covered by a multitude of bruises in various stages of healing, a virtual rainbow of discoloration, from red to black and blue, and ultimately fading to a jaundiced yellow.

Jaime Jo turned her head away in shame. "Billy, don't."

"How did this happen?

"It's no big deal," she answered, unwilling to look him in the eye.

"No big deal? It could be broken. Did you have it checked out?"

"I'm sorry, Billy. I just don't want to talk about it." She turned to leave.

To stop her, Billy grabbed her by the other arm. And when she winced in pain again, he pulled up her other sleeve, yielding a view identical to the first.

"Oh my God," he said more to himself than anyone. "I'm such an idiot." Grabbing the bottom of her sweater, he pulled it up to examine her back. More of the same.

Billy lowered the sweater and gently took his limp and crying friend in his arms and soon they were crying together. Billy wanted to soothe her in his arms but he was unsure where he could place them without touching a wound and adding to Jaime Jo's pain.

After Billy'd cried enough, he felt outrage rising in his throat.

"Who, Jaime Jo? Who did this to you?"

Jaime Jo just shook her head in silence.

"Come on, now. You can tell me. It's your Billy."

She just shook her head again.

"Are you afraid to tell? You know I can keep a secret. Come on, we'll work this out together. You can't do this alone."

Jaime Jo looked at Billy, considering his offer for a moment, only to turn away again.

Billy was frustrated. "Jaime Jo, come on." Then, more calmly, even though it was unimaginable, he had to ask, "Is it Tommy? Is Tommy Harris hurting you?"

Jaime Jo immediately turned back to Billy with a look of horror on her face, opened her mouth to say something, but then caught herself again, and lowered her head in silence.

Billy couldn't believe it. She didn't have to say it. The look on her face said it all. He'd easily guessed her secret, as only a close friend could. Tommy Harris.

Billy'd guessed it, all right, but that didn't mean he could comprehend it. It just didn't add up. Not the Tommy Harris Billy Sawchuck loved and adored. Not *his* Tommy.

Billy felt like the wind had been knocked out of him. But he knew that was nothing compared to the pain Jaime Jo'd been enduring. Billy had to act. With a hand under her chin, he raised Jaime Jo's face so he could look her in the eye.

"We're going to the police."

Her eyes went wide, and then she began shaking her head back and forth emphatically.

"I... I can't," she said.

"But why? Are you afraid of him?" Then Billy stopped, slapping himself in the forehead. "I'm such an idiot? Of course, you're afraid of him. What about your father?"

Jaime Jo gasped, eyes wide, and in them Billy witnessed fear like he'd never seen before.

"But he'll know what to do. You have to tell him."

Jaime Jo's fear turned to anger. "No, I don't."

"But why?"

Jaime Jo looked him square in the eye. "He already knows."

Now Billy was at a loss for words. Maybe he hadn't heard right. "Your father already knows?"

She nodded her head yes, wiping tears from her eyes.

"So it's done then. Your father went to the police, right? He put a stop to it," he added, taking her in his arms again.

Jaime Jo just lowered her head, shaking it no.

"What do you mean? Why doesn't he stop it?"

"God's will," she muttered.

"God's will?" asked a bewildered Billy. "What's that supposed to mean?"

"He says I deserve it, as punishment for my sins."

"Sins? What sins?"

Jaime Jo lowered her head, embarrassed. "You know. For being interested in boys. For them being interested in me."

Billy looked at her as if she were speaking in tongues. "But that's normal. That's no sin. And even if it were, it doesn't justify allowing someone to be beaten to death."

Jaime Jo just sat there, cradling her battered body, unconsciously rocking back and forth.

"Jaime Jo. You have to report it. You have to put an end to it."

"I can't." It came out more as a feeble squeak than anything, as she started crying again. "I can't."

"Well I can. I'm talking to Tommy Harris."

And so he had. He'd talked to Tommy Harris about it back when it all started. Tommy didn't really fess up to anything. But he never denied any of it either. Said that was Jaime Jo's call.

Well, here they were again. No sooner did Tommy Harris come home from the war than Jaime Jo began turning up black and blue again. Billy didn't know where it would all end. But he didn't think it would be in a good place.

Chapter 10

Tommy Harris looked at the dilapidated trailer he shared with his father. It wasn't even good enough for a trailer park. Instead, it was just parked on an empty patch of dirt someone let them use. Appearances no longer mattered to Tommy's dad once his mom died. And liquor used up any money that might have gone into a better place. Besides, it was within hiking distance of Chezzy's. Like Tommy's father always said, location, location, location. But it was all Tommy'd ever known growing up. He was used to it. Tommy'd grown used to a lot of things.

Like the expression on his father's face when Tommy walked through the door. It was that same look someone gives a dog that isn't quite house-trained and leaves a present for you on the kitchen floor. Disappointment.

Tommy knew his father could always tell when something had happened, as if he could smell Tommy's guilt and frustration. Never mind that the man was a broken alcoholic. That only made it worse, that one from such a low vantage point could still manage to look down upon him.

Tommy'd nearly been arrested for assault and battery upon Jaime Jo Tremper, a predicament not unfamiliar to him. But unlike that first time around, two years ago, he was used to his father's looks. The accusatory looks from others hardly affected him anymore.

"Where you been?" his father asked, trying to keep the whiskey-induced tremor from spilling his cup of coffee. He hadn't been home much longer than Tommy. But Tommy'd left the bar much earlier than he had. So when Jimmy'd finally managed to drag himself home from Chezzy's long after sun up, he'd expected to find the boy already in bed.

Jimmy Harris's memory wasn't so good anymore. But he still remembered those nights a couple of years ago when his boy managed to get himself all tangled up with the preacher's daughter. Jimmy Harris knew that when he got home before his son did, trouble would surely follow. It was just a matter of time.

"Nowhere," Tommy replied from the kitchen sink, trying to wash off his bloody hand without his father seeing.

"Nowhere, huh? Is that where she lives now?"

"Who?"

"You know who. The Tremper girl."

"What makes you think I was over at her place?"

"Just an educated guess."

Damn him. "And when did you get so educated?"

Jimmy Harris put his cup down before he spilled it. "No need to get all uppity with me, Son. You know I'm only lookin' out for you."

Tommy turned off the faucet and turned to his father. "I'm sorry, Dad. I didn't mean nothin' by it. I know you're just concerned."

"And do I have reason to be?"

The two stared at each other, one waiting for an answer, the other wondering what it was.

Tommy wanted to tell his father he had nothing to worry about, that the whole thing with the preacher's daughter was behind him, ancient history. But he couldn't. He didn't honestly know. Oh, he knew he still had feelings for the girl. Always did. Always would. But he was older now. He'd seen a few things. He wasn't a kid anymore.

And Jaime Jo? She'd had to grow up pretty fast too, being a mother and all. Tommy had no idea where Jaime Jo stood on things. But he didn't want to do anything that would hurt her. Never had. He still remembered the day Billy Sawchuck confronted him about the situation.

Billy appeared out of nowhere, shoving Tommy roughly in the chest. Tommy had just returned from the football field where he'd made a halfhearted tryout for the team. That was back when he still had thoughts of trying to impress his father, before he'd decided that earning the respect of a man who had so little for himself wasn't worth the trouble. He didn't even make it through the whole tryout, instead stopping for a smoke out at the bleachers after the coach pissed him off. Oh, he knew the whole idea was ridiculous. Tommy's aversion to authority and pack mentality would always sabotage any effort at fitting in on a team. That was something only the military had the tenacity to instill in him.

He was still wearing his shoulder pads and it must have looked comical, scrawny Billy Sawchuck with the swish in his walk, shoving the tall prospective linebacker. Tommy thought maybe it was one of Billy's jokes.

"What did you do to her?" Billy demanded in a high-pitched voice, his face all screwed up like he was going to cry.

"Nothing you'd be interested in. Why? Are you jealous?"

Normally, Billy would have come back with a line about how he was jealous of Jaime Jo, not Tommy, but not this time. "Fuck you!"

Tommy good-naturedly picked his friend up in a bear hug to drop him in the towel bin, but Billy wasn't playing around this time, and struggling, managing to scratch Tommy in the face.

"Whoa there, big fella," said Tommy, putting Billy down. "You're serious. What's going on?"

"You tell me," answered Billy. "Why are you doing it?"

Tommy was confused. "Doing what?"

"I saw them," Billy began. "I saw the bruises. She's got them all over. Don't play dumb with me."

Suddenly Tommy realized what it was all about. But he wasn't prepared to have that conversation. "I don't want to talk about it." He turned to walk away.

Billy grabbed him by the back of the jersey. "That's it? You don't want to talk about it?"

"That's right," answered Tommy, swiping Billy's hand away. "It's none of your business."

"None of my business? She's my best friend in the world. Whose business is it?"

Tommy stopped walking for a second, hoping something would come to him. But nothing did. "Just drop it, Billy. It's got nothing to do with you. Get lost."

Billy wasn't going anywhere. "So you know all about it. You admit it."

"Yeah, I know all about it. How could anyone not see what's happening to her?" He paused, holding back tears. Tears of sadness? Or of shame?

Billy came to accuse Tommy, never really expecting to have his suspicion confirmed. So now that he'd heard Tommy's admission of guilt, at first he couldn't believe it. But then he found himself saying something he never thought he'd hear coming from his lips.

"Leave her alone, or I'll kill you." Billy Sawchuck was prepared to fight over a girl.

Tommy didn't know what to say. He had no intention of fighting Billy.

Billy smelled weakness and took advantage to press his attack. "You have to stop it."

Tommy raised his arms and squeezed his head in his hands out of frustration. "I don't know how."

Billy wasn't letting him off that easy. "Then you have to get help. You have to tell someone."

Fear crossed Tommy's face. Then sadness. "I can't."

Billy was dumbfounded. "Well if you won't, I will."

Tommy looked like a wild boar cornered by a pack of hounds, eyes wild, adrenaline pumping, the moment when they're most dangerous. Tommy lunged at Billy.

Billy flinched, thinking Tommy was striking out at him. But Billy wasn't Tommy's target. It was the water fountain next to him. Tommy ran into it with his shoulder in perfect linebacker form. It bent halfway to the ground. Then Tommy kicked the battered stainless box to the ground, water shooting from its ruptured pipes.

Then he turned to Billy, still in a rage. "No! She won't allow it!"

Billy was frightened by Tommy. But not so much he'd give up on Jaime Jo. Was Jaime Jo so in love with this monster that she wouldn't let anyone know what was going on for fear of losing him? Billy just couldn't accept that. That was a load of horseshit.

"*She* won't allow it? *She* won't? Or *you* won't? What about *you*, Tommy?"

Tommy was calming down, having taken it out on the water fountain, now battered and bleeding on the ground. "I'm sorry, Billy. But I swore I wouldn't say anything."

Tommy still remembered the look on Billy Sawchuck's face. Disbelief. Disenchantment. Disappointment. It was the same look Tommy'd given his father, watching him stagger through the door every morning reeking of whiskey. It was the same look his father was giving him now.

"Don't worry about me, Dad. You just worry about yourself."

"It just don't work that way, son. A man never stops worrying about his kid. Don't think I wasn't thinkin' about you everyday over there in Nam. Ain't enough whiskey in the world can wash those thoughts down."

"Don't blame your drinking on me."

"That's not what I'm sayin' and you know it. I'm just praying you'll stay clean. Don't let that girl ruin you, boy."

Tommy looked at his father, the man telling him not to let a girl ruin his life, a man barely able to hold a cup of coffee. He was looking at a ruined man, ruined by a girl, Tommy's mother. She was the world to Jimmy Harris. And when she passed, so did Jimmy. The faded shadow trembling at the kitchen table was all that remained. Well *his* girl had died. There was no helping that. But not Jaime Jo. She wasn't dead. And as long as she lived and breathed, there was still hope for Tommy. He knew that now. Looking at the remains of his father, he knew it. He wouldn't let the same thing happen to himself, no matter who stood in his way.

Tommy could see how people might see it that way, that he'd let that girl ruin his life, or more likely, that he'd ruined hers. But he knew better. He knew that's not what happened. Sure, he could see how it might look that way to the town of Pleasant Valley. Shit, he'd even believed it himself a couple of years ago. But that was then. He was just a stupid kid in love then. Maybe he was just as stupid now, stupid for coming back to this town at all, let alone to her. But at least he was older now. He wasn't a kid anymore.

And yet, was he ready to go down that path again? He felt as though he had no choice. He'd walked away last time. He took their offer, a way out. But that seemed a lifetime ago. He'd spent two years in goddamned Vietnam. He was tougher now. He never ran from a fight in Nam. He wouldn't do so now. He'd do whatever he had to, whatever it took.

But would *she*? That was the question. He needed to know. Was *she* tough enough? Would she walk through hell *with* him? That's all he needed to know. Would she look past the repulsive scars he'd earned in Nam and still see the prince that came to save her? Because if she would, if she'd follow him through hell, he'd take her there. He'd take her there, and right out the other side. As long as she loved him. If she did, there'd be no stopping him. He could do anything. Hell would be a walk through the park. They'd come out the other side in no time, and never look back. As long as she loved him. And that's what Tommy aimed to find out.

He grabbed the keys to the Camaro and headed for the door.

"Where do you think you're goin'? Tommy, don't—"

His father's plea was cut off by the slamming screen door. Tommy gave the old man left standing anxiously at the door a wave as he left the trailer in a cloud of dust.

Chapter 11

She couldn't just sit there all day watching Billy do her job for her. Maybe if she got up and made herself useful it would take her mind off the pain, both physically and mentally. Like the athletes say, maybe she could walk it off. The least she could do was serve the coffee. Yet even that seemed to come at a cost. Simply serving coffee brought her face to face with the town of Pleasant Valley.

If Jaime Jo held a grudge against every customer at the diner who'd rubbed her the wrong way at one time or another, she'd have to set a torch to Frank's place. But the sad fact was that a preacher's pay didn't support a grown daughter and her baby. Jaime Jo needed the work.

It seemed every gossiping biddy in Pleasant Valley managed to wander into Frank's at some point in the day, if for no other reason than to check out the latest goings on with Jaime Jo Tremper. There wasn't a whole lot that went on in Pleasant Valley, North Carolina. But if something were going to happen, they all knew it would start with the preacher's daughter. Jaime Jo could feel them eying her as if she were that two-headed calf at the county fair.

But she'd grown used to all that. Let them gawk and pray she did something wild and dangerous. Maybe she would someday. Someday… Maybe someday she'd pull a shotgun out from behind the counter and blow them all away, her childlike face frozen in a wicked grin as she picked them off one by one.

But so much for wishful thinking. She knew she didn't have it in her. The Lord just wouldn't have it. Besides, the old biddies weren't the only customers that left a bad taste in her mouth. There were things worse than gossip. And one of them was sitting at a window seat.

So she swallowed her pride and served Jo Bob Buckner his coffee just like everyone else. Of course his role in Tommy Harris's deportation to Vietnam had a lot to do with it, but that wasn't the only thing. She knew he had a job to do, and at the end of the day, it probably saved her life. She wouldn't have lasted much longer if someone hadn't intervened. No, that wasn't it. Even without that, Sheriff Buckner had plenty going against him in Jaime Jo's book.

The man was a pig. And not the messy kind. No, he was the kind of pig that never seemed to be embarrassed when a waitress caught him trying to peek down her blouse as she brought the check, or up her skirt when she reached for supplies on the upper shelf. And she'd catch him looking all the time. But instead of turning away like an embarrassed schoolboy caught cheating off of someone else's exam, he'd look right back into her eyes with a dumb grin on his face as if he'd won at some game only he knew the rules to, daring her to go best out of three.

Today was different, though. When Jaime Jo placed the cup in front of him, he didn't even seem to notice her. He was distracted. He was staring out the window of the diner like a starving man eying a steak dinner, like there was either an eight-point buck waiting to be shot and mounted over the sheriff's mantle, or there was a wet T-shirt contest going on. But that wasn't it. Jaime Jo saw exactly what it was as soon as she followed his gaze outside.

Tommy Harris's Camaro was parked across the street.

Jaime Jo almost spilled the coffee as her hands started to shake and she felt her guts twist. She hoped briefly that it was just his father Jimmy that drove the car into town. But no such luck. He was in there, all right. She could see him, just sitting there behind the wheel, staring, staring across the street, right through Frank's window, into her eyes, right down to her soul. And she could feel it, his stare, just as if it were a bullet.

She'd seen his car at her house the other night, lurking in the darkness. But this was broad daylight. Shameless. No fear of what anyone might think. She wondered if he'd come into the diner. She hoped he wouldn't. She hoped he would just go away.

She felt gossiping eyes boring into the back of her head.

"Looks like you have an admirer," the sheriff said to Jaime Jo, without turning from the window.

Jaime Jo didn't feel the need to respond. But that didn't mean others wouldn't. She could hear the murmurs behind her back.

"In broad daylight."

"The boy's got no shame."

"Someone ought to do something."

"No choice but to put a rabid dog down."

Jaime Jo thought maybe if she ignored the situation it would go away. So she turned and went to refill the coffee pot, feeling the eyes boring holes in her sore back. But when she got back to the kitchen, her knees suddenly wouldn't hold her up anymore and she had to sit down before they gave way.

Jo Bob Buckner watched Jaime Jo Tremper's ass as she turned for the kitchen. Damn, they grow up fast. He couldn't really blame Tommy Harris for wanting a piece of that. Just why couldn't he do it without all the rough stuff? Sure would make Jo Bob's life a lot easier.

He wasn't deaf, after all. He could hear the murmurs too. And he knew what they meant. Why wasn't he doing something about all this? Why didn't he get up off his fat ass and do his job? Those nagging old biddies. It reminded Jo Bob why he'd never married. Yet here he was having to put up with the nagging of not just one woman, but a whole town full. Couldn't a man enjoy a cup of coffee in peace?

The perfect shape of Jaime Jo Tremper's ass driven from his mind by the images of old biddies, he turned back to the window, hoping the Camaro was gone. No such luck. Damn, that boy was persistent.

Well, there just wasn't any way around it. He figured he'd better go take care of business before he changed his mind. Jo Bob Buckner was apt to change his mind when it meant avoiding responsibility.

When did taking care of such a small town like Pleasant Valley become such a chore? The answer, he knew, certainly seemed to have something to do with that boy parked across the street. And sometimes the best path to the goal line wasn't an end around but a run straight at the opposing player.

Jo Bob could feel the eyes prodding him from behind as he left the front door of Frank's and ambled across the street. He had hoped the boy would take off at the site of an approaching sheriff. No such luck. Apparently this wasn't the same kid that let the sheriff lead him by the ear onto a bus bound for war. No, this kid was made from tougher stock than that. He'd been trained for battle and thoroughly tested. It wasn't exactly clear how well he'd handled the testing part. But he was here after all. He'd survived. And there were only two grades in war. Pass and fail. Tommy Harris made it back alive. He'd passed. And hardened by the experience, he wouldn't give ground just because some small town sheriff was approaching to give him a hard time. The kid was tough.

"Sure is a fine morning, ain't it?" Jo Bob began, leaning against the boy's car, trying not to let the facial scars intimidate him.

"Can't argue with you there, Sheriff," answered Tommy.

"No, I don't suppose you could." Jo Bob was deliberately taking things slowly. Calmly. "Well, at least we can agree on something. That's good."

Tommy continued staring across the street at Frank's.

Jo Bob turned toward Frank's to follow Tommy's gaze. "And that Jaime Jo sure has grown into a fine young woman, hasn't she? Can we agree on that?"

No reply from Tommy.

Time for Jo Bob to step it up. "I said, can we agree on that?"

Tommy finally turned to the sheriff. "A little on the young side for you, don't you think, Sheriff?"

"Can't argue with you there, boy. Nevertheless, her being so fine and all, what do you say we agree to leave her that way... in one piece... if you know what I mean?"

Tommy narrowed his eyes at the sheriff. "No, Sheriff, I don't know what you mean."

"All's I'm sayin' is it'd seem such a shame to spoil somethin' so pretty, you know, ruin it. Like stompin' through a bed of flowers. Or bruising a perfect fresh peach. Can you agree with that?"

"Oh, I imagine I like a pretty flower or a succulent peach as much as the next man, all right, but I'll be damned if I know what the hell you're gettin' at."

Jo Bob began to see the boy was going to be difficult. So much for the nonconfrontational approach. Time for plan B. He didn't really have a plan B, but Jo Bob could be quick on his feet when the situation called for it.

So he leaned down toward the window of the Camaro and spoke quietly. "What I'm gettin' at is this. What do you say, you just leave that poor girl alone?" Seeing his words barely register on the boy, Jo Bob's hopes of a rapid resolution to the problem quickly dissipated.

"I'm just sittin' here in my car, Sheriff," Tommy finally replied.

Well, so much for the direct approach, thought Jo Bob. Rapidly advancing to plan C, the in your face approach, he responded, "And I've got no problem with that. Just why don't you go sit in it somewhere else?"

"But this is a public street, Sheriff. And I'm properly parked, not bothering anybody. Is that a crime?"

Jo Bob's blood began to rise. He wasn't ready to reach for his gun yet, but his temper had already skipped several plans and was rapidly approaching plan Z.

"Now I've asked you nicely. So why don't you just take my advice, throw this thing into gear, and move on out o' here?"

Tommy took a moment to look the sheriff in the eye and size up the threat. "I'll thank you for the kindly advice, Sheriff, but I'm afraid I'll have to decline it. I'm not breakin' any laws sittin' here. It's a free country."

The boy certainly had changed, realized Jo Bob. This was no scared young kid starin' him in the eye. Not any more. Jo Bob could feel it. Tommy Harris must have seen some real shit over there in Nam. And he wasn't about to be intimidated by some small town sheriff. Jo Bob didn't know whether to reach for his handcuffs... or his gun.

But he quickly realized his momentary indecision was a mistake, a sign of weakness, as Tommy Harris took the lead.

"So why don't you mind your own business and go finish your coffee, maybe have another donut?"

Jo Bob swore he could feel a vein popping somewhere in his brain as he backed off the window and his right hand involuntarily came to rest over the gun in his holster. He soon found he'd lost that quiet let's be reasonable tone to his voice.

"Mind my own business? Now you listen to me, boy. *You* are my business. That young girl in there is my business. This town is my business. And I'm beginning to agree with more than a few folks around here sayin' maybe you never shoulda' come back. But seeyin' as you're already here, maybe it's time you moved on."

Despite the escalation in tension in Jo Bob's voice, Tommy maintained his cool, if not cold, demeanor. "I'm afraid I'm unable to oblige you there, Sheriff. It seems I've still got some unfinished business to take care of."

Well, Jo Bob tried. He did his best to try and settle things peaceful like. He'd gone through all the plans he had, A through Z, but all to no avail. The time had come for action. Jo Bob didn't need any dumb plan for that. All a man needed for that was a big ol' pair o' balls. And Jo Bob could feel his twitchin' for a fight.

"Just who the hell do you think you are, boy? I'm givin' you an order." Kicking the car door with his boot, "Now take this piece of shit out of here or I'll have it towed with you in it right out of town!"

Tommy's calm deliberate manner of talking cut right through Jo Bob like a knife, and that knife seemed to be poised right up against those big ol' balls of his. "You touch me or this piece of shit, and I won't be responsible for what happens to your fat ass, Sheriff, *sir*."

Jo Bob felt briefly confused. He never expected something like that. Why would he? No one had ever dared speak to him that way before. But none of that mattered. It didn't matter what he'd expected or thought about. Because all the plans were over. He was working on raw instinct now. And those balls of his were runnin' the show.

Jo Bob stepped away from the car, pulling his forty-five from its holster, finger at the trigger, taking a bead right between the boy's eyes. "Now you listen to me, you pathetic psycho—"

The bang that followed shook the car.

Chapter 12

Shock was exactly the effect Jaime Jo meant to have on the two men when she slammed the passenger door of the Camaro closed. She never knew, however, just how close the startled sheriff's itchy trigger finger'd come to accidentally blowing Tommy Harris away as a result.

She saw both men turn, wide-eyed, to find her sitting there in the passenger seat. She saw the fear in both their eyes, balls or no balls. The fear, however, quickly turned to confusion, silently asking what the hell she thought she was doing in Tommy Harris's car?

That was the same question she was asking herself. She hadn't exactly taken the time to think it all out. She'd just acted.

Resting her wobbly legs back in Frank's kitchen, she'd heard the usual morning customer chatter turn funny. First it got kind of quiet, as though the whole place were suddenly distracted by something. Then the normally whispered and murmured remarks resumed, only at a much louder level, as if meant for everyone's ears.

"This is gonna be good."

"'Bout time that sheriff got up off his ass and did somethin' 'bout that boy."

"Lookit now. He's gone and pissed Jo Bob off."

"I don't like the looks of this. Someone's gonna' get hurt."

That's when Jaime Jo decided she'd better get back out there and see what was going on.

They were all gathered about Frank's window, pushing and shoving each other for position, craning their necks for a better view. Jaime Jo approached the window to see just what all the commotion was about. When people noticed Jaime Jo, they practically parted for her as if she were royalty. They knew she was as much a part of the spectacle out on Main Street as the two rutting bucks locking horns out at the Camaro. Everyone knew Jaime Jo was the spark to the fireworks. She deserved a front row seat.

And she knew they were staring at her. They wanted to see her reaction to the events out on the street. It must have been a real treat for them to finally see Jaime Jo Tremper and Tommy Harris in the same scene again after all these years. Things had gotten exceedingly dull in Pleasant Valley without Jaime Jo and Tommy to stir things up.

But Jaime Jo didn't care about all that. She'd grown used to being a source of entertainment for those with no lives of their own. What concerned her more were the events unfolding across the street. She never expected to see Tommy Harris again after they shoved him onto that bus to Vietnam. And when she'd heard like everyone else that he was coming home, she'd wished it weren't true.

Yet there he was, not 50 feet from her. He'd changed. Even seated inside his car, he seemed bigger, colder, more... dangerous. And even from a distance, she could see something had happened to his face. But he was still Tommy. Jaime Jo saw right through the muscle, the wild unkempt hair, and the scars, to see the same 18-year-old boy that stepped on that bus out of town three years before, the same boy that couldn't live without her, the one she herself couldn't walk away from.

She quickly saw something else unchanged, the fact that whenever she and Tommy Harris were near, someone was going to get hurt. And as she saw the sheriff rest his hand on his holstered firearm, she sensed this time it would be Tommy Harris.

That was the last thought she remembered. Because when the sheriff drew his gun and aimed it at Tommy, Jaime Jo'd already stopped thinking. It wasn't a conscious decision she'd made. Her legs decided for her. And her legs decided to give the crowd just what they'd come for. A show.

"Where you going?" shouted Billy as she ran for the front door to Frank's.

"Take care of Scarlet," she shouted, without turning back.

The crowd at Frank's closed ranks about the window again when they saw Jaime Jo Tremper bolt through the front door.

She didn't know what she was about to do. Would she tackle the sheriff? Would she jump in front of the gun? Or would she grab it, shoot Tommy Harris and then herself in a double murder suicide and never be troubled by the whole thing again? That'd be some show for the crowd at Frank's window, wouldn't it? She didn't know what she was going to do. She just did it.

She jumped in the passenger door of the Camaro and slammed it shut. Seeing the confusion in the two men's eyes, she reached across the car and turned the key in the ignition. Hearing the souped-up chariot's 400 horses roar to life, she sat calmly back in her seat and said, "Take me out of here."

The two men remained frozen for an instant.

"Now!" she ordered.

Tommy looked back at the sheriff's gun drooping from neglect, put the car in gear, and followed orders. He took one last look in his rear view mirror at Jo Bob Buckner, standing in the middle of Main Street confused as all hell, before crossing the bridge out of town.

As the car carried them away from town, they both sat silently staring straight ahead, like two strangers on a bus. They hadn't spoken for three years. And there was a whole world they'd left unsaid since parting. Still, they'd never exactly been the introspective conversationalists, and neither imagined they'd be able to start right back where they'd left off only to navigate those dark and treacherous waters again.

That's certainly not what Jaime Jo wanted. Sure, she'd acted on instinct when she extricated Tommy from the brink of disaster back in town. And her heart ached to reach out and touch his face as soon as she first saw the disfiguring scars up close, her Tommy's beautiful face left behind in some filthy cave halfway around the world.

But that didn't mean she intended to let Tommy Harris creep back into her life. That life was over. She'd survived it somehow, battered and bruised, physically and mentally. But that was then. She'd moved on. And she had no intention of going back.

At least that was the plan, as the town behind them faded into the countryside, and the world became less and less civilized.

* * * *

No face is perfect. They've all got their blemishes, a mole, a freckle, a pockmark. Yet, for those who know the face, those blemishes are all part of what makes that face unique, able to be discerned from a crowd. And so it is with small towns, whether it be a rusty abandoned water tower, a weathered barn that leaned too far over one day and collapsed, or a stretch of old railroad track from some bygone era running along the edge of town like a poorly healed scar. Folks would pass by these remnants of town history without a thought for why they were there or for removing them. They just were.

The old quarry on the outskirts of Pleasant Valley just was. A gaping ulcer in the wilderness with an access road winding along one edge to the quarry floor, it looked as if some developer had planned a man-made lake, but running out of money, lost interest in the project and forgot to add the water.

No one even recalled what its purpose was, what was pulled from that hole in the ground. But looking at it now, one could see what it had become, what purpose it had taken on. Mostly, it had become a junkyard, a place to abandon things no longer wanted, mangled cars long ago stripped for parts, assorted refrigerators, washers and dryers, their white porcelain skins reflecting the harsh morning sunlight, even a few of the very bulldozers and backhoes that created the quarry sat glued to its floor like prehistoric dinosaurs caught in a tar pit. Splatters of rust clung everywhere, like cancer, slowly consuming its victims.

There were, however, some signs of life, hints at a new purpose. In some areas, the floor of the quarry'd become more glass than dirt, broken and shattered glass, a sparkling testament to those who'd come before, mostly beer bottles, a sign of times both good and bad, eventually used for target practice, seasoned with a spattering of empty bullet casings and shotgun shells.

And clothes, assorted undergarments draped here and there, forgotten amid the beer and the heat of long summer nights, a testament to those with no place of their own to share their love. Jaime Jo Tremper and Tommy Harris had been to the quarry before.

But that seemed a lifetime ago. It all looked so different to her now, no longer their private place under the starlit night. Now, in the harsh light of day, she saw it for what it was. A grave. A hole in the ground where things came to die and be forgotten.

And maybe that's how Jaime Jo Tremper felt about Tommy Harris and herself, their time together, the relationship they'd had. A dead thing. A thing of the past, to be laid to rest, buried and forgotten.

Tommy couldn't be sure how Jaime Jo felt. Yet, as he parked the Camaro at the quarry floor, coming to rest with a crunch of shattered glass, he heard the old quarry speaking to him, as it did to Jaime Jo. Only he saw things a little differently. He saw the pain and despair of shattered glass and shotgun shells. He saw the rusting metal of passing time, time lost forever. But he didn't see death. He didn't see a grave. Oh, he could appreciate the lowness of the place, dug deep in the ground. But he saw it more as a bottom than a grave. Just a bottom, a place stripped down to rock, where one couldn't drop any further. But hitting bottom, there was no place to go but up. And that's what he intended to do, to stop falling. He'd found the bottom, and now it was time to change direction, to pick himself up, dust himself off, and look upward, toward blue sky, once again. That's what he'd decided to do, to find his way up and out.

But not alone. He knew he hadn't reached bottom alone. He'd found it with Jaime Jo. They'd hit bottom together. And that's how he'd rise up, with his Jaime Jo. Together.

She stared out at the harsh landscape of the quarry and asked, "Why?" summing up all her questions in one word.

Tommy hesitated, unsure what she was asking, but he loved her, and he thought that would probably explain why he'd done anything over the past four years, ever since first laying eyes on her.

So before he could reply, Jaime Jo made it easy for him, narrowing down the inquiry. "Why did you have to come back?"

Tommy felt a wave of relief. That was an easy one, despite the fact that he'd never actually thought it out before. He'd never seriously considered any other option. As soon as he stepped on that bus to Vietnam, he knew he'd be back, not necessarily to Pleasant Valley, it didn't matter where, but back to his Jaime Jo, wherever she was. Even if, in his absence, she'd left town for parts unknown, escaped, he'd track her down. Like a champion coonhound, he'd locate the scent and wouldn't rest until he'd found his prize and cornered it, or run it up a tree.

Well, here he was. And here she was. She'd made it easy. She stayed put. And when he approached, she didn't run. She came to him.

"Where else would I go?" he replied.

Jaime Jo didn't hesitate. "Anywhere but here."

Tommy reached for her hand, "But—"

"No. Don't." She pulled her hand away. "I can't do this."

The melancholy buzz of cicadas filled the painful silence like moans of anguish.

"You can," he began, tentatively. "You can do this."

"No... I can't." And she lowered her head in despair.

Tommy went to put his arms about her, but she slipped away, slamming her shoulder against the door of the Camaro and bolting from the car. She thought of running, but conflicted, stopped and leaned her back against the door.

Tommy calmly exited the car and went around to her side. He approached her as he would a skittish colt. He didn't bring her there only to drive her away.

"It doesn't have to be that way," he said, keeping some distance. Jaime Jo looked at him as if he were speaking in tongues. She didn't understand how he'd come to that conclusion. Of course it had to be "that way." She'd never known it any other way. He couldn't understand. He'd never exchanged an innocent date for a concussion. He'd never traded kisses for crutches. He'd never woken up in the hospital wondering how he'd gotten there and how many bones had been broken.

"There's never been any other way," she insisted, looking him in the eye. "I don't know another way."

"That was before," he said. "We were just kids then."

Jaime Jo wished she could understand. "I don't feel any different," she began. "Nothing's changed for me. Have you changed? Are you saying you've changed?"

Tommy took a moment to think, to ponder her question. But it didn't take long. The answer came to him immediately. Yet he didn't want to give an automatic reply, in case his reflex was wrong. He wanted to be sure. He didn't want to deceive her. He wanted to mean it.

Jaime Jo took his pause, his deliberation, as doubt. So when he answered her question, she wasn't ready to believe him.

"Yes," he replied.

She couldn't contain a small cynical chuckle. "Right. And how's that? How have you changed?"

This time there was no hesitation. Tommy didn't have to think. He wasn't a kid anymore. He was much stronger this time. He'd been tested. He couldn't really say he'd won that battle over in Nam. But he'd survived, come home alive. And that had to count for something. Yes, he'd changed. He'd definitely changed. Tommy Harris was done taking orders. No one was going to tell him what to do. It would take more balls than Jo Bob Buckner's to put him on a bus now, more balls than you could count in all of Pleasant Valley. Not that he wanted to stay. He didn't give a shit about Pleasant

Valley. He'd almost stayed on that bus from Fort Bragg and kept going right on out the other end of town. But that would have been *his* choice. The more they wanted him to leave, the deeper he'd dig in his heels. Maybe if they elected him mayor and got on their fucking knees begging him to stay, that's when he'd go. But no one was going to run Tommy Harris out of town. Oh, and one more thing. This time, when he did finally decide to go, he'd take what was his with him.

"How've I changed? I'll tell you how. This time, when I leave this shithole of a town, I'm taking you with me."

Jaime Jo was taken aback. She'd never seriously thought of leaving Pleasant Valley, just running away, simply because she knew her father would never let it happen.

"Just up and leave?" she began. "That's your solution?" She looked him in the eye. "What about my father?"

Tommy looked away under the intensity of her gaze. He looked somewhere off in the distance. When Jaime Jo tried to see what he was looking at, she didn't see anything there. But she could tell he was looking at something. And it had his undivided attention, like an alert hunting dog that smells or hears something its human master cannot, when it senses its prey. She was about to repeat her question when he replied.

"Your father?" The words came from Tommy's mouth, but to Jaime Jo it sounded like someone else speaking, like someone else occupied his body, channeling their thoughts through him. It was a cold voice.

"Your father?" the voice repeated with a chuckle. Then, after an eerie smile formed on his lips, "If your father comes between us again, I'll kill him. Then he can go rot in that hell of his he likes preaching about so much all the time."

Silence filled the quarry. Jaime Jo had no words, caught completely off guard.

He had changed. She never thought she'd ever leave Pleasant Valley, that someone would take her away. Ever since her mother died, she'd never thought of leaving the nest. She'd had her father and the church. Then Billy. Everything was OK. For a while. Then Tommy came. And everything fell to pieces.

She'd always melted in his arms. He could have led her off a cliff and she'd have followed, smiling. And in a way, that's just what they'd done. They'd walked right off that cliff. But he never asked. They just did it. Together. Without a thought, without a word, they walked hand in hand right over the edge. And when he was shipped off to Vietnam, that's where she was left, battered and bleeding at the foot of the cliff.

But this was different. This time they knew what they were getting into. They weren't blind anymore. They could see the cliff this time. And here was Tommy, holding out his hand, and asking her to follow, to trust him. Maybe he thought he was leading her away from that cliff. But she saw it differently. With Tommy Harris, she saw only cliffs... in every direction. She didn't see any way down.

So when he told her he'd kill her father and take her away, she panicked. She didn't think. She just ran. Jaime Jo ran from the car, from Tommy Harris.

He hadn't expected her to run. Why would she? He hadn't even touched her. Was it the scars? He sometimes forgot the profound effect they had on people, the ability they had to make people turn away from him in disgust.

But he never expected that from Jaime Jo. He never expected her to run from him. Besides, there wasn't anywhere to go. They were in the quarry, after all. She couldn't get away. And he wasn't done with her yet. He hadn't told her yet how much he still loved her, hadn't had the chance to ask if she felt the same. And he needed to know. Because if she didn't, if she didn't love him anymore, he was prepared to end it right there, to bury their love right there in that quarry.

So when he saw her bolt, as much as he wanted to take her in his arms, he didn't immediately chase after her. He thought he'd wait a moment, maybe have a smoke. He'd allow her a head start. Maybe she'd cool off when she realized there was no escaping the quarry.

Tommy Harris took the keys from the Camaro's ignition before setting off at a walk after Jaime Jo Tremper.

Chapter 13

Jo Bob Buckner was a man of many theories, and considered himself a scholar on the human condition. The way Jo Bob saw it, a man's ego was a force of energy. And like most forms of energy, it ebbed and flowed over time. One day, that energy might be high, ready to overflow, threatening to literally burst from a man, as measured by the turgor of the wood between his legs. On other days, that energy might be virtually depleted, leaving a man so deflated as to forget his very reason for being, his raison d'être.

That's where the sheriff's run in with Tommy Harris had left him, his balls so drained of energy that Jo Bob could barely get out of bed in the morning. And he wouldn't be the same until he could reenergize, tap into some source that could reinflate his ego.

That's where Charlotte Sawchuck came in. It took a woman. Not any woman. Just certain ones. Every man knows who they are, which ones harbor the energy they need. And Charlotte Sawchuck had it to spare. Jo Bob just had to tap into that source and his ego would be restored. Well he'd been tapping Charlotte Sawchuck all night. So by morning, ridden hard and put away wet, his body may have been weary— after all, he wasn't a young man anymore— but his ego'd been replenished to the brim. Jo Bob Buckner was ready to go back out, face the world, and kick some ass, preferably Tommy Harris's.

The rumors began to fly as soon as the boy'd driven off with Jaime Jo Tremper, rumors that she'd been abducted, possibly even murdered. Soon the word about town was that Tommy Harris stormed the diner, dragging his struggling victim out into the street by the hair as she screamed for help.

And the rumors didn't stop there. After all, the whole abduction took place right under Sheriff Buckner's nose. The man just let it happen. They all saw it from the window of Frank's, the sheriff's inability to intervene when duty called, just when the sleepy little town of Pleasant Valley finally needed the protection they all paid him for. Seeing the Camaro ride out of town with their Jaime Jo, they all stared in disbelief at their sheriff left standing alone in the middle of Main Street, his limp and drooping 45 a testament to his impotence.

Jo Bob Buckner's fierce reputation on the football field had long ago faded. But he'd continued to walk about town with that gun at his hip. That still counted for something. Yet now, it appeared, even that was just for show. As his waist slowly expanded from too many donuts at Frank's, and beers at Chezzy's, the sheriff's gun wasn't the only thing hanging below the man's waist that began to look small by comparison.

But it was time to stop wallowing in defeat, crying about it like a little girl. Jo Bob's mojo replenished, thanks to Charlotte Sawchuck's magic, it was time he addressed the problem head on. It was time to deal with Tommy Harris.

Jo Bob's first stop would be the preacher's place. Best make sure the girl was OK. After all, she hadn't been seen in a week. Jo Bob assumed she'd be there, otherwise her father would have said something, reported her missing.

The drive out to the Tremper home wasn't so bad, Jo Bob still feeling the effects of Charlotte Sawchuck as his sheriff's cruiser came to a stop amid the crunch of driveway gravel. Yet, as soon as he exited the vehicle and saw Warren Tremper open the front door, the euphoria of the previous night quickly dissipated. Time to get back to work.

Warren Tremper stood, arms folded, with his back against the front door. Jo Bob wasn't feeling the love. But then he never did around the preacher.

"Hey, Warren," Jo Bob opened pleasantly.

"Hey, yourself," the preacher answered mechanically.

Jo Bob noticed the man didn't move to invite him into the house.

"You'll have to excuse my absence from church this week," began Jo Bob. "You know how it is."

Apparently the preacher didn't. "No, Jo Bob, I don't know how it is. Why don't you tell me?"

What an asshole, thought Jo Bob. Even small talk turned into a jousting match with the man. He ignored the question.

"Well, you know I'm never missed over at the church. But your Jaime Jo's another story entirely. The whole town's talking."

Jo Bob thought he could see the hair on the back of Warren Tremper's neck stand up.

"What business is that of theirs?" asked the preacher. "Do they come to church to find salvation or gossip?"

Just no talking with the man, thought Jo Bob.

"Now Warren, they all know about the little show in front of the diner the other day. I'm sure you could understand how they'd be concerned about her welfare. After all, no one's seen the girl for a week."

"And what's it to you?"

Jo Bob was feeling about as welcome as a snake down a muskrat hole.

"Look Warren, is the girl home or not?"

Warren Tremper clearly didn't like being pushed.

"I don't think I like your tone, Sheriff." He paused to watch the color in the sheriff's face rise. "Yeah, she's home. I haven't let her out for a week."

"You haven't let her out?"

"Let's just say she's under protective custody."

Jo Bob wasn't sure he liked the sound of it. Something told Jo Bob he'd better see the girl for himself.

"Well if something's happened to her, it's my job to get to the bottom of it, take a statement against the boy."

"I must confess, I'm not moved by your concern. Is it true that animal snatched her right from under your nose and you didn't stop him?"

Jo Bob was taken aback by the insinuation. After all, the girl jumped in the car of her own free will.

"That's not exactly what happened. Your daughter—"

"My daughter was abducted by a vicious animal and you didn't lift a finger."

"Now just hold on there. I—"

"You what? You watch my daughter dragged from the middle of town in broad daylight and you show up here over a week later wondering if she ever turned up?"

Jo Bob knew enough not to attempt a reply. Let the man have his say, get it out of his system. He did his best to take it like a man with a minimum of eye rolling.

"What would you like me to say, Sheriff? What is it you want to hear? What if I told you she was dead? That would solve all your problems, wouldn't it? I mean, you seem so concerned. I'm sorry my girl's caused you so much trouble, put you out and all. And here you could have been sleeping in this morning. How is Ms. Sawchuck these days?"

That was it. Jo Bob had given him plenty of line, but comes a time to start reeling things back in under control. He'd naturally been startled by the preacher's talk of his daughter being dead, but it took a jab at Charlotte Sawchuck to snap him out of his inaction.

"Warren, is your daughter dead?"

Jo Bob felt a shiver down his spine when he saw an eerie smile form on the preacher's face.

"You'd like that, wouldn't you? Make your life a whole lot easier."

Jo Bob stood his ground and waited, but the preacher just looked right through him, smiling.

"Warren, I asked you a question."

Warren Tremper hesitated another moment, enjoying the sheriff's discomfort.

"Well, Sheriff, you'll be sorry to hear my daughter's alive. No thanks to you. I wasn't so sure a week ago. I could hardly recognize her, she'd been beaten so badly."

Jo Bob felt his gut twist. He could have done something. He could have gone after them. He shouldn't have allowed himself disarmed by the girl's apparent willingness to go along with the boy. Jo Bob Buckner had plenty of theories on women, but they were just theories. He never claimed to actually understand them. Even years ago, when the whole trouble started, Jo Bob's instincts told him the boy wouldn't hurt that girl. And yet, he'd been wrong then. Now those same instincts had failed him again when they kept him from shooting out the Camaro's tires as it fled the diner last week. He had to make things right.

"I'd like to have a word with her, get a statement against the boy."

The preacher seemed to be weighing his options.

"She's not taking visitors just yet."

Jo Bob felt bad about what happened, but not so bad as to let someone interfere with an investigation.

"Are you saying she won't talk to me?"

"Oh, she'll do what I tell her."

"I don't doubt that. But look here. How do you expect me to do my job if you won't cooperate?"

Jo Bob waited for a reply, watching the gears in Warren Tremper's head turn.

The preacher finally pushed the door behind him open, but held a finger up in front of the sheriff's face.

"You wait here. I'll see if she's up to it."

A few minutes later, the preacher stopped short coming back downstairs when he found the sheriff in his parlor snooping around.

"I thought I told you to wait outside."

"Oh, the sun's starting to heat up out there, Warren. I didn't think you'd mind."

"Well I do."

"So how's your girl?" asked Jo Bob, ignoring the preacher's protest over his trespass.

"She'll do the best she can. But don't take long. You'll see she's pretty poorly just yet."

"You know me, Warren. Gentle as a lamb," as Jo Bob followed him up the stairs to the daughter's room.

Even though the preacher had informed the sheriff that the girl'd suffered some damage, Jo Bob couldn't help but stop dead in his tracks when actually confronted by the situation. He quickly tried to compose himself at the first site of Jaime Jo Tremper. Out of simple courtesy, he tried to hide the disgust he felt at the first site of the girl's ravaged face. But Jo Bob Buckner was no actor and the girl immediately looked away out of embarrassment.

She wore no makeup this time, no illusions of health, no attempt to hide the truth. And the truth was written, more like beaten, all over her face. The swelling hadn't receded yet. But the initial shades of black and blue had taken on rims of yellow gray with the first attempts at healing.

Jo Bob couldn't be sure if any broken bones were involved, but everything seemed to be straight and roughly where it belonged. He thought he could make out two eyes, but one was so swollen shut, he couldn't be sure. It was the swelling and discoloration that transformed her from sweet young girl to something nightmares were made of. Still, he knew she'd heal in time. This was nothing he hadn't seen before... on that very face. He was reminded of that time, before escorting Tommy Harris out of town, when people forgot what Jaime Jo Tremper was supposed to look like. And yet, she'd healed then, healed up just fine, at least physically.

Despite the fact that her father'd warned her the sheriff was coming up to speak with her, she practically jumped out of the bed at first site of the two men entering her room. Skittish as a hen in a fox's den, she pulled the covers about her as if it were a shield of armor, knowing there would be no escape.

She clutched a bible in one arm, an ancient Raggedy Ann doll cradled in the other, an undersized replica of herself, years of wear and tear evident on its sad little stitched-up face.

Jo Bob had some difficulty finding words. Nothing rattles a big man like a little girl's suffering.

"Jaime Jo, darlin'," he began, "I'm sorry this had to happen to you. But if you'll help me, I can make sure it don't happen again."

Jaime Jo gave no response.

Jo Bob looked over at her father, wondering if the reason was physical or emotional. "Can she speak?"

The preacher nodded his head.

The sheriff looked back at the witness. "Jaime Jo, just tell me what happened."

As soon as the words left his mouth, Jo Bob was sorry he'd said them. A look of sheer terror crossed the girl's ravaged face. As if she wasn't in enough pain, Jo Bob's question only seemed to twist the knife. He felt like he was trying to cross the thin surface of a lake covered by the first ice of winter. Every step his heavy boot took seemed to send out hairline cracks, threatening to completely shatter the delicate surface.

He was so uptight about possibly adding to the girl's pain that he barely even noticed her glance over at her father. But when Jo Bob followed her gaze, the preacher seemed more angry than sad. Jo Bob felt only sad. But he supposed a father had every right to be angry, given the circumstances.

"Don't look at me," said the father to his daughter, losing his patience. "You know what to say. You know exactly what the sheriff needs to hear. How many times we been over this?"

Jo Bob wasn't feeling the love. The man was scolding his daughter. True, she'd gotten herself into this situation. But then again, she didn't beat herself up. Someone else played that role.

He turned back to the girl, who'd turned her swollen face into the pillow, crying. Visibly squeezing the bible and her doll, Jo Bob thought he heard her mumble something. He looked to her father.

"Speak up, Jaime Jo. The man needs to hear it."

Jo Bob looked back at the girl. She wouldn't turn to look at either man, but she managed her two-word confession more clearly this time.

"I'm sorry."

Jo Bob didn't get it. "What do you mean, you're sorry?"

"I'm sorry I sinned. I let the Lord down. I never should have gone with that boy."

Jo Bob wanted to take the poor thing in his arms. "Don't you worry about that, little girl. Just tell me what that Harris boy did."

Now she turned toward the sheriff in protest. "But I deserved it. Everything." She said it with the conviction of a true believer. "I'm a sinner. I knew what would happen. But I went with him anyway."

"But—" began Jo Bob, shaking his head.

"The devil's in me!" she shouted, interrupting him. She suddenly sat up in bed. "Don't you see it, Sheriff? Look at me."

Jo Bob couldn't help involuntarily looking away from the sight confronting him.

"That's the devil, Sheriff. He's written all over my face."

Jo Bob didn't know what to say. The girl just wasn't right. He turned to her father. The preacher almost had a smile on his face, a look of victory, as if the girl had finally seen the light, and perhaps salvation wasn't yet out of reach.

Yet, out of instinct, without thinking, Jo Bob turned back to the witness. She hadn't answered his question. "Did Tommy Harris do this to you?"

In a flash, the religious trance left her, and she seemed to return to Earth. Yet, she glanced again at her father.

"Don't be an idiot, Sheriff," the preacher interrupted. "Of course he did."

"I'm not sayin' he didn't," Jo Bob replied. "I just need *her* to say it."

"What difference does it make if—"

"It was *my* fault!" shouted Jaime Jo. "Don't blame Tommy. *I'm* to blame."

Jo Bob looked to her father once more. At first, the preacher looked angry. Then, feeling the sheriff's gaze, his expression softened.

"Now, Jaime Jo," the preacher began, "it pleases me to see you've learned something, that you're taking responsibility for letting the devil walk into your life. But that's only half the story.

Now it's the sheriff's job to deal with the devil. Stop protecting him. We've gone over this."

It seemed to Jo Bob that the girl'd done pretty well reciting her lines. Yet she couldn't quite stick to the script. She just couldn't utter the words implicating the boy. Her face went suddenly blank. And just as quickly as she'd come down to Earth, she was gone again, gone to a place only she could see.

Frustrated by her silence, the preacher turned to Jo Bob. "Sheriff, I'd like a word with you outside."

Jo Bob took one last look at Jaime Jo Tremper as he followed her father out of the room. Her bible had fallen to the floor and she lay there curled in a ball, clutching her doll.

Then he followed the preacher down the stairs and soon felt relieved to be out on the porch in the fresh air. His relief was brief, however, as the preacher still had something on his mind.

"I've been thinking, Sheriff. She was just fine all this time the boy was overseas fighting for his country. I think another tour of duty might just solve all our problems. What do you say?"

Jo Bob hadn't anticipated the preacher's problem solving skills. Yet despite his desire to make this problem go away, Jo Bob felt jail time was preferable to another ticket to Nam. After all, the boy'd survived one death sentence. It just didn't seem fair to give death another shot.

"Now, Warren, if the boy's responsible for this mess, he ought to be locked up. Two years in Nam doesn't seem to have changed a thing."

"Would if he didn't come back."

"Now that doesn't sound very Christian of you, Preacher. Besides, I don't think they'd take him back."

The preacher looked confused. "They won't take him back? Why, is the war going so well they're turning down able-bodied men?"

"That's just it, Warren. They're taking able-bodied men. The way I hear it, his brain ain't so able-bodied no more. The stress and all. They say he sort of snapped."

The preacher's eyes widened. "Well don't you think we'd all be safer with him snapped over in Nam than here in Pleasant Valley?"

The preacher had a point. Yet it still just didn't seem right. "Warren, the army wouldn't have let the boy loose if they didn't think it was safe."

"You don't think so, Sheriff? I think that's precisely what they'd do. They dumped him on us. He's our problem now."

"Well that may be, but—"

"But nothin'. I think you'd better place a call to Fort Bragg. Maybe talk to a shrink over there. See just exactly what we're dealin' with here. Seems the least you could do. Before he snaps on someone else."

Jo Bob had to stop to scratch his head. The man had a point. A little information couldn't hurt. Might even be helpful in figuring out how to handle the situation. Maybe some kind of medication was in order. Somethin' to calm the boy down, take the edge off. And if they didn't have anything for the boy, maybe they'd have something for himself. Jo Bob wasn't used to all the upheaval. His bowels weren't even regular no more. And Jo Bob's bowels were normally as regular as one o' them Swiss clocks.

"All right, Warren. You win. Don't see why the town couldn't afford a dime for a phone call over to Fort Bragg."

Warren Tremper couldn't hide his smile as he reached in his pocket and pulled out a dime. "Here you go, Sheriff. Just in case the petty cash is short." He tossed the dime to Jo Bob, who caught it before it could hit him in the face.

Jo Bob placed the dime in his shirt pocket and turned to walk to his car.

"The town of Pleasant Valley thanks you, Warren." Without turning around he added, "Will you be needin' a receipt?"

Jo Bob felt bad about the man's daughter and all, but that didn't change the fact that he just didn't like Warren Tremper. Never did.

Chapter 14

Jo Bob wasn't the only one needing his batteries recharged.

Billy Sawchuck couldn't help but notice the sheriff's frequent visits to the house over the beauty shop, to his mother Charlotte to be exact. The man couldn't help himself. Billy knew his mom was a fox. And in a town like Pleasant Valley, she might as well have been Miss America.

It didn't help matters that Charlotte Sawchuck was oblivious to her effect on men. She had a little side job to help make ends meet. She'd bought a secondhand hot dog stand and would tow it to the side of the highway outside of town at lunchtime. Passersby would stop for a quick lunch. Charlotte never noticed that only men stopped. She also never noticed how short her shorts were, and saw nothing wrong with working on her bikini tan on warm days. A five-dollar tip on a dollar hot dog seemed awfully generous, but she'd picked a good location and sold only all beef dogs, so she chalked it up to her good business sense and left it at that.

Sometimes Billy felt sorry for the sheriff. The man couldn't help it, like all those dogs humping trees when the neighborhood bitch was in heat. Billy even took mercy on the man on those occasions when the sheriff had pissed his mother off and wasn't getting any. The matchmaker in him just naturally took over. He considered himself cupid's accomplice. Sometimes Billy's assistance took the form of helpful suggestions for the sheriff's wardrobe. The man simply had no fashion sense and appreciated any advice Billy could give him. Other times, something as basic as a refresher course in the hygienic effects of showering, or a simple reminder on the proper application of deodorant was all it took. After all, Charlotte Sawchuck had never been exactly hard to get.

So Billy didn't hold the sheriff's weakness against him. After all, a man's got needs. So did Billy. He was a man too, after all. He may have been gay, but he wasn't a eunuch. He wasn't dead.

Being gay in 1972 simply wasn't acceptable. But that didn't mean it didn't exist. With sex being the strange and often uncontrollable compulsion it is, people have probably been screwing it up since the beginning of time. Men with men, women with women, parent with child, even shepherd with sheep. You name it, it's been tried.

Billy Sawchuck stopped thinking about it long ago. There wasn't any rhyme or reason. He just did what came naturally... to him, anyway. And as odd as someone might feel himself or herself to be, they soon find they aren't alone. Odd may be unusual, but it's never unique. There are always more where that one came from. Even in a small town. You just have to look harder.

Billy Sawchuck'd looked everywhere. And sure enough, there was a place outside of town, a place people chose to ignore. Like that big ol' wart standing in defiance on the end of Aunt Edna's nose, etiquette dictated that people simply pretend it wasn't there.

It wasn't exactly what Billy was looking for. But it would have to do in a pinch. After all, there weren't many places for someone like Billy to go when he felt lonely.

About ten miles outside of Pleasant Valley, the Adult Junction was a rectangular box of cinder blocks wedged between an old truck stop and a run down motel. The truck stop sold mostly diesel fuel and Slim Jims. The Adult Juction sold most everything else. The motel? Well, let's just say most people didn't stay longer than the required hour minimum.

After Billy'd heard about the latest beating Jaime Jo'd suffered, he knew for sure that the bad old times were back. When he'd gone to drop little Scarlet off from Frank's that day her momma ran off with Tommy Harris, Jaime Jo's father wouldn't even let Billy see her. He said she was in no condition for visitors. That's when Billy knew it was bad.

The whole thing left Billy feeling depressed and powerless to help. So like Jo Bob Buckner, Billy Sawchuck needed his batteries recharged as well. That's when he found himself parking his yellow Gremlin at the Adult Junction.

Nothing like sex to help forget your troubles. Billy loved sex, or anything close to it. Unlike Jaime Jo. Well, Billy could never be sure of what exactly went on between her and Tommy Harris. He could never really get a straight answer out of her. Billy certainly knew what *he'd* like to do with Tommy. And he wasn't shy about letting Jaime Jo know, much to her embarrassment. She'd get all flustered and red in the face.

Billy knew she loved Tommy, but whenever he tried to pull any dirt out of her, it seemed he'd get the same old speech, as if it came right from her daddy the preacher's lips, about how sex was a vile and evil thing, and how Jaime Jo simply didn't see what Billy saw in it, what the big deal was all about.

Well, Billy Sawchuck knew what the big deal was all about. He may not have known about love yet. But sex? He knew all about that. Oh, he knew he'd never find true love at the Adult Junction. After all, the boys and men he found there were more horny than gay. And that meant there was often some buyer's remorse after the deed, after some hard-up farm boy realized what he'd just done. Sometimes that remorse brought with it a threat of violence, but Billy would never put up with anything like that. Not like Jaime Jo. Why she put up with it was anyone's guess, why she wouldn't turn Tommy in to the authorities and be done with it. But that was Jaime Jo's call, her own deep dark secret.

Everyone had secrets at the Adult Junction. The parking was out back, so passersby might not notice where both the postman and the mayor spent there lunch breaks, or which teenagers had given in to the lure of two-dimensional sex, where they could find those magazines that picked up where the Sears catalog left off. The place had a glass front door, but the glass was obscured by wallpaper so no one could see what was going on inside, or who was doing it.

Billy always entered with a sense of exhilaration, a sense that he was about to experience something completely alien to his existence in Pleasant Valley. The strong smell of cleaning ammonia only added to the effect, like smelling salts, awakening something in Billy that was asleep and unconscious, something repressed and too long caged up.

Billy welcomed, like old friends, the magazines lining the shelves along the walls and stacked on the tables in between. Pornography. Despite what Preacher might have to say on the subject, that is if he were capable of the conversation, Billy rationalized that there wasn't anything wrong with it, that it must have been around since the beginning of time. He imagined cavemen painting obscenely posed nudes on the wall of their caves using mammoth blood.

And yet, every year, it seemed, the subject matter grew more and more graphic. The original pretty smiling pinup girls in skimpy outfits soon morphed into totally nude tattooed sluts posed performing acts that would have killed their parents. Eventually, with Billy's wholehearted approval, men began showing up on the glossy pages right along with the women. And it was only a matter of time before things turned really kinky. The evolution to fetish was inevitable, as leather and restraints began turning up everywhere. And finally, the pinnacle, at least to Billy, had been reached when gay porn began finding its way to one out of the way corner of the Adult Junction.

He wasn't alone after all. If a market for gay porn existed, then there truly must be others of his own kind somewhere out there. And yet, not everyone was as in touch with his feminine side as Billy Sawchuck. Whoever was buying the stuff at the Adult Junction must have been so deep in the closet they'd never find their way out.

And it must have been a pretty big closet, because judging by the content of some of the kinkier stuff at The Junction, there must have been quite a few folks around town with dirty secrets. After all, Billy didn't see anything wrong with a little leather or soft bondage, but who was buying all those magazines depicting hard-core sadism, with young women bruised and bloodied by whips and canes? Who could find pleasure in treating people that way? Who was into that kind of shit? Billy found it all more than a little disturbing as Jaime Jo's situation came to mind.

If he'd asked that question of the folks from Pleasant Valley, all eyes would turn to Tommy Harris. But Billy knew better. He couldn't accept the idea that Tommy was that way. Yet what of Jaime Jo? What kind of woman would stand for that kind of abuse? Well that, Billy feared, was much more complicated, as women usually were. It always seemed so easy from those on the outside. No one ought stand that sort of treatment. Simple to just pack up and walk away. Or better yet, forget the packing all together and just run for your life.

But to the woman on the end of those beatings, things were never so clear. In fact, the only clear thing was that leaving was impossible. Only an act of God could extricate them from their plight. Unfortunately, more often than not, that act was their last.

Billy received a knowing look from Lou, the middle-aged proprietor behind the counter. Despite the fact that the man was always friendly to Billy, maybe too friendly, there was just something off about him. Pale pasty skin with hair unnaturally black, like the Ray Ban sunglasses he was never without, the man reminded Billy of Roy Orbison. But Billy couldn't quite figure him out. Despite the odd attraction the man seemed to have for him, Billy was certain he wasn't gay. As of yet, Billy'd remained unacquainted with the concept of pedophilia. Lou, on the other hand, had not.

Lou's wife, Sue, also worked at the Junction, filling in for Lou. She was thin and hard, with short, cropped hair, too many earrings, and never a touch of makeup. Now Sue might have been gay, but Billy's experience was as limited with lesbians as it was with pedophiles. Let's just say Lou and Sue made for an interesting couple.

Billy went right past the sex toys at the back of the place, to gay corner. He wasn't trying to hide anything. On the contrary, he kept hoping someone with similar tastes might find him there. But that had yet to happen. Oh, they existed all right. Of that, Billy was certain. Like raccoons that came in the dark of night to upset trash cans, Billy saw the signs. The magazines in gay corner were well worn and dog-eared. And that wasn't just from Billy's hand. Oh they were out there, all right, somewhere, like the ever-elusive Sasquatch.

But not today. No, after perusing the pages of his favorite Boy Blue magazine for a while, Billy conceded it would be a lonely existence in gay corner that day. So he scanned the room out of the corner of his eye to find two other customers in the store. The first to catch his eye was a cute little thing Billy wouldn't mind getting to know better. But when Billy nonchalantly wandered over to the magazines next to his prey, even before Billy could open his mouth, the boy made his intentions perfectly clear.

"You come an inch closer to me and I'll have to kill you, faggot."

Billy let him be. There were other fish in the sea. In fact, one was standing on the other side of the store right now, a big ol' farm boy glued to a Playboy honoring college girls of spring break. And from the looks of things, he liked what he saw, unconsciously rubbing himself through his pants.

Thinking he might lend a hand, Billy made his move. Grabbing a magazine from the neighboring shelf, Billy could smell the alcohol. That was a good sign. Billy always found heavy mid-afternoon consumption of beer to be somewhat of an aphrodisiac for farm boys. It also helped ease their inhibitions, helped them focus more on getting off than on any silly objections they might have to the gender of the other party.

"Ever been in the back room?" Billy asked, nonchalantly, without looking up from his magazine.

Unlike the homophobe across the store, at least farm boy wasn't antisocial.

"Back room? What's that?"

"You should check it out. They've got 8mm movies back there. Better than this stuff," Billy added, putting his magazine back on the shelf.

The boy was obviously interested, trying to peer through the hanging curtain of beads at the back of the store into the darkness beyond.

"What do you mean, like a movie theater?"

"Well, no. More like individual booths. Private. You'll need some quarters. It's a quarter a minute."

"Hey, thanks."

Billy'd peaked his interest. He saw the boy pulling four quarters from the pocket of his jeans before easing his way through the curtain at the back of the store.

Billy felt optimistic about the prospects. He quickly made his way up to the counter, trading Lou a ten-dollar bill for a roll of quarters.

Lou had to admire the boy's tenacity, as he watched Billy follow the larger boy into the back room in search of love. Lou'd never been a big game hunter himself.

Chapter 15

Used to be Jo Bob Buckner could get some serious fishin' done before eight in the morning, before the catfish had a chance to have their breakfast and start turnin' up their noses at Jo Bob's bait. Not lately though. Not since that Tommy Harris came back. Since that boy showed up, seemed there was always something got Jo Bob out on the road at some ungodly hour doing the town's business, and it was beginning to take a toll on the man. This sheriffing stuff was beginning to seem like a full time job. So much so that he began to suspect even Charlotte was beginning to feel neglected. And Jo Bob instinctively knew that a man who couldn't keep his woman satisfied under the sheets would soon lose her to some other stud. The sooner he resolved this Tommy Harris business the better for all concerned, especially Jo Bob Buckner.

That's why he found himself on the interstate so early in the morning headed for Fayetteville, North Carolina to speak with that shrink over at Fort Bragg. Oh, he tried his best to save some gas and take care of things over the phone. But they wouldn't give him the time of day, some horseshit about confidentiality and how discussions concerning the medical records of soldiers had to take place in person.

It wasn't like the sheriff was asking how many times the kid caught the clap over there in Nam. He just wanted to know if he was a danger to the community, and, by the way, could they please take him back, if for no other reason, so that Jo Bob could get back to screwin' and fishin' in the morning again. What was the point of wakin' up at all without knowin' there'd be some screwin' and fishin'?

Jo Bob had long ago polished off the last of the box of doughnuts that sustained him on his trek, and was having second thoughts, thinking of turning around and going back to Charlotte's bed, when he saw the first road signs for the army base and figured he'd come all this way, too late to change course now.

Fort Bragg was a huge sprawling complex that could swallow up the whole town of Pleasant Valley without leaving a trace. Didn't seem like asking too much for it to just swallow up one damn person. Tommy Harris. And yet, judging by the sentries out front and the barbed wire fence, it wasn't clear whether they were trying to keep people out or in.

Jo Bob took his pass from the guard and followed the man's directions to the base's medical facility, where he was escorted to the office of one Colonel Henry Baker and offered a cup of coffee from a male military secretary of some sort. Jo Bob accepted the offer, thinking to himself that if someone was going to provide *him* with a secretary, it had better be some buxom blonde wearing a skirt. And that went for any nurse that might have to give him a sponge bath as well.

Jo Bob wasn't exactly sure what to expect from a shrink, seeing as he'd never had the need, but Colonel Baker soon arrived in a whirl of white coat and stethoscope. Jo Bob stood up out of respect.

"Hey, you're like a real doctor or something."

"That's right," replied the colonel with a knowing smile as he took his seat behind his desk.

"But I thought you were just a shr—, a psychiatrist."

"Psychiatrists *are* doctors," answered the colonel, pointing over his shoulder with his thumb at the degrees hanging from the wall behind him.

"They are?"

"What can I do for you, Sheriff, uh, Buckner?"

Jo Bob could take a hint. Time to get down to business.

"I'm here on official business, as sheriff, from the town of Pleasant Valley, North Carolina."

"What sort of business, Sheriff?"

"It concerns a soldier of yours, one Tommy Harris."

"Yes, I know. I've reviewed his file in anticipation of your visit."

"Good. Good. Well, here's the thing... uh... we'd like you to take him back."

The colonel eyed the sheriff a moment, trying to understand his request.

"So you mean, you'd like to send him back to Vietnam?"

Jo Bob, feeling a certain amount of guilt, couldn't look the colonel in the eye.

"Yeah... well... the thing is, the boy's quite a handful for a small town, and... uh... we were hoping he might be more useful serving his Uncle Sam."

The colonel paused again, staring right through Jo Bob, looking for the truth, in that way psychiatrists do.

"Look, Sheriff," he began, lazily thumbing through the soldier's file, "I told you all about Thomas Harris when I called you a couple of weeks ago to warn you he might be coming home."

Something about the way the shrink said "warn" piqued Jo Bob's interest.

"Yeah, well, you said he'd had some issues dealing with the trauma of war and all that. Now I ain't no shrink, but having dealt with the boy a week or so now, seems to me he'd be much better suited killing gooks over in Nam than reeking havoc in my little town."

Colonel Baker couldn't help but sympathize with the sheriff.

"So his flashbacks persist? Yes, I can see how that might be a problem. I was hoping they might stop once he got home."

Jo Bob looked confused. "I don't know nothin' about no flashbacks, whatever that is, but the boy's sure been stirring things up."

"Have you considered some anger management classes for him?"

"Anger what?" Jo Bob was beginning to grow angry himself. "Look here, Doctor… uh Colonel… or whatever you call yourself, we got us a real tiger by the tail situation here, more than a little ol' town like Pleasant Valley can hang onto. We'd like to get the boy signed up again for another tour of duty."

The colonel could certainly see the sheriff's point. Yet the military was no depository for delinquent young men. "You can't," he replied.

"We can't? What do you mean?"

The colonel wasn't one to play with the truth. "You can't sign him up, because he's already signed up."

Did Jo Bob hear right? Was his problem already solved? It seemed too good to be true. "You mean he's already signed up for another tour?"

"That's not what I said," corrected the colonel.

Jo Bob just blinked, not knowing what to say. He knew there had to be a catch.

The colonel tried to fill in the gaps. "He's never been officially discharged."

Jo Bob couldn't help smiling over his good fortune. "So he's just on leave or something? When's he due back?"

"Thomas Harris is *not* on leave," stated Colonel Baker. Then, looking for the right words, "He's… um… eloped."

Jo Bob was confused. "Eloped? Tommy Harris is married?"

Colonel Baker couldn't help but chuckle at the sheriff. "No, no. That's not what I meant. Elope is a term we use when patients escape."

Jo Bob's head was beginning to hurt. This was taking much more thinking than he was accustomed to. "Escaped? You make it sound like he was some kind of prisoner."

"Well, in a way he was, though I wouldn't use the term."

Jo Bob didn't like this game. "Well, was he a prisoner or not? Did he kill someone? You're telling me he's escaped from the brig?"

"Thomas Harris was never in the brig, and no he didn't kill anyone, at least not anyone he wasn't supposed to kill."

A frustrated Jo Bob leaned back in his chair, trying to keep his cool. "Look, Colonel, I'm a simple man, if you haven't noticed. Could you kindly tell me what's going on?"

The colonel pondered the situation a moment, weighing how much information he was obligated to impart to the sheriff. He measured his words. "Sheriff Buckner, your Thomas Harris was a superb soldier. He served his country well. But he was very young when he signed up, more a boy than a man, and the war's taken its toll on him, as it has on many of our young men. In some cases that toll is paid physically, in other cases, mentally. In Thomas Harris's case, he's paid both. He was initially brought stateside to deal with his facial burns, but it soon became evident his suffering was more than just the physical kind. Let's just say, Thomas Harris was having some... uh... issues, that led him to be a patient on our psychiatric ward."

Jo Bob never imagined the military dealt with that sort of thing. And frankly, the boy didn't seem any crazier than when he left Pleasant Valley. Bigger and tougher, maybe, but no crazier.

"You said he... uh... eloped. So Tommy Harris has escaped from some kind of nut house... or uh... mental ward? Is that what you're telling me?"

The colonel came to the point. "Private Harris is A.W.O.L."

It took more than a moment for it to settle in before Jo Bob knew what to say. But it seemed to Jo Bob that this was a positive development. "Well that's... uh... great then," tried Jo Bob. "Just loan me a couple of strong MP's and we'll go collect him for ya'."

"Sheriff Buckner, if the military wanted Thomas Harris back, we'd have been waiting for him when he got off the bus in Pleasant Valley."

"If?" Jo Bob was trying to understand. "You mean to say you've got an A.W.O.L recruit and you don't want him back? Seems to me you could use all the help you can get over there in Vietnam."

Colonel Baker decided it was time to stop beating about the bush, time to give the sheriff a dose of reality. "Normally, I'd be in agreement, Sheriff, but we've got enough *healthy* boys gone A.W.O.L. to keep us busy gathering them up. Thomas Harris served, and served bravely. But like a lot of once fine soldier's, he's as damaged now as if he'd had a limb blown off. We can't have boys like that walking around carrying dangerous weapons, experiencing flashbacks so they don't know where they are or who they're fighting. Believe me, we keep them in the field of battle as long as they represent an asset. But at some point, they become a liability, more likely to get our own boys killed than take out the enemy. That's when we do our best to treat them here at the base. But if they take it upon themselves to elope and head for home, we're not inclined to waste precious resources chasing after them. We've barely enough resources for those that actually *want* our help. We're not going to waste time and money chasing down those that don't. Besides, they usually calm down and more or less blend in once they're home, in a familiar stress-free environment. That's why I called to give you a heads up."

Jo Bob was at a loss for words. He'd never heard such a load of crap in his life. Yet the colonel had nothing to add.

"So, Colonel," Jo Bob began, "what you're saying is I've got a dangerous hallucinating psycho, escaped from your loony bin, now on the loose, in *my* town?"

The colonel found the sheriff's dramatic characterization somewhat amusing, but couldn't entirely disagree with it. "Well, I don't know that your choice of words does the situation justice. As I said, we almost never hear of any problems once they're home. But yes, under certain circumstances... you know... stressful situations, situations where he might feel cornered, there could be some danger."

Stressful situations? Seemed to Jo Bob Buckner, anywhere Tommy Harris went resulted in a stressful situation. Jo Bob was feeling pretty damned stressed right now. "So you're saying the boy could murder us in our sleep if he has a bad day?"

"That's hardly what I'm—"

"Just how did he escape?" interrupted Jo Bob in frustration. "Seems like there ought to be adequate security on a military base."

Colonel Baker sat in silence, reluctant to say more. Yet, recalling how he'd found the hapless military police bound and trussed in straight Jackets, tucked away in psych. unit beds as if they'd belonged there all along, his conscience convinced him he'd better let the sheriff know what he was dealing with.

"Your Thomas Harris is no ordinary infantryman, Sheriff. As I told you, he was a fine soldier. More than that. He was exemplary. Because of that, he was chosen for and trained to serve in our Special Forces unit, the Army Rangers. That's what Fort Bragg is all about."

Jo Bob didn't like the sound of this. "Special Forces, huh. Special, in what way?"

"Highly trained. Highly disciplined. Highly resourceful. Expert in using lethal force and evading capture. Thomas Harris could survive in the Carolina mountains indefinitely with nothing more than a nail file."

"That is until I rounded up a posse to bring his ass in."

"Sheriff, I don't think you understand what I'm trying to tell you. No one's bringing Thomas Harris's ass in unless Thomas Harris brings it in himself."

"But—"

"And if you and your posse are foolish enough to go up into the mountains after him, you'd best pray he doesn't have access to as much as a pea shooter, because that boy is just about the best sniper I've had the honor of knowing."

Jo Bob sat in silence for a moment, trying to absorb exactly what the colonel was telling him. "So I've got a trained assassin having hallucinations on the loose in *my* town?" Jo Bob looked at his watch, beginning to wonder what the hell he'd find upon his return to Pleasant Valley, what carnage might await him. He stood up without waiting for a reply. "Seems like I ought to be getting back. And if the place ain't completely burned to the ground, we ought to at least get all the firearms locked up."

"Now, Sheriff," began the colonel, "like I said, I think you're blowing things a little out of proportion. We almost never—"

Jo Bob had already risen from his chair and wasn't listening. But he interrupted the colonel with one more question. "Colonel Baker, the boy was getting treatment here for this, uh, war-induced nervousness. Do you know why he felt it was necessary to... uh... elope and head for Pleasant Valley, North Carolina?"

"Well, I can't say for sure. It was sometimes difficult to know when he was grounded in reality or simply hallucinating. But he kept talking about some hometown girl he'd left behind. How he'd had some sort of unfinished business with her." Colonel Baker began leafing through Thomas Harris's file in hopes of finding the girl's name, thinking it might be of some help to the sheriff. But only moments later, when he'd located the name of Jaime Jo Tremper, and looked up to relay it to the sheriff, the colonel saw the door to his office slamming behind Jo Bob Buckner already running for his car.

Chapter 16

"He's gone," Jimmy Harris offered before the sheriff could even enter the trailer for a look around.

But Jo Bob Buckner would need to see for himself. This wasn't a game anymore. Not after hearing what the colonel at Fort Bragg had to say. He all but shoved Jimmy aside, squeezing through the door.

"Suit yourself," Jimmy added, seeing that Jo Bob was committed to searching the place anyway. "Packed up his stuff a couple of days ago and hit the road."

The trailer was pretty damn sparse to begin with. Practically the only thing filling the place was the smell of booze on Jimmy Harris's breath. But Jo Bob couldn't seem to find any signs of Tommy Harris at all.

"Everything the boy had was in that duffle bag of his," his father began. "That and the Camaro. And they're both gone."

True enough, Jo Bob noticed the car was gone.

"You thinking he's moved on?" asked Jo Bob, wishfully.

"I'm guessin' so," answered Jimmy. "Ain't nothin' holdin' that boy in Pleasant Valley."

Nothin' but trouble, thought Jo Bob, poking his nose out the trailer door like a hound trying to pick up a scent. He thought of heading over to the preacher's place, thinking how often he'd found a hunted animal unwilling to leave its caged mate.

But then he remembered something the colonel had warned about. Jo Bob turned slowly back to look at the wall over the TV set, afraid of what he might find, or not find. Sure enough, there was a bright line in the paint above two nails where years of smoke and dust had not had a chance to light.

"Hey Jimmy, I know your hands shake too much to use that fine hunting rifle you kept on the wall. Don't tell me you finally pawned it just to buy some hooch?"

Jimmy looked over at the wall, noticing for the first time in his own home what the sheriff had detected in only ten minutes of snooping around. He felt the sheriff's eyes on the back of his head as he tried to make sense of it.

"You still think your boy's gone for good?" asked Jo Bob, too impatient for Jimmy's pickled thoughts to swim to the surface on their own.

"Guess maybe he's just gone hunting after all," answered Jimmy.

And that was exactly what Jo Bob feared. "You had a scope on that rifle, didn't you?"

"Sure did. A fine one, too."

"What do you think he's huntin' for?"

Jimmy racked his brain, but couldn't think of any major game that was in season. Of course, there was always rabbit, squirrel, or bird. Nothing you'd use that high-powered rifle with a scope for. He was about to say as much to Jo Bob, but when he turned to do so, the sheriff was already gone.

* * * *

Tommy Harris didn't mind the rifle's weight. He'd grown used to lugging the extra pounds around with him in Vietnam. It had become just another appendage to his body as he wandered the jungles of Southeast Asia. A sniper's rifle was as much a part of him as stripes to a tiger. In fact, he'd come to feel naked and vulnerable without one since he'd been home.

He knew all the larger prey were out of season this time of year, but he hadn't decided how long he'd spend up in the mountains and had no desire to starve. He'd made no itinerary. He just knew he had to get out, clear his head.

His talk with Jaime Jo hadn't gone exactly as planned. He thought for sure they'd be on the road by now... to a new life... together. It didn't matter where. Just so long as it wasn't Pleasant Valley.

Every minute over in Vietnam, both waking and sleeping, he'd thought of his Jaime Jo, of coming home to rescue her from Pleasant Valley. But now that he'd come back to collect her, she'd balked at the idea. Like one of those donkeys strapped to a gristmill, walking in the same circular rut day in and day out, she knew no other path. Still under her father's roof, she trusted in God more than herself, and certainly more than Tommy.

He hadn't expected it to be this way. He'd always thought they'd fly away the minute he returned. And when she hopped into the Camaro in front of Frank's the other day, he thought his dream had come true. He thought they'd crossed that bridge out of Pleasant Valley for the last time.

But that's not how it turned out. Maybe it was never meant to be after all. Maybe her father, his church, their God, had won in the end. Jaime Jo'd rejected him. She said she couldn't do it. She couldn't really explain it. Or if she did, he simply couldn't hear it. But he knew it had a lot to do with her father and his power over her, his control.

None of that mattered now. She'd asked him to leave, told him she'd wished he'd never come back. Tommy Harris was no Einstein, but he understood plain English. He got the message, loud and clear.

So he grabbed his stuff and headed up into the mountains to think things through. With him, he carried the only friend he'd had all that time over in Vietnam, a high-powered rifle, and all the ammo he could carry. One should always be prepared for any eventuality.

He'd done plenty of camping up in those mountains as a kid. The trees, fresh air, and birdsong always brought a welcome change from peeling paint, the smell of whiskey, and the sound of puking in the early morning hours, as those were the comforts of home he'd come to expect at the trailer he shared with his father.

From his youth in the woods, he'd come to know every path, stream, cave, and cliff as if he'd been raised by wolves, while his father couldn't have survived a whole night away from Chezzy's. Tommy'd wished he *was* raised by wolves, by anyone other than his own father. He'd always felt more at peace up in those mountains than with the people that lived down in Pleasant Valley, where he'd always felt the outcast, the motherless boy with the wino for an old man. Maybe the motherless part is what drew him to Jaime Jo, a shared chasm that bound them, each looking to fill the void. They each played the hand they'd been dealt in different ways. She'd veiled her flaw with religion, accepting her loss by replacing her mother with God. Tommy, however, responded differently, refusing to give in to fate, fighting back, acting out against the world. Jaime Jo'd been the flexible reed bending with the wind, while Tommy'd been the immobile oak that would splinter and shatter before giving an inch.

As pleasant as the past two days in the woods had been, there'd been precious little progress in forming any plan of action concerning Jaime Jo. One thing he knew. She didn't want him anymore. Given that, there wasn't much cause to stick around Pleasant Valley. With her or without her, he knew he had to go. Where he went didn't matter. There were only two prerequisites. It had to be someplace that didn't know him, someplace that hadn't already labeled him a troublemaker. And it had to be someplace far from Jaime Jo, far enough that he'd forget any silly notions of love, forget once and for all any possibility of happiness. How far that might be, if such a place even existed at all, Tommy Harris didn't know.

Tommy almost wished he'd never met Jaime Jo Tremper. He knew that was a crazy thing to think, yet he couldn't help wondering how things might have turned out. He might have finished high school, found a job, and settled down with a different girl, one that didn't bring the law down on him for no good reason. Maybe then he'd never have ended up in Vietnam killing people he didn't know, seeing things he wished he'd never seen and never wanted to see again, things he couldn't stop seeing, even though they no longer existed, things that lived on in his mind, haunting him daily. Maybe he'd have been able to get through a whole day without forgetting where he was, seeing things that weren't there at all.

He wondered what his life would have been like had Jaime Jo Tremper never existed. So it was quite the twist of fate when he came to a small meadow at the edge of the woods and saw her. Her back was to him, but her head was turned, eyes fixed on his. She'd frozen in indecision, the seconds ticking off in slow motion as she struggled to decide whether it was safe to stay or whether she should turn and run for her life from the man holding the rifle.

He almost hadn't even noticed her, distracted as he was, her brown coat blending nearly perfectly with the brush at the opposite edge of the meadow. Why'd she come at all? Was she only spying on him? Or had she come to confront him, to get the final word? How dare she show up just to torture him, to play some sick game? He wished she would just go away and leave him be. But she didn't, even after she saw him. She just stood there staring, her eyes locked on his, taunting him. But why? She'd asked him to leave and he did. Yet there she stood, teasing him, testing his willpower, his self-control. And Tommy didn't appreciate it. Not one bit.

He felt his surprise and confusion fade, replaced by anger. Did she think he was a fool? She wasn't the only one to have read the bible. And Tommy Harris had no intention of biting from her apple. He knew the work of the devil when he saw it. And that's exactly who was staring at him from across the meadow. And Tommy'd had just about enough. He wouldn't take it anymore.

Feeling his hands tighten on the rifle, he just wished she would turn and run. But she wouldn't, daring him, just daring him to do something about it. Why didn't she just run? Did she *want* to die? Maybe that was her game after all. Maybe she was doing them both a favor.

Tommy raised the rifle to his shoulder, placing her square in his sites. He didn't even need the scope. She wasn't that far. It was an easy shot.

He hesitated, giving her one last chance, a chance to change her mind and save herself, to stop tormenting him and finally leave him be.

But she didn't. She held her ground, welcoming her fate. And Tommy knew what he had to do. He just knew it. He had to be the brave one, the strong one. It was all up to him. He had to do it. He had to end this thing once and for all.

Her eyes never left his. Her legs never moved. She just stood there, defiantly. There was barely a twitch of the skin as the bullet penetrated, tearing through her chest and ripping into her heart. Tommy Harris hadn't lost his touch since leaving the military, still deadly accurate. Those last few heartbeats seemed to stretch into eternity, as if she were immune to the effects of the bullet, as if, by sheer will, she would deny her own mortality. But death would not be denied forever, and her legs finally gave out, collapsing under the inevitable weight of reality. She was dead before she hit the ground.

Chapter 17

Despite what some might have thought, Tommy Harris respected the law. Yet the laws of nature always trump the laws of man. He hadn't eaten a thing for two days. And hunger was a law that couldn't be ignored. So despite the threat of a stiff fine for hunting out of season, he knew what he had to do when he saw that doe staring at him from the other side of the clearing. He took the shot.

He hauled the carcass to his campsite, ate his fill, and thought he'd preserve the rest for later, unsure how long he'd be up in the mountains. Yet once his hunger was sated, he sat staring at the campfire, mesmerized by the flames dancing in the night. His mind slowly regained a sense of clarity, and turning inward, he knew what he had to do. He had to leave. He had to leave Pleasant Valley, Jaime Jo, the whole mess. Comes a certain point where defeat can no longer be denied. He could have fought her father, the sheriff, the whole damn town if need be. But not alone. Not without Jaime Jo. At this point even she had deserted him. And without her by his side, what was the point? Where was the payoff? Nothing mattered without her.

Even so, simply admitting defeat didn't stop the pain, didn't bring the suffering to an end. No, that wouldn't stop until all ties were severed, until one of them was gone.

So, in the morning, with a full stomach and a clear head, Tommy Harris decided to pack up his gear, sling his rifle over his shoulder, and head back down the mountain. Game over. It was time to say goodbye to Jaime Jo Tremper.

* * * *

Jo Bob Buckner knew his troubles weren't over when Tommy Harris disappeared. The empty space on Jimmy Harris's wall where that rifle had been stored for years put an end to that fantasy. No, Jo Bob knew his troubles were far from over. If anything, they were just beginning. Things had gone from annoying to serious. And as uncomfortable as it might have been having Tommy Harris under foot, having to keep an eye on him, it was a damn site worse not knowing where he was at all.

It didn't take Jo Bob long to find the Camaro parked at the side of the road. The trailhead up into the mountains was well known. But he'd be a damned fool to strike out after him, into the wilderness, alone. Only an idiot would be dumb enough to do that, to go stumbling after a dangerous sniper on his own turf. No, Jo Bob wasn't ready to go up into the mountains after him yet. Instead, he'd stick to familiar ground, out in the open. He'd wait him out.

The first thing he had to do was round up some deputies and strategically spread them around town to keep an eye out for the fugitive. It wasn't easy. Not very many men were willing to put their lives on the line without some big reward to look forward to. And Jo Bob didn't have the funds for that sort of thing. But he did eventually manage to scrape together a handful of righteous citizens. It was an odd combination of boys who went to high school with Tommy, Neanderthals from the football team who still held a grudge against Tommy's independence, and a few yahoos from Chezzy's who couldn't pass up a chance to legally hunt two-legged mammal.

Jo Bob wasn't too comfortable with the thought of sending his motley crew out into public, armed, but desperate times called for desperate measures.

* * * *

Tommy Harris had no idea he was a hunted man, not until he reached inside the driver's side window of the Camaro to open the door and a bullet ricocheted off the roof inches from his head. Even then, it didn't occur to him that he was actually the target of the assault. But that didn't matter. Reflexes picked up in Vietnam immediately kicked in as he abandoned the car and darted back into the woods for cover.

Was it just a stray bullet from some irresponsible hunter after a squirrel? Or could it be something more sinister? This wasn't the first time Tommy Harris had taken fire. And just because you're paranoid don't mean they ain't out to get you.

Tommy quietly circled through the woods toward the direction where the shot came from. It didn't take long for him to catch up to an out of breath Buford Higgins making quite a ruckus tramping through the woods to report his findings back to Sheriff Buckner.

Buford knew damn well that shooting wasn't part of the plan, not unless absolutely necessary. But Buford figured better safe than sorry. Better a hero than a corpse. Besides, he never had any patience for white trash like Tommy Harris or his drunkard father anyway. Tommy was the loser the whole team liked to pick on. And when they heard he was taking it out on that poor defenseless Tremper girl, it only served to justify their actions.

But back then, the team always had the advantage of strength and numbers. None of them had seen how Tommy Harris had filled out since heading off to war. He'd grown as big as any of his tormentors, who, since high school, no longer traveled as a pack.

Buford hadn't thought things through. He hadn't thought of a contingency plan should he miss his target. He hadn't thought the hunter and the pray might switch roles. He hadn't expected Tommy Harris to come after him, not until he watched his bullet ricochet harmlessly off the roof of the Camaro. Only then did he realize he'd better run for town.

But Buford was out of shape. He'd run his last lap around the football field a couple of years ago. Since then, the only laps Buford had taken were the ones involving his tongue and a can of Bud.

Tommy Harris, on the other hand, had maintained his military conditioning. It didn't take him long to run down an ex-front lineman like Buford Higgins. Any sound of Tommy's approach was drowned out by the racket Buford made stampeding through the woods like a spooked elephant. Buford never saw what hit him as he landed face down in the leaves, Tommy Harris on his back like a load of bricks.

Tommy quickly disarmed Buford, tossing his rifle aside. He then rolled him over onto his back and straddled his chest, holding the point of his hunting knife to Buford's jugular.

"What the hell's this all about?" Tommy demanded.

Buford wanted to talk, but couldn't catch his breath. And the point of Tommy's knife poking his neck with every gasp for air only made it worse.

Tommy gave him a chance, but his patience was limited. "Well? What were you thinkin', Buford?"

He'd almost caught his breath when he began to feel nauseous from running too hard. If he didn't get Tommy Harris off his chest soon, he was going to puke all over himself.

"I didn't mean to shoot. It was an accident," he lied.

Tommy knew it was a lie. But he wanted information, not a debate. "What are you doin' out here? You never been much of the outdoorsy type."

"It was the sheriff. He wanted us to find you for him."

"Us? Who's us?" Tommy asked, beginning to wonder just how serious things were.

"Everyone. The whole town's out looking for you."

"Me? Why me?"

"Oh come on, Tommy, you know what this is about."

"No, I'm afraid I don't." Then bringing some more pressure on Buford's neck with the knife, "Why don't you tell me?"

Buford didn't know what kind of game Tommy was playing, but with that knife at his throat, Buford was ready to play. "Well, after what you did to Jaime Jo—"

Interrupted by a sudden increase in pressure exerted by the knife at his throat, Buford didn't know what was more concerning, the knife or the look in Tommy Harris's eye.

"What about Jaime Jo?" insisted Tommy.

Buford was truly confused. "What do you mean?"

"What happened to Jaime Jo?"

Buford felt a trickle of blood start down the side of his neck. At this point he'd say whatever Tommy Harris wanted to hear. So what if it meant telling him something he already knew. "You really beat the shit out of her this time. She's hurt real bad."

Buford's last conscious thought was that the man with the knife at his throat truly looked as if the beating of Jaime Jo Tremper was news to him. Then the butt of Tommy Harris's knife came down between his eyes, and the lights went out.

Tommy Harris was trained to evade capture, to see without being seen. He naively thought he'd seen his last mission back in Nam. Yet here he was on a brand new assignment, one more important than killing a bunch of communists in some jungle on the other side of the world. No, this one was right here in Pleasant Valley, and it was personal.

How did he ever think he could leave her? As if that would solve everything. Did he really believe the trouble would stop when he was gone? That's what Jaime Jo believed. But Tommy knew better. He knew that was a load of horseshit. He knew it in his heart.

She didn't know what was good for her. She'd been in this situation so long she didn't see any other way. She didn't know that all she had to do was walk away. She couldn't do it herself. She needed him. Jaime Jo was hurt, and contrary to what the folks of Pleasant Valley might believe, it was up to Tommy Harris to get her out of harm's way.

He traveled on foot, through the woods, couldn't risk driving the roads. If Buford's account were accurate, they'd be waiting for him. His first stop would be the trailer, to stock up on ammo. No telling what sort of resistance he might come up against.

Sure enough, as he came over the hill just above the trailer, under cover of trees, he saw the sentry parked up the road a bit. That was Clinton Lewter's truck. Clinton was one of the Chezzy regulars, always ready to make a quick buck to buy his next beer. And most of Clinton's income came off of thievin'. They didn't have much of a fox problem in Pleasant Valley, but whenever some chickens turned up missing, chances were Clinton made a recent delivery to the butcher.

So now Buckner was hiring chicken thieves. Tommy wondered what the sheriff was paying, as he inched his way toward the old rusted pickup. Turns out he didn't need to get very close. He could make out the rhythmic bobbing of Clinton's head as he slept off the effects of the previous night at Chezzy's. With that small bit of reconnaissance, Tommy felt safe entering the trailer to collect his supplies, even if it was right under Clinton Lewter's watchful eye.

Jimmy Harris wasn't as sound a sleeper as Clinton Lewter. Either that, or he ran out of funds before he could do any serious damage over at Chezzy's. Because when Tommy opened the cabinet where the rifle ammo was stored and started shoving it into his pack, his father got up to investigate.

Tommy had his hunting knife at the man's throat before he realized who it was that sneaked up on him from behind.

"Go ahead. Slit my throat," his father calmly requested. "Better that than have to watch you go down."

"I ain't goin' down," Tommy responded, turning back to the task at hand and grabbing the last of the rifle shells.

"But Buckner's got the whole town lookin' for you."

"Well then the whole town's goin' down. Too bad for them."

Jimmy Harris knew when his son's mind was made up. He went to make some coffee. "You got enough supplies? Food? You know you've worn out your welcome around these parts. Whatever you're thinkin' of doin', you're on your own."

"Nothin' new about that," Tommy replied, throwing a jab at his old man for crawling into a bottle after his mom passed.

Jimmy put down the coffee. "You know, son, there's more than one way to ruin your life. Certain people just have bad karma. That's what Chezzy calls it. Seems to run in our family. You and I just handle it differently. I run *from* it. But you, Tommy, you run *to* it. I guess we'll find out who's got the better approach."

Tommy stopped at the front door, without turning to his father. "I guess you're right about that. We'll find out soon enough."

The screen door slammed behind him, leaving Jimmy Harris wondering if he'd ever see his boy again.

Chapter 18

He came for her in the night.

Jaime Jo Tremper prayed for sleep. Sleep was what she lived for. Because only in her dreams did the torment of the real world abate. So she lived in her dreams. That was her reality. Or so she chose to believe, because it was only in her waking hours that the nightmares dwelled.

Flying. That was Jaime Jo's dream. It was always some variation of flying. This night she was flying over Pleasant Valley. The sky was blue. The sun was warm. Flying, she felt none of the pain that was ever present as she walked the earth with legs almost too weak to carry her weight. But it was different when she was flying. Her wings felt strong, as though they could carry her as far away as she wanted to go, all the way to heaven, if she so desired. And that's exactly where she wanted to be, in His arms, the arms of the Lord, where she could finally find peace. If only he would have her. If only he would.

But she knew better than that. She'd spent enough time in church to know He'd never have her. No sinners allowed. And she was a sinner, one of the worst kinds. Everything that happened to her, she'd brought upon herself. She deserved every beating, every bruise. It was she who tempted the devil, as women will do. It wasn't Tommy Harris's fault. He was only a man, after all. He couldn't help himself, defenseless against a siren's temptation. Her daddy was right. It was all her doing, just like Eve, in the Garden of Eden. So she deserved whatever she got. And she'd never be granted sanctuary behind those pearly gates.

That was only the stuff of dreams. Yet anything was possible in her dreams. And so she flapped her wings, ascending higher and higher, away from Pleasant Valley, toward heaven. Maybe this time she'd make it, and never have to return to Earth.

But Jaime Jo knew better than that. She knew she'd never reach her goal. She'd had this dream many times before. And it always ended the same way, with something ultimately holding her back to foil her escape. What would it be this time? That was the only question. Not if she'd make it. That would never be. But why not? What would stop her this time?

Scarlet, her baby girl. Where was Scarlet? She couldn't leave without her. She turned to look back toward Earth, toward the house she'd flown from, through the shingled roof and into her room. There she was. She'd walked from her own room to Jaime Jo's, looking for her, searching in the night for her mother. But her mother's bed was empty.

Jaime Jo felt the tug on her heart. She felt her wings grow weary. So that was it. Scarlet. This time it was Scarlet that bound her to the Earth below. Now she knew. There was no surprise or disappointment. Jaime Jo knew it was only a matter of time. She knew she wouldn't make it all the way to heaven. Maybe next time. Maybe next time.

She was falling, falling to Earth. Her wings were gone. She saw Pleasant Valley rushing up to meet her. Soon she could make her house out of the darkness. She wasn't afraid of falling. It happened every time. That's how the dream always ended, falling into her bed with a jolt. Only this time, when she opened her eyes, she wasn't alone.

He held the sleeping little girl in his arms. Tommy Harris stood over Jaime Jo's bed gently cradling the child. He wore army boots, bloody camouflage fatigues, and a rifle strapped to his back. Scarlet looked like an innocent cherub in the big fighting man's arms. He seemed to be assessing Jaime Jo, checking what kind of condition she was in.

Jaime Jo had to pull herself together. She sat bolt upright in the bed. "What are you doing with her?"

Tommy was pleased she could sit up. She didn't seem as bad as Buford had led on. Her bruises seemed to be healing, not that it relieved him of the responsibility he felt for her condition, after their encounter out at the quarry. He should have known what it would lead to. On the other hand, he never asked her to get in the car back at the diner. Nevertheless, that was then and this was now. He needed to know her status. "Can you walk?"

"Yeah, I can walk," she answered, finding nothing unusual about the question. "Why?"

"Then let's go," came his reply.

"Go? Go where?"

"Away. Come on. There's no time."

"Away? Are you crazy? How did you get in here? Don't you know Buckner's parked out front?"

"Then it's a good thing for him I came through the back. Now get dressed. We're leaving."

"I don't understand."

"There's nothing to understand. It's simple. I'm taking you away. The both of you," he added, looking down at the sleeping toddler.

Jaime Jo felt the first faint glimmer of hope, hope that maybe she could surrender to this man, go with him, just follow his lead and everything would turn out all right. But the glimmer didn't last. That spark was quickly extinguished in the stiff wind of reality. "They'll hunt us down."

"Then they better hope they don't find us. Cause I'm just about through running. And they don't want to be around when that happens."

Jaime Jo had hoped this was just another dream, that Scarlet was still in her own bed and Tommy Harris had stayed gone. But she could still tell fantasy from reality. He was here all right. So she had to make a decision. She wanted to refuse, to stand up to him, to tell him to go to hell. But she knew that's not how it would go. She'd never been able to say no to Tommy Harris. That's exactly why she lay battered and bruised, conversing with the maniac who'd snatched her child from it's bed in the middle of the night with plans to shoot his way out of the house, if necessary, and take them both out into the wilderness. He held some irresistible power over her, a power she'd never been able to fight. Yet she wanted to. She wanted to take control of her life. She was bone weary of men telling her what to do all the time. And now all she had to do was say no for once.

"I'll have to pack some things," she pleaded.

"No time for that. We ain't goin' to the Ritz. Just put on some pants and boots."

She never took her eyes off of his as she did so, like the mouse hypnotized by the cobra. "I'll have to get clothes for Scarlet. She can't go out like that."

Tommy reluctantly handed her the child, knowing time was short. Satisfied to see she seemed mobile enough, he turned and went downstairs on the lookout for the sheriff or her father.

* * * *

Asleep at the wheel of his sheriff's cruiser parked out front of the Tremper place, Jo Bob had run through a whole thermos of coffee hours ago. It hadn't succeeded in keeping him awake and alert. What it did do, however, was stretch his bladder beyond its recommended capacity, finally forcing him from a sound slumber out into the night to take a leak. Barely alert enough to avoid the ever-growing puddle of urine forming at his feet on the pavement outside his cruiser, Jo Bob looked up at the moon, shaking his head at the fact that he was sleeping in his car instead of with Charlotte Sawchuck. As he shook the last drop of coffee from his Johnson with a shiver, he glanced up at the Tremper girl's window.

It was probably nothing. And yet, he couldn't help wondering what the hell was going on up there at this hour when he made out the motion of silhouettes through the drawn curtain. Maybe, like him, she'd gotten up to use the bathroom. Then he finally figured it out when he noticed her shadow moving about the child's room. She'd just gone to check on the baby. Thank God. Just a false alarm. He had to stop letting his mind get the better of him. Tommy Harris was no fool. He had to know they'd be watching the Tremper place. That boy was probably as far away from Jaime Jo Tremper as a man could get.

Jo Bob zipped his fly, got back in the car, and pulled his sheriff's cap down over his face. No reason to lose any more sleep over Tommy Harris.

* * * *

What does one pack for a two-year-old being taken up into the mountains on the run from the law? That's what Jaime Jo wondered as she stared into the child's clothing drawer. Hell, she only had three outfits. Choosing one wasn't the problem. The current situation was the problem. The whole thing was crazy. Where would they go? What would happen? When would she get even a glimpse of a normal life? These were only the most basic of questions that ran through her mind in the short time she had. But she didn't dwell on them, or the million other questions yet unasked. She never had. She'd learned long ago not to expect any answers. She could question, think, and plan all she liked. None of it mattered. Jaime Jo Tremper'd come to believe it was all out of her hands. No matter what she did, she always found herself back on the same path she'd been headed down her whole life. It was a journey over which she had no control, whether she was led by her father, Tommy, or the devil himself. All she could do was pray, pray that it was none of the above, pray that it was the Lord that guided her every move, the Lord that had some plan for her, the Lord that would see her safely home.

She only had time to grab one outfit and a pair of shoes for the baby when she heard Tommy's urgent whisper from downstairs. "Time to go. Buckner's awake and moving around."

She almost yelled back down to him that she was ready, but didn't want to rouse her father. It only took a couple of seconds to make her way down the stairs to meet him waiting impatiently at the back door of the kitchen.

"Where's Scarlet?" he demanded with hushed urgency.

"Isn't she with you? I put her down to grab her clothes and when I turned around you'd already taken her."

"I didn't take her," he cursed, bounding up the steps three at a time to check for the wandering toddler.

He was back down in seconds. "She's not there."

"What do you mean, she's not—"

She was interrupted by the sound of footsteps somewhere inside the house. Had the sheriff come in to look around? She looked to Tommy for instructions. He grabbed her by the wrist and lurched toward the back door.

But what about Scarlet? She couldn't leave without her. Jaime Jo's feet were firmly planted in the house. Tommy could have dragged her after him, or easily thrown her over his shoulder. But he didn't. That's not how it worked between them.

She looked into his eyes, begging his understanding, and he didn't disappoint. He dutifully let her hand drop.

"You'd better go," she said tenderly, as she heard the sheriff's footsteps approaching. She expected him to turn and head for the woods, but didn't know what to think when, instead, he raised his rifle and aimed it in her direction.

Initially startled that the gun was pointed in her direction, she quickly surmised that Tommy had decided to shoot the sheriff as he entered the kitchen. That would have been the last thing she wanted, Tommy on the run for murdering a police officer. She thought of running to warn Sheriff Buckner. But when she turned around toward the front of the house, she saw what Tommy was really aiming at.

It wasn't the sheriff. It was her father. He didn't have his baseball bat this time. But he was armed, her baby, little Scarlet, fallen back asleep in one arm, a kitchen knife in the other. He stood there holding the little girl, staring Tommy Harris down, a maniacal grin on his face bragging that he'd won the day.

"I hope you're as good a shot as you think," Warren Tremper dared, shielding himself with the child, bringing the knife to her throat.

"No!" screamed Jaime Jo, reaching for her baby.

But he kicked at her, keeping her out of reach. Then he laughed at Tommy, enjoying the upper hand.

Jaime Jo looked frantically back and forth between the two of them, her baby's life hanging in the balance. "Please," she begged, suddenly crying, unsure to whom she pleaded, whether her father, her Tommy, or her God.

Warren Tremper, however, seemed to enjoy nothing more than riling the man with the rifle. "Go ahead. Do it. Shoot. Maybe you'll hit me. Maybe the child. No matter. Either way, at least then they'll finally do something about you. Even if they don't hang you, at least they'll lock you up and throw away the key. Problem solved."

Tommy grew impatient. Then, keeping the preacher in his sites, "Put the girl down. Cause I *will* shoot. And I *won't* be hittin' no baby."

"I'll take that bet," the preacher answered, calling what he believed to be a bluff.

"That's your call," Tommy calmly replied. "Jaime Jo. After I kill your daddy—"

"No, don't—" she began.

"Jaime Jo!" he repeated. "After I kill your daddy, I want you to grab your things and walk out this door."

Jaime Jo was frantic at the site of the rifle pointed at her father and daughter.

"But—"

"And don't you worry about Scarlet gettin' hit by no stray bullet either," he replied. "Cause I don't plan on wastin' a perfectly good bullet on your daddy. I plan to use my bare hands."

The preacher's poker face seemed to waiver at Tommy's confidence, a bead of sweat visible on his brow. He tightened his grip on the knife in readiness.

As much as Jaime Jo wanted to turn and run, she knew she couldn't. She wasn't sure she could stop him. But she had to try.

Whatever he'd become, she knew she couldn't let him become a murderer. She couldn't run away with him, wanted for murder. They'd only hunt him down. Both of them. And even if they got away, they couldn't hide. Not from God. They'd never be able to hide from Him.

Jaime Jo walked over to Tommy, put her arms around his waist, her head on his chest, and she hugged him. Tommy remained stiff and unyielding as he kept his rifle trained on the enemy. Then she backed away from him toward her father and child. She looked Tommy in the eyes and slowly shook her head, no. She'd made up her mind. She wouldn't be going with him. Not this way.

Tommy could have seen the smug grin return to the preacher's face. But he didn't. None of that mattered. All he saw was his Jaime Jo. She'd made up her mind, made her choice. He'd lost again. He'd come to claim what was his. But once again, he'd be leaving empty handed. There was no reason to prolong things.

Tommy Harris was nearly halfway across the back yard to the woods already when her father roughly dropped her daughter and turned toward the front door to fetch the sheriff.

But something held him back. He turned to find his daughter sprawled on the floor, her arms wrapped firmly about his ankle. Unable to kick her free, he began to drag her across the kitchen floor with him. Yet, before he could reach the front door, he glanced over his shoulder and realized it was no use. Tommy Harris had vanished, back into the wild from which he'd briefly emerged.

"God damn you, girl!" he cursed, kicking her off him.

But Jaime Jo didn't hear or feel a thing. She'd already scrambled back to Scarlet, where she sat on the floor hugging her little girl and rocking back and forth, her mind already in another place.

It was her dream all over again. She'd almost made it this time. Heaven stood only a few yards from the back of the house. She could still see the line of trees guarding the entrance. But once again, she'd been pulled back to Earth, bound to it by the child, her precious Scarlet. And now, instead of heaven, she'd awoken with a jolt, on the hard kitchen floor at her father's feet, feeling his fury, closer to hell than she'd ever been.

Chapter 19

In a town the size of Pleasant Valley, it doesn't take long for news to spread. And Charlotte's Beauty Salon & Bridal Shoppe was indeed the epicenter of all that was newsworthy. Since the return of Tommy Harris and the prophesized trouble with the Tremper girl, Charlotte's business had more than doubled, just from the curious starving for any scraps of intel.

Charlotte herself frowned upon such gossip, but business was business. Besides, some things were just too big to ignore. So when Charlotte heard first hand from Jo Bob what went down at the Tremper place that night, she considered it her civic duty to report it.

Mid-wash, mid-curl, mid-color, all action had stopped, as the particularly graphic account demanded everyone's full attention.

"It's all just so sad," replied June Parker to Charlotte's revelation.

"Not like anyone didn't see it coming," stated Sally Wright. "Right, Dot? You predicted the whole thing."

"Well, I'll be damned," answered Dot Elliot, impressed with herself. "But even *I* didn't think it would come to *this*."

"I thought they said he'd changed," offered a disillusioned June.

"Right, Deary, and do you also believe in the tooth fairy? Then again, apparently he has changed," Dot replied. "For the worse."

"It just sounds like somethin' from the picture shows. Some kind of horror flick about the criminally insane," Sally added with a shiver. "You wouldn't make somethin' like this up, Charlotte, now would you? Cause that'd be pretty sick if you did. You say the blood was everywhere?"

"Everywhere," confirmed Charlotte. "They'll never get the stains out of that kitchen linoleum." Soon the tears began to flow again. "That poor girl. I remember when they were younger. My Billy was always the best of friends with the both of them. They were good kids. What's this world coming to?"

"That Tommy Harris weren't no good kid," Dot corrected. "Damn white trash. Worse than that no good daddy of his. Least Jimmy's harmless enough. But the boy? Born trouble. And don't nobody try and sugarcoat it."

Then Sally spoke up in confusion. "But I thought Jo Bob was out there all night guarding the place. Explain to me again why he couldn't prevent the whole mess."

Charlotte felt a bit indignant at the insinuation and came to Jo Bob's defense. "He *did* stop it. He was parked right out front. But he's only one man. Can't one man surround a place," she protested, parroting Jo Bob's words to her. "Tommy must have come through the back. By the time Jo Bob heard the screams and broke the front door down, the damage was done. The boy was gone. All he found was poor Jaime Jo in her father's arms."

June had to put in her two cents. "And poor little Scarlet must have seen the whole thing. She's still in shock. They say she won't even let her own grandfather touch her without going into hysterics. Had to bring in a sitter to help out while Jaime Jo's laid up at the hospital. Does Scarlet even know that Tommy Harris is her daddy? I mean, that it was her own daddy beat up her momma?"

Sally had an opinion on that. "Well I know Jaime Jo's never admitted who the daddy was one way or another, even though the whole world knows it's the Harris boy. So maybe just as well the little girl be spared the sordid details." Then, as an afterthought, "That poor preacher. You know, for a man of the Lord, he's certainly seen his share."

"Something tells me he ain't seen the last of it either," Dot added. "That boy's still out there in them woods somewhere. Gone commando."

"God preserve us all," June prayed. "Any word from the hospital? How's poor Jaime Jo fairing?"

"My Billy's been to see her," answered Charlotte.

"And?" inquired Sally, hungry for details.

Charlotte wanted to answer, but her throat seemed to tighten up every time the image Billy painted came to mind. Finally, swallowing back tears, she did the best she could in fits and starts. "She's still... unconscious. He says... he says she's got... got a broken arm. And... and her face... it's all bruised and swollen... like she'd been in a car wreck. They're still waiting to see if there's any internal damage."

"Jeez," offered June.

"Sounds like old times to me," stated Dot.

"There's more," continued Charlotte, now crying freely.

"More?" from Sally and June in unison.

Charlotte nodded, trying to find her voice. "He... he cut her."

"Cut her? What do you mean? How?"

Charlotte had to take some deep breaths before she could go on. "On the chest... with a kitchen knife."

"Oh, no. On the chest?"

Charlotte couldn't stop now, not after she'd come this far. She'd get the rest out, and be done with it. "It was a number."

"A number? What kind o' number?" asked Dot.

"Just three six's," answered Charlotte.

Sally and June looked at each other. "Three sixes? What's that supposed to mean?"

Charlotte just nodded her head, unable to continue.

"That sick motherfucker," answered Dot.

"What?! What does it mean?!" yelled June and Sally in confusion.

Dot looked at them like they were idiots. "It's all in The Book of Revelation. Number of the beast. Sign of the devil."

June and Sally looked over at Charlotte for confirmation. "Are you sayin' he carved the sign of the devil..." But Charlotte was in tears, unable to speak. They turned back to Dot.

"Right on her chest," she said, confirming what they'd already heard from Charlotte.

June Parker had to excuse herself as she ran to the ladies room to vomit.

* * * *

Billy Sawchuck had heard enough. He'd seen it first hand. He certainly didn't need to hear it over and over again. Once was plenty. Now he was ready to forget the whole mess. He didn't want to deal with this shit anymore. He needed some air. He needed to get away. The back door to the Bridal Shoppe slammed behind him as he ran out to the parking lot and hopped into Tinkerbell.

Speeding over the bridge heading out of town, he didn't even notice Otis Williams fishing, suddenly forced to jump for his life out of the path of Billy's speeding car. Otis would probably thank the Lord and call it a day. Safer to stay in his makeshift home under the bridge 'till morning when the traffic was lighter.

It didn't matter that Billy could barely see through his tears. He wasn't sure where he was headed anyhow. Away. That's where. Just away. Away from Jaime Jo and the pain she was in. Away from Tommy Harris and all the pain he'd caused. Billy'd hoped the nightmare of a couple of years ago was over. They'd said Tommy'd changed. Billy now knew it was just wishful thinking after all. Far as he could tell, nothing had changed. If anything, it seemed worse than ever.

The one person who actually had the power to end it hadn't changed either. Jaime Jo was still protecting him. She wouldn't accuse Tommy. She wouldn't file a complaint. Billy didn't really understand why it mattered. Everyone knew Tommy was the one that was beating her. Her own father'd witnessed it more than once. Didn't that count for something? Why did they need to hear it from Jaime Jo's lips? Billy knew that would never happen. She would die first. And apparently that's where things were headed. Blame it on love. Must be a powerful thing, love, to drive two people as crazy as Jaime Jo Tremper and Tommy Harris. And that was something Billy Sawchuck knew he'd never experience.

So, for now, he just wanted to get away from all of it. But mostly he wanted to get away from himself, from being all alone. Billy Sawchuck should have left Pleasant Valley to find a life for himself long ago. But he didn't. And he wouldn't this time either. Once again, he'd settle for something less. Less than whole. Less than real. Less than true.

Before he knew it, he found himself pulling into that familiar parking lot out back. The Adult Junction was the closest to salvation Billy Sawchuck would ever get. A place where he could be himself, where he could find comfort in the arms of another. He knew it was a lie, that he was only fooling himself. But it was all he knew. And in a pinch, it would have to do.

So would the half bottle of Boone's Farm he'd found at the back of his mother's fridge. No wine cellar to be found at the Sawchuck residence. But after the first couple of swigs, it went down as smoothly as the finest champagne. By the time he'd drained the bottle, watching the sun set from the back of The Junction, his nerves had settled, he'd put the problems of home behind him, and he was ready for some action. Nothing like a wine buzz to transform a local hayseed into a prince charming.

Billy took a moment to pull himself together. He wiped the tears from his eyes and checked his hair out in the rearview mirror to make sure he looked presentable.

The room was barely spinning as he entered the place with a nod to Lou. Lou seemed to nod back with the assurance of a man who knew everyone's secrets. He seemed particularly full of himself at the moment, sporting an eerie smirk vaguely resembling a smile, as if he were the guardian of an extra special secret that night.

Billy wasn't the only one looking for salvation at the Junction that evening. A quick scan of the room revealed a familiar boy's face, a former conquest of his, leading Billy to wonder if that was the source of Lou's smirk. You never could tell with Lou. So Billy eased his way over toward the boy, hoping for the best. He took it slow, not wanting to spook the prey. Closing in, he smelled alcohol. That was a good sign, improving his odds.

The negotiation went smoothly enough. Apparently, the boy still hadn't found a girlfriend, and more importantly, harbored no regrets over his prior moment of weakness with Billy. In fact, they were both so eager to get down to business that they had to suffer an embarrassing reminder from Lou to come get some quarters before proceeding to the back room.

* * * *

Billy soon found himself alone again in the sticky booth in the Junction's back room. His courtships were uniformly short-lived, boyfriends of convenience quickly pulling themselves together in a flurry of buttons and zippers, hard-pressed to escape before the warm glow of release could wear off, inevitably replaced by the shameful weight of regret.

It was different for Billy, though. He always took his time, time to catch his breath, pull himself together, send his emotions back into hiding. He wouldn't give Lou the satisfaction of seeing him cry.

He was just wiping his eyes with his sleeve when he heard something disturbing coming from the booth next to his. Over the years he'd heard all sorts of moans and cries of ecstasy coming from the videos as well as the occupants of neighboring booths. But this was different, both the sounds coming from the video and from the occupant of the booth.

Billy'd seen the magazines out on the racks, the sick ones with the grainy black and white images of tied and cuffed women being beaten and tortured. But he'd never seen or heard such a thing on video. Now that he had, he was sure he'd never forget it. The sound of a crying girl begging and pleading for mercy at the hands of some sadist. It was a sound no one should hear, an image no one should see. What kind of sick fuck could possibly get off on something like that?

Billy only meant it as a rhetorical question. So when the answer instantly popped into his head unexpectedly, he felt a chill shake him to the bone.

His first thought was to run. Run before his suspicion could be confirmed. Just bury this moment at the Junction along with all the others he'd long forgotten. Did he really want final confirmation of his worst fears, that Tommy Harris truly was the monster everyone knew him to be? Everything good he'd ever felt for Tommy was screaming for him to run out the door and never look back.

But then he heard the screams of the girl in the video. And he could tell she was no actress. It was for real. And it was heartbreaking. He couldn't turn from it. He had to know.

Billy could just make out the flicker of light from the video coming through the hole in the wall between the booths. The hole was just the right size for peepers who preferred watching live action. It also happened to be just the right size for those who went the extra mile by bravely slipping a fifth extremity through the same hole in hopes of some anonymous interactive participation. Billy soon found himself bending to eye level with the peephole.

He first made out part of the video screen, catching bits and pieces of the action taking place there, and finding, as he expected, that the video was even more nauseating than the audio. He didn't know which would turn out worse, watching the video, or turning his gaze from it to confirm just who the audience was for such a thing.

But then, between the screams, he heard it. The whispering. Billy suffered a moment of panic, thinking maybe the viewer was whispering to him, that he'd been discovered. He pulled back from the peephole in fear. Yet the whispers continued. It sounded like some sort of chanting. Billy listened harder to decipher the words between the helpless cries for mercy.

It was the same thing over and over. "Lead us not into temptation but deliver us from evil. Lead us not into temptation but deliver us from evil. Lead us not—"

Billy had to look again. He bent to the peephole once more. The first thing that struck him were the hands. The viewer wasn't even beating off. His hands were clenched in fists at his sides, fighting the urge with all his might.

Soon Billy was straining to look upward through the limitations of the small hole. And as he adjusted his head to get a better angle he saw them. The eyes. Staring straight ahead, locked on the scene playing out on the small screen in front of them. Cold and piercing. Barely human. Yes, more bird-like than human. A bird of prey. The eyes of a hawk, locked on a small field mouse, every born instinct sending it hurtling downward, talons extended, ready to pounce on its victim.

Billy was mesmerized by those eyes, unable to turn away until it was too late. Something, maybe just the movement of Billy's own peeping eye in the hawk's peripheral vision had caught its attention, the bird eyes turning in unison to lock on his. And it was in that moment, before he'd even recognized the face, that Billy knew he'd become the field mouse, the hunted.

Billy's heart jumped in his chest as he fell backward against the opposite wall of the booth. He had to get out. He had to run. And he knew he'd be running for his life. He scrambled to his feet, lunging through the booth's curtain and bursting through the beaded one leading to the front part of the store. He didn't need to turn back to see if he was being pursued. His legs already knew. They knew it was time to run for his life. The magazine-lined walls went by in a blur as Billy bolted for the exit to the parking lot. He caught the look on Lou's face as he shot through the door. He wasn't looking at Billy. He was looking behind him, at his pursuer. And it only served to validate Billy's panic. It wasn't the first time Lou'd seen evil. But it was the first time he'd seen it bent on committing the ultimate act.

Billy was glad he hadn't locked Tinkerbell. He needed every second for his getaway. But when he fumbled for his keys and dropped them to the floor of the car he cursed himself for drinking all that wine. Yet, God must have felt sorry for him, for when he reached blindly downward for the keys they were instantly in his grasp. He jammed them in the ignition and Tinkerbell's four little cylinders sputtered to life. He still hadn't looked back at the Junction to see if he'd been followed. But as he threw the transmission into reverse, he felt the talons come through the open window clawing at his shoulder.

Billy's foot stomped on the accelerator, sending Tinkerbell lunging backward. The grasp of the talons almost yanked Billy through the window, until he felt the thud of the creature slamming into the driver's door panel as it fell to the graveled pavement, freeing Billy from it's grip.

Billy didn't look back until he'd managed to get Tinkerbell out of the parking lot and pointed toward Pleasant Valley. Only then did he dare glance up into the rearview mirror to see exactly what was hunting him. It looked smaller in the rearview. And yet, Billy knew the danger it held for him. It only stood still for a moment, just long enough to be sure it knew which direction Billy was headed. That's when it turned for its own car and Billy knew it was coming after him. The preacher was coming after him.

Chapter 20

Billy pressed Tinkerbell's gas pedal all the way to the floor, yet it wasn't far enough. Her tiny motor whined under the stress, but she would only go so fast. Would it be fast enough? Billy knew it was a matter of life and death. He saw it in the man's eyes. His secret would die with Billy Sawchuck.

If Billy could just get into town, he figured he'd be OK. At first, he thought maybe he should have stayed back at The Junction. But something told him the preacher's rage was too much to be denied by someone so anonymous as Lou. No, he had to get home. The preacher wouldn't try anything there, in front of people they both knew. He wouldn't blow his cover. If Billy could just make it home...

Even through the panic, his mind searched for meaning. One thing was clear to Billy. They'd all misjudged Tommy Harris. Billy just knew it. Tommy never had it in him. Not the Tommy Billy knew.

It was all a mistake. Now everything seemed to click into place about Jaime Jo. About why she'd never accused Tommy, about why she was always found beaten at home, how her father seemed to be the only witness. It was her father all along, not Tommy. But she was too afraid of the man to report it. And poor Tommy, sent off to Vietnam for nothing, he knew what was really going on, but didn't say a thing, out of loyalty to Jaime Jo, and fear for her life.

Just catching the preacher drooling over that video made everything clear. The bastard was probably jealous of what Tommy and Jaime Jo had, and took it out on her. But it was worse than some perverted kind of revenge. The man obviously took pleasure in it. The sick fuck actually got off on it, enjoyed beating his own daughter. Or worse. Could he have been doing anything else to her? The thought made Billy suddenly nauseous and he couldn't think about that or he wouldn't be able to drive

This was one secret that had outlived its usefulness. It was obvious to Billy that things weren't working out this way for either of them, Tommy now a hunted man, and Jaime Jo laid up at the hospital. No, better to let the truth out and be done with it. At least get her out of that house. Sure, he still had no hard evidence, and chances were a lot of folks wouldn't believe him. But Billy was never more sure of anything in his life. And if he could at least plant the seed of doubt concerning Tommy, and raise the possibility of the preacher's involvement, he knew the whole sordid thing would unravel. Shit, as it stood now, no one even imagined the preacher was the source of the problem. Well, all that was about to change. Billy Sawchuck would see to that. If he could only make it home…

As Tinkerbell barely managed to grip the country road over every bump and turn with her little tires, Billy kept dreaming that his pursuer had given up the chase. Yet every time he glanced in his rearview, the telltale headlights persisted, glowing like the preacher's eyes back at The Junction. Billy almost lost control a couple of times, screeching around the unlit bends in the road. After all, Tinkerbell wasn't exactly designed for NASCAR. And that bottle of Boone's Farm wasn't helping either.

He thought he'd been driving all night when he saw the bridge into town just up ahead. He thought of driving through town to the sheriff's place but knew better than that. The place to find the sheriff was at Billy's house, with his mom. Just as well. That wasn't far from the bridge, right on Main Street.

That was the plan, when suddenly he thought he heard a motor rev. But when he looked in the rearview, he wondered where that damn car'd gone. He didn't see any headlights. But feeling

Tinkerbell lurch, he suddenly knew why. The preacher's car was too close to see his lights. He was right on Billy's bumper. And as Tinkerbell began to sway out of control, Billy realized the preacher was pushing him off the road. He jammed on his brakes as he saw the edge of the ravine at the side of the bridge approaching. No one could survive a fall like that into the river below.

Billy didn't have time to think of a way out. Whether it was his own reflexes or Tinkerbell's he didn't know. But somehow, the last thing Billy remembered before coming to was that lone tree at the edge of the ravine miraculously jumping in the way to catch him.

He was only out for a couple of seconds, his head bleeding over the dashboard covered in shattered glass. At first he didn't know where he was, or why. But he was alive, which was more than he could say for poor Tinkerbell. A tree trunk seemed to be growing out of where her motor used to be.

When he looked away and saw the beginning of the bridge only a few feet away, he remembered he had to cross it into town. But he couldn't remember why. What was so urgent? Couldn't he just sit in the car and catch his breath? He didn't think so. His heart was starting to pound again. Something was telling him to run. Get out and run.

Blood was running down his forehead into his eyes. He raised his arm to brush it away but something grabbed it. Someone was opening the door and dragging him out of the car. Why? Billy tried to stand, but one leg buckled when he put weight on it. He thought maybe it was broken. But at least someone was helping him up. Billy put his arm around the man's shoulders as he supported Billy about the waist. He noticed it had begun to rain as they started to hobble across the bridge toward town. Billy knew it wasn't far to the salon. His mother would take care of everything, get him to a doctor, have Tinkerbell towed. Thank God there was some Good Samaritan to help him home. He didn't think he'd be able to make it on his own.

He was beginning to feel the pain throb in his leg as the adrenaline wore off. And just where was all the blood coming from? Other than red, he couldn't see very much. The rain was washing it into his eyes. He didn't think he could handle the throbbing in his leg much more, when he was allowed to rest midway across the bridge. Billy wanted to sit down. But his rescuer wouldn't let him. Billy thought maybe things were serious enough that he wanted to forge on into town, but when he felt himself pushed up against the bridge railing, he began to think something wasn't right. And when he felt his feet leave the pavement as he was bent backward over the rail, panic returned. What was happening? His arms shot out, grabbing the man around the shoulders, before he could be forced over the rail. The man tried to shake him off, but Billy grasped at the back of the man's neck to save himself. Then he rubbed his eyes on the man's shoulder to clear the blood away.

That's when he saw the preacher's face and everything came rushing back. The preacher was trying to kill him. He'd helped him out onto the bridge only to throw him over the railing to his death in the river below.

But Billy wasn't ready to go. Billy Sawchuck had plenty of reasons to hate his life. Always had. But that didn't mean he was ready to give up on it just yet. If nothing else, there was Jaime Jo to think of. She wouldn't speak up for herself. It was up to him to save her.

Billy Sawchuck was no gladiator. And he was hurt. And he was drunk. But he was young. And he was good. And that had to count for something. Billy decided to fight back.

"No!" he shouted at his attacker, finding his voice amid the first clap of thunder. He shoved the preacher away, regaining his feet as the pain shot up his broken leg.

The preacher was momentarily taken aback by the force of the scrawny young man. "You think a little faggot like you can stop me?" he countered, lunging back at his prey.

But Billy stepped aside, letting the preacher run into the railing. His first impulse was to run for it, but he knew his leg wouldn't carry him. Then he thought of yelling for help, but they were still too far from town, with no one about at night. No, he'd have to make a final stand at the bridge.

The preacher was on him again, manhandling him toward the railing of the bridge. With only one leg to support him, Billy was hard pressed to resist. His back to the rail again for support, he was able to fight back, throwing off the older man. But his brief success was met with a right cross, the preacher's fist adding stars to the blood already obscuring Billy's vision. Billy'd never been in a fistfight in his life. He was shocked and frankly disoriented by the violence of the strike to the jaw.

"Shit," the preacher laughed. "My Jaime Jo can take a better punch than that. Then again, she's had more practice."

He went after Billy again, but Billy shook off the effects of the punch just in time to avoid going over the rail. He threw his arms about the man to keep from falling backward over the edge, and when the preacher attempted to extricate himself from Billy's grip, Billy clawed at his eyes, drawing blood.

"Damn," the preacher remarked, dabbing at the blood on his face with the back of his hand. "You even fight like a girl. But that won't do you any good. Didn't help Jaime Jo. She tried that a couple of times at first, but I broke her of the habit. She accepts her punishment now. You see, women can be trained over time. Being practically a woman yourself, I'm sure I'd have equal success in your case. Unfortunately for you, I just don't have the time."

The boy was putting up more of a fight than he'd expected. Oh, he had no doubt he'd eventually wear down the wounded prey. But the clock was ticking. No telling when someone might decide to come cross the bridge in the middle of their dance. He'd better end it sooner than later.

The first thought Billy had when he saw the man back away was that maybe he'd changed his mind. Maybe Billy's resistance convinced him he wasn't worth the trouble. But when he looked into those hawk eyes aglow in a flash of lightning, he knew he'd been mistaken. Billy knew there'd be no stopping until one of them was dead. But Billy had no idea how to kill a man.

Warren Tremper had no such problem. He began to lecture Billy as he placed one hand in his coat pocket. "You can't win this, Billy Sawchuck, because I have the Lord at my side. You don't think I'd descend into a den of iniquity such as that sin-peddling smut shop you frequent without the Lord as my protector. You never know what manner of evil one might confront."

Billy didn't know what the man was getting at, but he was beginning to sound as crazy as he looked. Billy knew this was it. Whatever was going to happen, this was it. He thought briefly of jumping over the bridge railing into the river. But it was a long way down and the swift running river was full of jagged boulders. So when he saw what the preacher pulled from his pocket, all he could think to do was pray.

Only it wasn't his own words he heard through the thunder and lightning. It was the preacher's, calm and eerie. "Yea, though I walk through the valley of the shadow of death, I will fear no evil, for thou art with me. Thy rod and thy staff, they comfort me."

That's when Billy turned to make one last feeble run for his life.

Chapter 21

Jaime Jo was already mad at Billy Sawchuck for not coming to visit her at the hospital for three whole days. But she'd have forgiven him if he'd at least come to give her a ride home when she got discharged. But Billy was nowhere to be found.

Now she'd have to wait around for her father while he took his sweet time. She sorely missed her Scarlet. No one but Billy had brought her to the hospital to visit. She'd been left with a sitter most of the hospitalization. That was the usual routine, as she couldn't count on her father to do right by her.

Finally she got tired of sitting around the hospital lobby waiting, so when she saw one of her nurses leaving after her shift, Jaime Jo thought she'd hitch a ride at least into town. There she stopped at the Beauty Shoppe looking for a ride from Billy, only to find a worried Charlotte, speculating that maybe her son had finally moved on, left Pleasant Valley for greener pastures. Funny how someone from Pleasant Valley could go suddenly missing for three days and people just assumed they'd had enough and lit out for parts unknown. That was Pleasant Valley for you. Jamie Jo couldn't blame him. At one time or another, most everyone in Pleasant Valley wished they'd had the gumption to up and do what Billy apparently had done. It wasn't like him, though, not to say goodbye.

Jaime Jo's first thought on the subject was, good for you, Billy Sawchuck. A successful escape from Pleasant Valley. That was a cause for celebration.

But the euphoria only lasted so long. She was soon confronted by the fallout from Billy's decision, for now Jaime Jo was alone. With Billy gone, she had no one. No one to get her through the day. No one to prop her up and make her laugh. Even with all her baggage, Billy still loved her unconditionally.

Oh, there was Tommy. No one could possibly love her more than Tommy. But that was just the problem. Tommy's unwillingness to let her go is exactly what led to all the trouble. If he would just accept the fact that they could never be, then things could go back to the way they were. Numb, but tolerable. At least she could breathe pain free, which was more than she could say at the moment.

Jaime Jo was feeling that pain as she placed one labored step after another down Main Street, toward the bridge. She didn't remember consciously deciding to head for the bridge. But that's where she wound up. She wondered if that's how it was with her mother those eight years ago. Did she consciously decide to take her own life? Did she weigh the pros and cons, plan it all out, down to the clothes they'd find her body in? Or was it like this? Did she just find herself alone at the bridge railing one day overwhelmed by a compelling urge to rest? Just rest, forever more.

That was just what Jaime Jo wanted. To rest. She was tired of the whole mess. Her father, Tommy, and the beatings that resulted, as if stirring the two men together led to some combustible chemical reaction. She guessed it was the beatings mostly that left her so weary. There comes a point where the soul gives way to the body, and the physical pain drowns out the emotional. There comes a time when even in the absence of pain, during those intervals between the beatings, the memory of it lives on undiminished, when life becomes a thing not lived, but suffered.

That's the place Jaime Jo found herself, standing at the bridge railing. And not for the first time either. She remembered back to the day Tommy'd left for Vietnam. She was pregnant with Scarlet at the time. And she never expected to see Tommy again. Coming back alive from Vietnam seemed to be the exception to the rule.

It was only Billy talked her out of it. He begged her not to leave him behind, all alone in Pleasant Valley. He told her things would get better now that Tommy was leaving. There was only one way to go once you hit bottom. And that was up. As much as she loved Tommy, things could only get better when he was gone.

Jaime Jo knew better. She knew something only she and Tommy knew. She never expected the beatings to cease on his departure. And yet, to her surprise, they had. Even though Tommy Harris was never the one inflicting the pain, he nevertheless appeared to be the trigger for it. It seemed Tommy's attention paid to Jaime Jo was precisely the thing that set her father off. Any reminder that she was becoming a woman only seemed to raise a flag of warning to the preacher. She was now fully capable of sin, committing it, or tempting others to do so themselves. As if becoming a sexual being in itself was the sin, and the uncontrollable feelings it stirred in her father were the natural result. Natural? Well that's what Jaime Jo was led to believe.

So when Tommy Harris left, and Jaime Jo was no longer seen as an object of desire, the beatings subsided. The healing process was already well along when she became a mother. And since that point, seen in a new light, her father had left her alone.

But then Tommy came back. And the whole cycle began again.

As a result, she found herself back at the bridge once more. Only this time, Billy'd left her behind. This time, there was no one to stop her, no one to talk her down.

Except the Lord. She hadn't spoken with him yet. And if ever there was a time to ask his opinion on a matter, this was it.

Jaime Jo knelt on the hard bridge pavement, her forehead pressed to the metal railing, and prayed. She didn't even know what to pray for. That was entirely up to Him. She was in his hands now.

"Just tell me what to do, Lord. I hold out my hand to you. Please take it and guide me. I beg you." She reached up to Him, anticipating his reply. She looked up into the morning sun, expecting a sign. But there was none to see. Nothing but silence.

Had even He deserted her? What did she expect? She knew He'd be disappointed. She knew his stance on suicide. Had He already given her over to the devil? Maybe her father was right. She could try to understand her father's actions toward her, how she bore responsibility for those actions. But what about God? What about *his* actions? Or inaction. Apparently He wasn't happy with her either. First her mother was taken. Then the whole business with Tommy. One thing after another. Even Job had it coming to him. She always knew it was of her own doing.

She remembered first hearing the truth about her mother, about how she'd surrendered all those years ago at the very spot Jaime Jo now knelt. At first, it made no sense to little Jaime Jo. Why would she do such a thing? But children are impatient. So the answer came to her much too quickly. It was the wrong answer. But it was an answer. At 11 years of age, a child's world still revolves about themselves. They are the center of the universe, the cause of everything good, and everything bad. It was all Jaime Jo's fault. She knew she was to blame for her mother's suicide. She wasn't sure how, whether she'd done something bad, or whether she simply wasn't good enough. Never mind. It didn't matter anymore. Her mother was gone. Because of her. And from that point on, anything bad that happened to her was her own fault. And so her destiny was clear. Like her mother's. The time had come. The time to go.

Except for one thing. Unlike herself, her Scarlet had done nothing wrong. Where was the blame for little Scarlet? Jaime Jo'd been left behind by her mother. But that was different. Jaime Jo deserved it. At least that's what she'd let herself believe. But she couldn't believe the same of innocent Scarlet. How would her baby feel when she learned her mother'd left her? Would she blame herself? As Jaime Jo'd done? Even the thought of it was ridiculous. Or was it? Who would be there to explain it to her, make sure she got it right? Who? Her grandfather?

That was hardly a comforting thought. Even worse than that, much worse, who would stand between Scarlet and her grandfather? Who would protect her from him once she came of age and he began to see the devil in her too? Jaime Jo vividly remembered praying to her mother in the beginning, when her father began abusing her. But her mother wasn't there. There was no one to hear her prayers, to hear her screams. She'd been left to the wolves.

Sure, God didn't come to her rescue either. But he must have had his reasons. He wasn't to blame for that. It was her mother. She was to blame. She was the one who'd abandoned her. Maybe the Lord wasn't done punishing Jaime Jo Tremper yet. Maybe he still had his pound of flesh to take from up in heaven. Well, let him have his pound, or two or three. But unlike her mother before her, Jaime Jo would take her punishment. She'd stay with her child and defend it from the evil still walking this Earth. Jaime Jo Tremper wouldn't be going anywhere. Looks like she had her answer after all.

Still a bit shaky, Jaime Jo stood up to turn away from the railing and head back into town. But before she turned, something caught her eye. Something down in the ravine, at the edge of the river, something, or someone, familiar.

Chapter 22

Otis Williams was barely short of incoherent on a good day. And today was anything but a good one. Distracted by the scene playing out up on the bridge, Jo Bob Buckner was having trouble questioning his witness down by the river's edge.

Up on the bridge, poor Charlotte Sawchuck was inconsolable. It had become clear that she refused to leave the bridge until her son's body was brought up to her. She'd run all the way from the salon as soon as she'd heard the news. She still had her work apron on when she spied the body from the railing and collapsed in the middle of the bridge. Her friends tried in vain to take her home. Doc Henderson, the local general practitioner, and medical examiner in a pinch, tried to have her sedated, but Charlotte wouldn't have it. She'd wait for her Billy to be brought up to her.

Jo Bob was not unsympathetic. In fact, it tore him up, seeing the state she was in, hearing her anguished cries all the way down at the river's edge. No mother should ever have to go through what Charlotte was going through. He didn't know how she'd ever get over the loss.

And God only knew when she'd ever be in the mood again. Jo Bob knew he was in for a lengthy dry spell. That right there was reason enough to catch the murderer. The man comes between Jo Bob Buckner and pussy was gonna' pay dearly.

It wasn't that Jo Bob was an unfeeling man. Just the opposite. He really liked Billy Sawchuck. He was a good boy. So what if the kid was queer? What was this world coming to when being queer was a crime? Was a time when queer was just... well... queer. Weren't nothin' to be afraid of, to be hated, to be snuffed out. Besides, Jo Bob would miss all of Billy's little pointers on how to impress the ladies. See, there he went again, making a joke out of things. But he didn't mean anything by it. That was just his way, how he dealt with stress and loss. He didn't want to think about it, about what it was doing to Charlotte, or the whole town for that matter, including poor Jaime Jo Tremper. As if things weren't bad enough for her already, now she'd lost her only friend in the world.

But all that emotional baggage was beyond Jo Bob's pay grade. Leave that to the biddies from the beauty salon. The best he could do was focus on the task at hand. He had a murder to solve.

Jo Bob wondered when Pleasant Valley had become the kind of town in which murders actually occurred. He'd never had a murder on his watch before. Talk about a pain in the ass. It wasn't supposed to be this way. That wasn't part of the deal. When the previous sheriff talked him into the job, the only requirement was to be big enough to intimidate any drunks might get out of hand down at Chezzy's. No one ever said nothin' about murder. As if this whole Tommy Harris business wasn't enough.

Like everyone else, Jo Bob initially assumed it was just another suicide off that damn bridge. That is, until Doc Henderson pulled that 38 slug out of the kid's back. That changed everything.

After the boys finally carried the body up to Charlotte, Jo Bob returned to his witness. It hadn't taken long for Jo Bob to spy Otis Williams fishing down river. The man was always lurking somewhere about the bridge. If there'd been anything to see thereabouts, Otis was your man. But getting anything more than incoherent babble out of him was the problem.

No one ever really knew what Otis's problem was. For all Jo Bob new, the man could have been a victim of that crazy new shit going around called LSD. But whatever it was, the man just never made no damn sense.

"Otis already told you, Sheriff Boss, Otis didn't see nuthin." Otis always referred to himself in the third person.

Jo Bob just responded with an eyeful of intimidation. He knew the man seated on the river rock next to him was just scared. Of course, he had good reason to be, the murdered body of a white man found practically in the black man's living room. Jo Bob had to feel sorry for the man. Not that he was any kind of civil rights activist. Nothing of the kind. He was just as prejudiced as the next redneck. The way he saw it, it was just a matter of fairness. There was just something unfair about being black. Like fishin' with dynamite, or huntin' cattle. Just didn't seem sportin'. Jo Bob thanked God he wasn't born black. Cause that would really suck.

Otis couldn't handle the sheriff's silent treatment. "This old nigger ain't see'd no evil, ain't heard none, and got none to speak of." He couldn't look Jo Bob in the eye.

"Look here, Otis," began Jo Bob, pointing his finger at the man, "don't you be callin' me stupid. You know better than that. This here's your home," he added gesturing to the whole area under the bridge. "Something like this happens in a man's home, a man's bound to know about it."

The black man just shook his head at his bad luck. Why'd he always have to be findin' dead white people down by the river? He found that sad lady years ago, too. She practically threw herself off that bridge. Flew right to heaven. But this boy, he was different. Oh, he sho' enough went to heaven, all right. But he weren't ready to go. He put up a fight, somethin' fierce. And afterward? Well, he was thrown off that bridge. Otis seen it with his own eyes. Why's Otis gots to be seein' everything?

"Otis don't know nuthin'," he insisted.

Jo Bob guessed it was time to turn up the heat. He bent over the seated man. "You listen to me, boy. If a man can't be responsible for what goes on in his own house," Jo Bob began, pointing up at the man's cardboard mansion tucked up under the bridge, "then maybe that house ought to be taken away from him. Maybe that man'd be better off livin' in a cell up at the prison."

That got his attention all right. Otis suddenly looked up at Jo Bob, the fear of God in his eyes. More than a few tears as well. "Oh please, Boss, don't be takin' Otis's home away. Otis wants to help." But he turned away, nervously scratching the back of his head.

"Then help," ordered Jo Bob. "Tell me what you saw, what you heard. You must have heard that car crash into the tree up there. You must have heard a gun go off. That must have gotten your attention. Don't tell me otherwise."

Otis began to wag his head back and forth in distress. "It was a thunderin' that night, Boss. Otis can't be sure what he heard."

"Well then how about what Otis saw?"

"Lordy Lordy, Boss. You's puttin' Otis in a tight spot. Otis scared to death."

Jo Bob thought to try a different approach. He sat down next to Otis, no simple task in itself. The man smelled something awful. Kind of a cross between dead fish and urine. Jo Bob just hoped there weren't no cooties lookin' to jump ship.

"Look here, Otis. You just tell me who did this and I'll put him away for good. Shit, I won't even let them waste no last meal on him. Just fry him directly in that big old chair over at the prison, the one with all the wires stickin' out of it. And you can bank on that. My Charlotte up there wouldn't settle for no less than that. Wouldn't have it no other way. So you don't have to worry about him. You've got my word on that. What do you say?"

Otis eyed the sheriff, considering his words. Then he took a deep breath, looked up at the bridge and started nervously rocking back and forth. "Yeah, Otis heard somethin' all right. Seen somethin' too."

Jo Bob wanted to slap himself on the back. This murder solving business was going to be a lot easier than he thought. "What, Otis? What'd you see?"

"Seen the Lord. Otis seen the Lord."

God damn it. Jo Bob wanted to scream in frustration. He wanted to slap the old nigger upside the head with the butt of his nightstick. But then he controlled himself, barely.

"Don't give me any of that religious mumbo jumbo. Can't you just pretend to be sane for five minutes? That's all I ask," begged Jo Bob, feeling desperate.

"Oh Boss, Otis be just as sane as the next man. Just as sure as he seen the light all them years ago, he seen the Lord take that boy's life up there on the bridge."

Jo Bob just stared at the crazy nigger. And he saw just where this interview was going. Nowhere. Even if, by some chance, the man actually saw what happened up on that bridge, Jo Bob would never be able to make heads nor tails of it. So, instead, he lay backward on the river rock, staring back up at the scene on the bridge. The last thing he wanted to do was to go back up there. But that's where his thoughts went, to Charlotte, and what he would tell her, what words could help ease her anguish.

As Jo Bob lay there, Otis Williams's blathering faded into the rush of the river. "The sound of it woke me up. Shook the ground. The Lord meant to take him when he ran his car into that tree. But that boy, he weren't ready. 'Tween you and me, Boss, when the Lord come for Otis, Otis take his hand and walk directly toward the light. But not that boy. No, he just weren't ready yet. So the Lord, he drags him out to the bridge to give him a little nudge, to help him on his way. But still that boy put up a fight. Wouldn't listen to no amount of reasonin' or passages from the scripture. I guess the Lord finally done run out of patience. I never seen nuthin' like it. Now it was a stormin' to be sure, but I seen a bolt of lighting spring directly from the Lord to the boy, right up on that bridge. From the hand of God Almighty himself. Seen it with my own eyes. Stopped that boy right in his tracks. Then, and only then, did that boy finally lie still enough for the Lord to help him on his way."

Otis told the truth, well, mostly. He only lied about one part. He hoped the sheriff didn't notice. All that talk of the Lord. He knew better than that. He knew it weren't the Lord at all. Otis Williams wasn't crazy like everyone thought. No, it weren't the Lord. Otis had eyes. And he knew the difference between the Lord and the devil. But he didn't say it. Otis was scared of the devil.

Otis Williams was still mumbling to himself when Jo Bob turned in frustration and made the steep climb back up to the bridge, huffing and puffing from the effort. Charlotte Sawchuck almost knocked him over when she fell into his arms, a total wreck. Seeing and touching her Billy's lifeless body hadn't helped matters.

At first she couldn't speak. She just shook against Jo Bob's chest, the tears and snot running right through his shirt.

Jo Bob never pretended to be an eloquent man, and he certainly had no words at the moment for Charlotte Sawchuck, as her entire posse from the beauty shop looked on helplessly. In fact, it wasn't long before Jo Bob had to turn from the onlookers himself so they wouldn't see his own tributary of tears joining Charlotte's to form a river down his chest.

Her first words came as a squeak. "You get him, Jo Bob. Promise me you'll get him."

He tried to comfort her, stroking her hair. "Now Charlotte, you know I'll do everything in my power to try to—"

But she shoved him away with surprising strength for something so petite. She just shoved him away and began screaming at him at the top of her lungs.

"Shut up! You just shut up, Jo Bob Buckner! I didn't ask you to *try* nothin', now did I!? I never asked you for nothin' in my life!" She didn't stop to take a breath as Jo Bob found himself stepping backward in fear. She followed him step for step, a finger wagging in his face, flames shooting from her swollen red eyes.

"And I'm not askin' you now either! I'm tellin' you! I'm tellin' you, Jo Bob! You get that son of a bitch! You get the animal what done this to my Billy!" Then, without any pause for reply from Jo Bob, Charlotte Sawchuck turned on her heel and marched back to her friends over by the body where she collapsed in their arms.

Jo Bob took one bewildered step in her direction but was stopped by Charlotte's voice again, once more diminished to the squeaky moan of a small broken woman.

"And don't you be coming around my bedroom door 'till you do." With that, she was lost to view as her friends closed ranks, engulfing her in the protection of the herd. So began the mission of getting Charlotte home.

Jo Bob was left standing there like a bad dog just rapped on the snout with the Sunday paper. Not another thought entered his head when he felt a pat on his back and an arm about his shoulder.

"Come on, Asshole. Sounds like we got some work to do." It was his old football buddy, Jimmy Harris.

Jo Bob looked at the man offering his help. He saw the bloodshot eyes and the tremor in his hands, the drawn unshaven face and unkempt hair. He saw a lot of things that didn't exactly instill the confidence a man would want in a deputy. But what he didn't see for the first time in a while was the glazed-over look of the drunkard. He didn't smell no booze neither. It was apparent to Jo Bob that Jimmy Harris had put some forethought and effort into his appearance at the bridge. The man seemed sincere enough. And Jo Bob could use all the help he could get.

"You sober?"

"A good 12 hours," Jimmy replied, proudly. "Word travels fast down to Chezzy's. Soon as I heard the Sawchuck boy turned up in a bad way, I suspected you'd be needing my assistance."

"I told you that you was on leave."

Jimmy looked disappointed. "But that was just concerning my boy. If you don't trust me to look into that bullshit about my own boy and the Tremper girl, that's one thing. Oh, I'm sure you need my help there too cause I just know you got it all wrong. There's more to that story than meets the eye. But at least I can see your point, my conflict of interest and all. You insist on messin' up that whole business about Tommy, you're on your own. But this is different. This has nothin' to do with my boy."

But Jo Bob wasn't so sure of that, and wasn't quite quick enough to hide the doubt questioning Jimmy's premise.

Jimmy pulled his arm from Jo Bob's shoulder and shoved him forcefully in the chest.

"Fuck you, Jo Bob Buckner. Bend you over and fuck you with a goddamned jackhammer. My boy's out there hidin' up in the mountains somewhere over somethin' don't make no sense, not to me anyhow, and now you're tellin' me you think he's involved in this too?"

Jo Bob hadn't time to think it through yet, but he had to admit he was having some trouble connecting those dots. "Now I never said no such thing, Jimmy. But I can't be seen excluding suspects just on your say so, now can I?"

Jimmy tried to calm himself. He noticed that was a lot harder to do without whiskey. His lips were beginning to feel awfully dry.

"Then don't do it on my say so. Do it cause it don't make no sense. Other than the Tremper girl, Charlotte's boy was Tommy's only friend. Why would Tommy want to kill him? It don't make no sense no how."

Jo Bob couldn't really argue with the man. Maybe Jimmy was right. On the other hand, was he to believe there were *two* violent maniacs running around little ol' Pleasant Valley, North Carolina? "The boy was shot, Jimmy."

"So what's that supposed to mean? Tommy never shot no one wasn't no Vietnamese. Just admit it, Jo Bob. Anything bad happens in this town, you assume my boy's behind it."

"Well, you got to admit—"

"I don't got to admit nothin'. Billy Sawchuck was shot in the back with a 38. Tommy never owned no 38 in his life. No good for huntin'. Besides, no matter what you think he's become, you've known my boy his whole life. Do you honestly think he'd shoot a friend in the back? You sure it's my boy and not yourself you're thinkin' of?" He'd never forget who sent Tommy to Vietnam.

It was a low blow. But Jo Bob guessed he deserved it. Jimmy was right. It wasn't Tommy Harris. Nothing about it made any sense. At this point he was only arguing for the sake of arguing. Besides, this sleepy little town had suddenly evolved into something more than one man could handle, and Jo Bob could use some real backup for a change. Not like those stupid kids he'd rounded up to watch out for Tommy, just boys pretending at doing a man's job. No, he had an urgent problem to solve and could use all the help he could get. For Charlotte's sake.

"You're right, Jimmy. I apologize." Jo Bob offered his hand to his friend to shake on it.

Jimmy Harris looked at the offering wearily. But life was short. Too short to stand on ceremony. He learned that today when they pulled that boy from the river. He shook his friend's hand.

"Where do we start?"

Jo Bob leaned against the bridge railing and looked down at the river below.

"Well, as much as it would have simplified things, we know it weren't no suicide. Kind of hard to shoot yourself in the back, let alone climb over the railing afterwards."

Both men saw the elephant in the room. But neither was comfortable with it. Finally Jimmy came at it from an angle.

"Jo Bob, I'm thinkin' this here was a crime of passion."

Jo Bob was grateful the other man brought it up. "I can't disagree with you there, Jimmy. The kid probably made some unwanted advances on the wrong fella'. You know, some good ol' boy don't take kindly to queers. A whatchacallem? Homophobian?"

"That's how I see it, pretty much," Jimmy agreed. "But that don't narrow things down much around these parts. The place is crawlin' with homophobians."

"True enough. Then I guess we ought to start at the beginning. What kind of place would Billy have been that he might make such a foolish move? Where might he expect to find someone of his own persuasion, or someone hard up enough in a pinch to switch hit?"

"That's got to be pretty hard up," offered Jimmy.

"No shit. In my day, used to be any fuzzy little sheep or some big ol' Hereford was good enough. But not now. No siree. Now you got boys doin' boys. Go figure. Sometimes I'm just glad to be gettin' old."

Chapter 23

They say blood is thicker than water. Maybe that's why the damn stuff is so hard to wash off. That's what Warren Tremper wondered when he first got home to clean up after the events out on the bridge that night. At least Jaime Jo wasn't there to start asking questions. He knew God must have had a plan when he made Warren land his own daughter in the hospital. He'd have had quite a time explaining away all that blood. But thankfully Jaime Jo was over at the hospital and Scarlet was with the sitter. That gave him plenty of time to clean up the mess. A little bleach went a long way toward making his car presentable. The clothes, he just burned. But he did forget one thing, at least at first. In all the rush to clean up the blood, he'd almost forgotten that he'd temporarily placed the 38 in his dresser drawer. It'd been a couple of days, but at least he'd finally remembered before it was too late and someone discovered it.

They said Jaime Jo'd left the hospital on her own, but she hadn't made it home yet. Probably stopped to pick the baby up from the sitter. This was his chance to put the gun back where it belonged. That's how he found himself over at the church talking to God the night the boy's body was finally found. He kept the lights off so as not to draw attention. Just a small sconce near the altar kept a crucified Jesus from falling into darkness.

Warren always felt a little sorry for himself when Jaime Jo and the baby were gone, leaving him alone. But they'd be back. As long as he knew they'd be back. His wife Ella wouldn't be back. The good Lord chose to take her early, eight years before, leaving him and his girl Jaime Jo, just eleven at the time, just the age at which a girl needed her momma. But as sweet innocent Jaime grew into her teenage years without Ella around, she just couldn't seem to find her way, led down the path of temptation by that devil of a boy, Tommy Harris. Warren did his best to keep them apart, a sort of house arrest. But it's hard to keep a beautiful bird locked up in a cage when she's ready to spread her wings and fly. She'd see that boy at school, and soon enough she was sneaking out of the house at night. And that was something Warren just couldn't abide.

That's when he had to take action. After all, he couldn't keep her locked up in the house forever. So he gave her some line. And what did she do? She hung herself with it. At first she'd just covered the bruises up with makeup. But soon they were everywhere and she just gave up, allowing all the world to see her shame. Why a girl would continue seeing a boy that would only lead to such abuse was beyond Warren. But he'd never been one to understand girls, or women for that matter. Way before Jaime Jo, it took a while for him and Ella to see eye to eye. Not that he'd ever really understood her either. But over time, she'd adapted, they came to an understanding, and things settled down. He didn't have that with Jaime Jo, an understanding. All because of that boy. The boy'd come between them.

Well he wasn't between them while he was over in Nam getting shot at. Warren made sure of that, as any father would. It took long enough, but the whole town finally couldn't ignore the damage that boy was apparently inflicting on Jaime Jo Tremper, all the result of his filthy propensities. And there was never any question in Warren's mind that the boy was the cause of Jamie Jo's wounds. Warren Tremper never blamed himself. No matter that it was by his own hands that his daughter suffered. In Warren's mind, that was merely a technicality. He'd had no choice. After all, what was a father to do? Everyone knows what happens when teenage boys and girls get together, the type of things got nothing to do with love. Nothing like the love Warren felt for Ella, and then, after Ella's passing, for Jaime Jo.

No, the girl had to be punished. And Warren assumed that would put an end to her sinful relationship with the boy. But it didn't. The sneaking around continued. The devil himself had Jaime Jo under his spell.

And the whole town agreed with Warren. They knew it was all the boy's fault. Tommy Harris was the reason Jaime Jo suffered. And when she turned up with child, with that abomination in her belly, well that was the last straw. The situation had to be remedied. And the military was just the place to do it, beat a little respect and humility into him. Even then, should the insolence persist, at least it would be overseas. And if the Lord, in his infinite wisdom, should decide to take vengeance on the boy through a Vietnamese bullet or landmine, then so be it. It's the Lord's prerogative, after all, to right all wrongs and bring home the wicked at the time of his choosing.

And there was plenty of wickedness to be dealt with as far as Warren Tremper was concerned. But that was nothing new to Warren. Even back when he was in high school, it seemed to be all around him. The goings on between boys and girls was an affront to all God holds dear. Rutting like animals in heat. Even without the girls, self-flagellation was rampant. It seemed fornication in one form or another was everywhere. Everyone was doing it. Everyone but Warren. Warren had to control himself. Warren Tremper had to stay pure.

Oh, he'd had his lapses, driven beyond reason by the temptation inflicted by all those young siren whores at school, finding himself in one compromising position or another in his moments of weakness. Yet he never touched anyone, or himself, for that matter. At least not until that boy turned his little girl into a slut. No, Warren Tremper believed his place in heaven was still safe. And he didn't expect to see people like Tommy Harris when he got there.

Warren Tremper was, after all, a preacher. He knew all too well the difference between heaven and hell. That was the easy part. But it was life on earth that perplexed him, that challenged him. Each and every day was a struggle to do the Lord's work. And so he looked forward to his time in church when he could be alone with the Lord, time when he could speak with him directly.

As he often did when he found himself alone with the Lord, the preacher approached the church alter, eyes closed, face to heaven, arms spread to either side, a crucified offering, waiting to be carried to his proper place alongside the Holy Father. Unfortunately, as usual, when he opened his eyes, he found himself right where he'd started, on the very Earth he'd spent his whole life, in that same sinful jungle the Lord saw fit to place him, locked in daily battle with the devil himself. The earthly demons were potent and plentiful. Satan's minions were perpetually on the move, both from without and within. Why he was chosen to fight the Lord's battles, he did not know. But he'd been chosen nevertheless. And there was so much to do. Each and every day was a struggle for Warren Tremper.

Warren was speaking directly to God as he stood alone at the pulpit looking heavenward.

"Things had been quiet around here, Lord. Once that boy was gone, everything went back to the way it was. Once the devil was cast out, I had my Jaime Jo back. That's all I ever asked for. And I've behaved my Lord. Even raised that little abomination as one of my own. Please don't forsake me now. Don't cast me out. I'm afraid, my Lord. Afraid I'm not strong enough, afraid I'll fail your test."

Yet Warren knew he'd already failed. He wanted to have faith in the Lord, faith that the Lord would reward those that walked the straight and narrow. But Warren couldn't wait. He'd suffered a moment of weakness. His temper got the better of him and he'd taken things into his own hands. Killing the Sawchuck boy was an act of passion. And passion was a thing Warren Tremper had struggled his whole life to control.

He glanced involuntarily at the floorboards behind the pulpit, drawn to the place where the gun normally rested for safekeeping. Catching himself, he quickly raised his face to heaven again, hoping the Lord hadn't noticed. Yet he knew he was merely kidding himself. God was all knowing and saw everything. Warren could never escape his eyes, his judgment. But why him? Why was God so forgiving of others, yet so harsh with him? Warren knew the answer to his own question. He knew that people of God were held to a higher standard. He always knew that. But that knowledge didn't make it any easier. Was he up to the task? It seemed every day of Warren Tremper's life was a test, a battle between the Lord and the demons within him.

"I know your decision to take the Sawchuck boy was the right one, Lord. And I thank you for it. He would have told. He would have told the whole world what he'd seen. Then the world would have known our secret. They'd have known it was me and not Tommy Harris that raised a hand to Jaime Jo. But someone had to do it. Someone had to keep her on the straight and narrow. And who but her father owned that responsibility? No one. But you already know that. I don't have to tell you."

Warren paused to collect his thoughts as his mind returned to the problem at hand. His grip tightened on the pistol in his pocket.

"I couldn't have done it without your help, Lord. The boy was stronger than I'd expected. I'm sure the devil played his part in that. But I know the Lord always provides for the needy."

Warren pulled the 38 from his pocket and held it up high to his Lord. "And I'm thankful for that, thankful you saw fit to provide me the tools to carry out your good work. It was only with your help, Lord, that I had the means to overcome that boy with the devil in him."

Warren Tremper remembered the last time he had such a conversation with God, eight years before. He was looking for absolution then too. "I know this isn't the first life I've taken. But surely you agree that sometimes the devil is so embedded within a soul that it's impossible to drive him out. That's when drastic measures must be taken."

Warren looked again at the gun in his hands. He had trouble raising his eyes to Jesus. He'd hoped hearing his own thoughts aloud would help him believe them himself. Yet he knew his words rang false. Warren Tremper was no stranger to the concept of guilt. He knew in his heart that he couldn't pull a fast one over the Lord. He knew he'd overstepped his authority back then, and now he'd done it once more. He just hoped the Lord would forgive him for taking things into his own hands again. After all, he'd had no other choice.

Warren walked tentatively forward to the altar, fearful that at any moment a bolt from above would reveal just how angry God was. He looked up once more at the figure of the Lord's son nailed to the cross. He forced himself to look into the face of Jesus, into the eyes of the one that died for all our sins. Did that include everyone? Did Jesus die for Warren Tremper's sins? Warren wasn't so sure. He continued to stare into those eyes. And soon the eyes were his own. The face was his. Warren Tremper was nailed up on that cross. That's when Warren knew. He knew Jesus hadn't died for him. Not Warren Tremper. No, Warren Tremper would have to pay his own way. At that moment, Warren Tremper knew in his heart he would die for his sins.

He felt a cold shiver run down his spine. But then it was gone. And Warren felt a calm peace spread over him, just reaffirming what he'd always known. His fate was in the hands of the Lord. As it should be. All was right in the world.

Warren stepped behind the altar and bent to one knee, carefully raising the loose floorboard to reveal a small hiding place. He gently placed the weapon in its dusty home and covered it over again with the board. He hoped he'd never see it again. But one never knew. No telling when it might be called upon again. That would be up to the Lord, as always.

Warren Tremper left the church and went back to the house, relieved that all the loose ends were finally tied up, all the evidence cleaned up and buried, nothing out of place.

Except one thing. He'd nearly forgotten one last loose end. Jaime Jo. He'd almost forgotten that night had fallen and she still hadn't made it home yet. But he didn't let it bother him. He was confident she'd find her way. His daughter was a lot tougher than people gave her credit for. Warren's fists could certainly attest to that. And he could certainly understand why she was in no rush to come home. She'd probably enjoyed her little vacation over at the hospital.

And Warren was right, about most of it, all except the part about Jaime Jo not being home. Earlier that morning, Jaime Jo'd been the one who'd discovered Billy Sawchuck's body in the very place she'd thought to throw her own. In shock, she'd run for help. Running on reflex and adrenaline, she'd just acted without thinking. She'd thought Billy'd taken his own life. And later, after a moment's reflection, she'd again forgotten all about her concern for leaving her daughter behind, and thought maybe she should have joined Billy right then and there, just hurled herself over the railing to land with a thud at his side.

But she didn't. She hadn't had time to think of herself. All her thoughts were with Billy. And then she'd heard what Doc Henderson and Sheriff Buckner had discovered. Billy hadn't taken his own life after all. He'd been murdered. Shot. In the back. Something about a 38.

And so Jaime Jo's thoughts shifted from suicide to confusion. Who would want to kill Billy Sawchuck? Nothing made sense anymore. So she didn't take her own life. Instead, she walked all the way home in a daze. She didn't remember the walk. She didn't remember how she'd cried the whole way. She just walked, something or someone leading her one foot in front of the other, toward home. But not exactly home. Next door. To the church.

She didn't know why. The church had ceased being a place of refuge and comfort for Jaime Jo Tremper long ago, ever since her mother'd passed away. Then when Tommy came into her life, her father told her that what she and Tommy Harris had was vile and sinful, that the resulting punishment was simply the will of God. And Jaime Jo believed him. Her father was, after all, not only her father, but a man of God. So instead of being a place of refuge, the church had become a frightful place, a place full of meanness, where constant battle raged, Satan pitted against the wrath of God. And Jaime Jo didn't know which was worse. And yet, long after the sun had set, when she'd finally stopped walking and looked up, she found herself in the church she'd come to fear. She sat in the last pew, all the way at the back, in the dark.

She didn't know why God brought her there. And she certainly had nothing to say to Him. So she just sat quietly, waiting for some kind of sign, some kind of answer. That's when she saw her father walk in.

For some reason he hadn't turned on the lights, so he walked right by her on his way toward the pulpit. He never noticed her sitting quietly in the dark. And Jaime Jo preferred it that way. She saw no reason to speak up.

Instead, she watched and listened in silence. She heard every word her father said, how he'd killed her best friend in cold blood. And then, as if that weren't bad enough, he had the nerve to thank the Lord for helping him. Billy Sawchuck loved everyone. And the idea that God could have had a hand in taking her sweet Billy's life was... well... grotesque. There was just no other word for it.

As she sat mutely listening to his confession, she felt her heart pound so hard that she thought it would burst from her chest, break free of her, and leave her dead where she sat. But it didn't. That would have been too easy. Instead, she sat in silence. Watching. Listening. And she stayed there long after he'd gone, letting it all sink in.

Back at the bridge, she couldn't imagine who would have wanted to kill poor Billy Sawchuck, sweet Billy who'd never hurt fly. Who would do such a thing? Well now she knew. Jaime Jo Tremper knew what her father'd done.

Chapter 24

Jaime Jo hadn't put a lot of thought into her actions lately. What would have been the point? It seemed her whole life had been one big storm, just a big old tornado blowing her all about like a mere fallen leaf, a speck of dust. Not much point in planning ahead when your roof's already been ripped off and you're flying through the air. Too late for that. At that point it becomes just a matter of survival. Cover your head, dodge the flying debris the best you can, and grab onto any stationary object within reach, something familiar with which to anchor yourself to Earth.

That's how Jaime Jo'd been living for quite some time now, in survival mode, acting on pure instinct. That's how she found herself sitting in Tommy Harris's Camaro that very night. No, Tommy wasn't with her. And she hadn't left town.

She'd spent most of the night walking. First to her house and up to her room where she'd overturned a dusty old flower vase to see if the keys were still there, the spare set of keys to the Camaro that Tommy'd left with her before he'd shipped out for Vietnam. He'd left her an escape, a way out, just in case.

They were there all right. She never thought she'd use them. Yet, when she squeezed them in her hands, it was like holding her Tommy. A soothing warmth spread from those keys, permeating her body and soul. To Jaime Jo, that small set of keys felt like a giant ship's anchor, securing her in rough seas, giving her hope in the midst of the storm.

Through all the trouble, since the beginning, she never thought of leaving town. She was only 15 when it started. Her mother'd been gone some time already. She only had her father, and the church. So when they both told her she was to blame, that the beatings were justified, she believed them. She didn't know a thing about love or sex. Yet she knew plenty about sin and guilt. So she accepted her punishment. She never thought to run, much less fight back.

She never told anyone. Not Billy. Not Tommy. Billy never really figured it out, not 'till the end. But Tommy knew. She didn't have to tell him. Tommy knew it all, even the parts Jaime Jo chose to forget, parts she'd tricked herself into believing never happened at all, things worse than beatings. Yes, there were things worse than that.

Tommy wanted to kill her father. And he'd have done it too, but for Jaime Jo. She couldn't let him spend the rest of his days in prison on her account. And she'd pleaded with him not to tell the world what was going on. So he didn't. For Jaime Jo. He'd have done anything for Jaime Jo.

But then Tommy was gone, a one-way ticket to Vietnam. That's when she briefly thought of telling everyone what her father'd been doing to her. That would have been the time too, when her life didn't matter anymore. No loss if he'd killed her for revealing his secret. But then Scarlet came, and everything changed. She once again had a reason to fear dying. She couldn't leave Scarlet behind... alone... with him.

So she held her silence. Besides, with Tommy out of the picture, her father seemed to let her be. Until Tommy came back. Then it began all over again. She didn't know how long she'd last. She didn't know what Tommy would do. But she didn't think about those things. After all, she was just a leaf in a twister.

Then they found Billy dead. He must have seen or heard something. And he would have told too. For Jaime Jo's sake. She couldn't control him the way she did Tommy. She didn't have that power over him. He wouldn't have kept her secret. He wouldn't have let things stand the way they were. And her father knew that. He knew Billy had to be stopped. So the monster she called Daddy did it. He killed Billy Sawchuck.

And now Jaime Jo had to go. She didn't know where. She had no money, no plan, and now with Tommy on the run, hunted, no help. She was on her own. Nevertheless, she had to go. Anywhere. Anywhere but under the same roof with that monster.

So she grabbed Tommy's keys and headed back out into the night on foot. It took most of the night till she reached the car at the side of the road where Tommy'd abandoned it. When she finally landed in the driver's seat, the torn vinyl felt good. It seemed she'd been on her feet since she left the hospital. But she wasn't done yet.

Nobody ever suspected Jaime Jo even knew how to drive. Nobody except Tommy. Initially, when he first got that car he was pretty particular about it and wouldn't let her behind the wheel. But eventually she'd worn him down and he took her out to the cow pasture where she couldn't do any damage. Before Tommy knew it, after a bit of painful wear and tear on the clutch, his girl could run that Camaro through a slalom course of cow patties like it was an Olympic event.

The babysitter didn't know what to make of it when Jaime Jo drove up in that hot rod at three in the morning to collect Scarlet. The whole thing was highly irregular. But Jaime Jo was the child's mother after all. And a good one at that. As long as she wasn't in the hospital.

It wasn't until the stars faded from the threat of a new day that Jaime Jo finally parked the Camaro at the quarry and nodded off to sleep with Scarlet in her arms.

* * * *

She'd been living in the Camaro, yet showing up at work, for three days before anyone even thought something was amiss. Frank hadn't minded fronting her paycheck when she said she was short on cash, and she'd always been welcome to free meals at the diner. But when it became apparent she was using the diner's bathroom sink as a shower, he could tell something was off.

Then her father showed up.

"Where's my daughter?"

"In the back," answered Frank, "prepping for the lunch crowd." He had nothing to hide.

"Could I speak with her, please?" asked the preacher.

"Course you can." Frank poked his head through the swinging door to the kitchen. "Jaime Jo, your daddy's here to see you." He turned back to the preacher with a smile. "She'll be right out," he assumed.

But she wasn't right out.

"Jaime Jo, did you hear me?" he tried again. "I said your daddy's here."

Jaime Jo looked up briefly from her work so Frank could see she'd heard him. Then she went right back to work.

"Ain't you comin' out?"

Jaime Jo just shook her head no and continued chopping potatoes for the hash browns.

"You ain't?"

She confirmed Frank's initial impression with another shake of her head.

Frank knew he was in the middle of something, a family matter that didn't concern him, when he turned back to the preacher and told him she wasn't coming out. The preacher remained cool, but not before a hint of overpowering rage briefly bubbled to the surface and crossed his face.

There were other folks at the diner that morning to witness the exchange, peaking the curiosity of more than one of the local busy bodies, such that Warren Tremper wasn't the only one to follow his daughter home from work one night to find out where she was staying. Well, if word that Jaime Jo wasn't on speaking terms with her daddy was news, then the fact that she was living in Tommy Harris's Camaro out at the quarry was front page. And before you knew it, the whole town knew Jaime Jo Tremper had lost her mind.

She'd gone crazy, they said. Snapped. Ever since her friend was found shot under the bridge. Poor thing. First her momma, then her best friend. And all the time, having the shit beat out of her by that Harris boy. It was all too predictable. Just a matter of time. But what about the little girl, Scarlet? That was no way to raise a child, in the back seat of a car. Something had to be done, for the child's sake. And what about the boy? That psychopath Tommy Harris was still out there, and up to no good for sure. Who would watch over the girls out there all alone? At least at home, her father was there to protect her.

More than one concerned citizen pulled Sheriff Buckner aside to put in their two cents on the matter. But Jo Bob tended to shy from family disputes and was unwilling on that basis to get involved. On the other hand, he still wanted to bring in the Harris boy. And maybe this was his chance. He just wished he could find bait could lure catfish out at the lake like Jaime Jo was likely to lure Tommy Harris out at the quarry. The way Jo Bob saw things, this new development only served to save him a world of hassle. Now he didn't have to chase that boy up into the mountains after all. Just like a cold morning sitting all cozy in a duck blind sipping coffee spiked with Jack, he could just wait out at the quarry for his prey to come to him. It was just a matter of time.

* * * *

Jaime Jo sensed Tommy Harris's presence right from the start. Just like the angel that used to come by each night after her momma died. She didn't have to see it. But each morning she'd wake up comforted in the knowledge that she'd been protected through the night.

The first morning she found a bunch of wildflowers on the hood of the car, she wondered how little Scarlet had managed to collect them. But she soon realized Scarlet had nothing to do with it after all. It was him. Each night, while she slept, he came by and left her fresh flowers. He was somewhere out there, watching over her.

So when she finally heard footsteps in the quarry gravel one night, she wasn't alarmed. She assumed it was only a visit from the florist, and closed her eyes again knowing she'd be safe and sound 'till morning again.

But this time it would be different. Apparently Tommy had something else entirely in mind. She'd been pleasantly dreaming of him when it happened. The approaching footsteps merged seamlessly with her dream. But things changed abruptly as she felt the rush of air being sucked from the car when the door was suddenly yanked open. It was all too real when she was jolted from her dream. She thought to chastise Tommy for her rude awakening, how he was going to wake Scarlet, how he shouldn't be out in the open or the sheriff might catch him.

But before her still-sleeping lips could form the words, she was forcibly dragged from the car by the hair, landing roughly on her back in the dirt and gravel. Opening her eyes didn't help. It was still too dark to see. In her half dream state, she didn't have the time to separate the Tommy of her dream from the man attacking her. They appeared to be one in the same. As did dream and reality. One in the same. Could it be? Despite the all too real pain of the gravel tearing at the skin of her back, that's what she prayed for, that she was still asleep, that it was all simply another dream turned nightmare.

The first kick to the ribs, however, assured her that, once more, her prayers would go unanswered. Oh, it was certainly a nightmare. But not the harmless kind. Not the kind where you wake up with nothing more than a cold sweat and maybe a little shortness of breath. No this was something entirely different. This was for real. Deadly real. This was Jaime Jo Tremper's life. And there was no waking from that nightmare.

She instinctively curled into a fetal ball with her arms about her head to protect what she could. But it wasn't a conscious reaction or any sort of strategy. She'd learned the futility of that over the years, the futility of a young girl trying to protect herself against the raw brutality of a grown man. No, it wasn't meant as a defense. It was just what she did. She couldn't help it. She just tried to curl up as small as she could get, hoping one day she could get so small as to disappear entirely, cease to exist, just go away.

So that's where she went as her skinny arms failed to shield her, and the fists fell repeatedly to her face. Pummeled relentlessly, she had no choice. She just went away, somewhere inside. She'd come back afterwards, when it was all over, like she always did. Until the time came when she absorbed one too many blows. The final one. Then she wouldn't come back anymore. She'd stay gone. And that would be OK too.

The stitches on her face and chest had opened up, and the blood flowed freely before the onslaught ceased as suddenly as it had started. She was asleep when it started. She was unconscious when it stopped, too far gone to notice.

But her attacker stopped neither out of mercy nor boredom. It didn't really matter. Not to Jaime Jo. Just so long as he stopped, before it was too late.

And it almost was. Jaime Jo was already on her way home, to her Lord. She saw the gates, and they were beautiful. Saint Peter was there waiting for her. Maybe she'd get to see her momma again. But at the last minute he raised his hand to stop her. She wouldn't be allowed through. Not yet, not this time.

Then she panicked. Was something wrong? Was she being sent somewhere else, that other place, where the sinners go, where there'd be no rest, no relief from perpetual torment, where the hell she'd known in this world would only continue into the next? But no, that wasn't it at all. Apparently the Lord had other plans for her. Jaime Jo Tremper wasn't going to hell just yet.

If she were, though, she'd have met someone along the way. Sharing her destination, she'd have met her attacker, because that's the path he walked. The same man that tried to drive her from the living was himself being sent to his final fiery destination.

That's why the beating had stopped. Someone had stopped it. Someone had pulled her attacker from what was left of her limp and bleeding body. And now, that same someone was pounding the man that attacked her with such force that he intended to send him directly through the gravel of the quarry floor, through the dirt and rocks below, through the Earth's very crust and magma beneath, straight to hell itself, straight where he belonged.

Yet Tommy Harris was no longer at the quarry. Not really, not anymore. He'd gone somewhere else, just about halfway 'round the world, even before he could pull the preacher off of Jaime Jo. It happened much faster than that. In fact, it was from the second he first saw Warren Tremper pull his daughter from the car that Tommy Harris was gone. For all appearances, to the rest of the world, he was still at the quarry, right where he'd stayed every night watching over his Jaime Jo. He was still there, physically. But mentally, he'd immediately gone to another place, a mean place, a fighting place, a place of swamp and bamboo, of sweat and blood.

Why the preacher kept showing up with him in Vietnam, Tommy couldn't say. But he was definitely there. Tommy could see him plain as day. He used to think it was a Vietnamese trick, some sort of disguise to play mind games on him. They were masters of psychological warfare, after all. But over time, Tommy began to realize it was no trick, no slight of hand. It was indeed the preacher himself. The traitor had joined the enemy. And that's not all. Even worse than that, he'd taken Jamie Jo, his own daughter, prisoner.

It was on Tommy's watch that night that it had happened. He'd observed the enemy's surprise attack on a sleeping Jaime Jo. At first he seemed to be torturing her, perhaps trying to extract some classified information. But in the seconds it took Tommy to spring into action, it became apparent the scene wasn't all that complicated. The man was killing her, plain and simple. The man was killing his own daughter.

So when Tommy yanked Warren Tremper off his daughter and threw him to the ground, Tommy intended to kill him. He would end this thing once and for all, with no regrets. And he'd have done it too. It would have been a simple matter really. Tommy was more than strong enough. And he'd been trained to do just that, quickly and efficiently. But Tommy never claimed to be the perfect soldier. Wound way too tightly, he more often than was prudent let his pent up emotions get the better of him. So this particular kill would not be a quick one. That would have been too easy on the enemy. He wanted this one to last.

Tommy Harris had never been religious, and since the day he met the preacher he knew he never would be. So forgiveness and redemption were concepts foreign and unknown to him. This would be no quick mercy killing. He wanted the preacher to suffer, like he'd done to Jaime Jo.

And that was Tommy's mistake. He could have broken the man's neck in an instant. But he didn't. He was playing with him. He intended to send him all the way to hell one fist at a time. And he was oh so close, so close Tommy could feel the heat, white hot.

That's when he was suddenly interrupted. The preacher was mere inches from hell when the sirens blew, announcing the air raid. Tommy looked skyward. He couldn't see them yet, but it was only a matter of seconds. His training automatically kicked in. He knew he had to take cover. As to the preacher, if he wasn't already dead— and Tommy couldn't honestly tell one way or another anymore— there'd be other opportunities. Tommy would just have to finish the job some other time.

Chapter 25

Jo Bob had tried everything he could to stay awake. He'd taken to sleeping all day and drinking coffee all night, just so he could keep an eye out for his fugitive. He knew he'd come for her. It was just a matter of time. But his daytime naps were less than satisfying. What with some kind of psycho on the loose and, worse than that, with Charlotte Sawchuck out of commission, he was as edgy as a tomcat under a full moon.

So after he'd drained his thermos of coffee dry that night parked out at the quarry, Charlotte was all he could think of, buck-naked and glistening with sweat. Jo Bob's raging hormones, and their effect on his nightstick, were better than any old caffeine. And they'd have carried him through the night too, but Jo Bob was a weakling when it came to self-deprivation, never much of an advocate for abstinence. So it was only a matter of time before he took things into his own hands, literally. It didn't take but a few moments and the edge was gone. Now he could put the image of Charlotte Sawchuck to bed and finally relax. In fact, he'd barely kissed his right hand goodnight before immediately falling sound asleep for the first time in days.

So just as Jaime Jo and Warren Tremper and Tommy Harris would dwell in other worlds that night, so would Jo Bob Buckner. He rocked gently in his rowboat out at the lake, dreaming of catching the biggest catfish he'd ever seen. And sure enough, as dreams will do, it wasn't long before he'd hooked the beast. He was trying to bring it up from the muddy bottom, but it kept ramming the bottom of his boat. It was almost rhythmic, a steady thumping he could feel through the hull of the car... uh, boat. No, car. Wait, he was in his car. What was a catfish doing under his car? It must have been just a dream. Yet he could hear and feel that catfish thumping through the floorboards of his police cruiser. Wait a second. What the hell was going on? He wasn't out at the lake at all. He was on watch at the quarry, waiting on the Harris boy. And that wasn't no catfish.

Jo Bob peered out his windshield and saw he had company. The preacher's car was parked just down a ways, probably hadn't seen the police cruiser tucked in among the brush at the side of the road. Must have come to check on his daughter. At four in the morning? That seemed awfully peculiar to Jo Bob.

Then there was the thumping echoing off the walls of the quarry that had awakened him. At first Jo Bob didn't know what to make of it. But fully awake again, it didn't take much concentration to pick up another sound accompanying the thumping stroke for stroke. It was a sort of grunt, someone exerting himself over and over, putting everything he had into that thumping.

Then Jo Bob had a sudden revelation. He'd heard that pairing of sounds before. Jo Bob had had to break up more than one ass-whupping in his life. Damn, in his younger days, he'd often been the one dolling it out. No, there was no mistaking that particular combination of sounds. Someone was kicking the shit out of someone else.

And from the sound of it, he hoped he wasn't too late. Jo Bob automatically flipped on his siren as he revved up the cruiser and made a beeline down into the quarry.

Jo Bob Buckner was a simple man, never made no claims to the contrary. And yet, when something didn't make sense to him, more often than not, there was usually a good reason. The whole Tommy Harris and Jaime Jo Tremper mess, for one. Tommy was Jimmy's kid. He'd raised his share of cane, but he was a good kid. And he loved that girl with all he had. It just didn't make no sense. And now the Sawchuck kid was dead. The two didn't seem related, yet Jo Bob wasn't a big fan of coincidence. Something just wasn't right.

So despite everything, he'd held out hope that everyone, including that shrink out at Fort Bragg, had had it all wrong about the boy, even if for no other reason than his old buddy Jimmy's sake. Maybe nothing was what it seemed after all.

And yet, there's something to be said for seeing a thing with your own eyes. Before even coming to a full stop, the cruiser's spotlight captured the scene all too clearly. Tommy Harris turned toward the car, fist frozen mid-swing, eyes aglow like a deer caught in the headlights. No, not a deer. More like a lion, caught devouring fresh kill. And in no time, its meal disturbed, the beast dropped what was left of the preacher and bounded off into the woods as wild animals will, blood still dripping from its jaws.

At first, Jo Bob thought to go after him, but his days of running down a younger man on foot were long gone. No, he'd better attend to the wounded, or dead. He wasn't sure exactly what kind of shit he'd stepped in.

As soon as he found the girl's pulse, he radioed for an ambulance. The preacher seemed to be coming around on his own.

Warren Tremper suddenly jerked back to life, raising his arms in an attempt to fend off blows that he imagined continued to rain down on him.

"He's gone, Warren!" shouted Jo Bob, trying to ease the man's mind.

But Warren Tremper had a ways to go yet before he could gather his wits about him.

"You belong to me," he mumbled through busted lips. "I won't let him have you. It's the devil who's come. And, Lord help me, it's the devil I'll beat out of you."

Jo Bob couldn't really follow the man's rambling, but he assumed it was Tommy Harris he talked of beating, not Jaime Jo.

"Warren! Wake up! He's gone! The devil's gone!"

But Warren wasn't done quite yet.

"He can't have you. You're mine. You belong to me, and only me, forever. He promised. The Lord promised me."

Jo Bob didn't know what to make of it, but began to wonder if the man had lost it for good when suddenly the preacher rejoined the living, opened his eyes, and looked right at him.

"What happened? Where is he? What did I say just now? What did you hear?"

"Well, you and your kid been beat to a pulp. He's gone. And I don't have a clue what you were babbling about."

It was the last statement that seemed to bring some calm to the preacher. He looked over at Jaime Jo, still unconscious on the ground nearby.

"Is she… is she going to be all right?"

"She's alive. Just like a dandelion, a pretty little weed that can't be killed. I called for an ambulance."

Then the preacher's face changed as the wheels began to turn. "Did you see him? Tommy Harris. Did you see him?"

"I seen him all right. He was about to finish you off when I crashed his party. He run off when he saw me."

"I'm not the only one he came for," the preacher added. "Look what he did to my daughter." He looked at the sheriff for confirmation of his power of suggestion.

"Well, I didn't see that part. It was just you and him when I—"

"Use your eyes, Sheriff," he demanded, pointing at Jaime Jo. "Look what he's done to her."

"What were you doing out here this time of night anyway?"

"Can't a man come check on his daughter? I thought that was *your* job, Sheriff. He'd have killed her if I didn't show up when I did."

Jo Bob did feel a momentary twinge of guilt. But it didn't last. After all, a man can't be expected to stay awake 24 hours a day.

Both men were interrupted by a child's cry. They turned to see Scarlet's face at the window of the Camaro. She'd lain silently hiding until she grew brave enough to peak out of the car and spy the sheriff, anyone but the man who killed her momma.

She thought Jaime Jo'd been killed. And she saw her grandpa do it. She never saw Tommy. She'd already seen enough and hidden her face in the rear seat of the car by the time he'd showed up. Now there was another man. She trusted him. He must have come to save her.

So when the sheriff opened the door to the Camaro, the little thing jumped at him, throwing her arms about his shoulders like a drowning man to a lifeguard. She continued her crying and Jo Bob couldn't pry her loose. He never imagined himself having a child, and yet his big strong arms and rough hands instinctively knew what to do. He comforted the little girl, rubbing her back and returning her hug as her tiny arms squeezed his fat neck with all their might, the sandpaper of his unshaven jaw rubbing her baby-soft cheek.

Jo Bob thought she'd finally calmed down enough for him to hand her over to her grandpa, but when the child saw that the monster was still there, and worse yet, the sheriff intended to feed her to it, she screamed as if she'd been stuck with a pitchfork, and clawed at the sheriff's clothes like a cat about to be given a bath.

"Whoa there, little girl," began a surprised Jo Bob with a chuckle. "I ain't gonna kill you." He let the frightened thing stay put, gently rocking her. "And don't you worry none about your momma. Your momma's just sleepin'. So 'till she wakes up, I was only tryin' to give you over to your grandpa for safe keeping, you silly thing."

After a while, when she'd calmed a bit, he tried to hand off the football again, but Scarlet wasn't having it, and clung to Jo Bob's neck with everything she had.

"I'll be damned," said Jo Bob with a smile. "I've never had a woman so enamored with me before. What's a man to do?"

Warren Tremper knew all too well what shaped the child's behavior. She must have seen the whole thing. But he couldn't let on.

"I'm thinkin' maybe it's all this blood," he offered, holding out his arms and looking at the streams of red that ran from his battered face down the front of his shirt.

"Maybe you're right," Jo Bob agreed. "Maybe I'll just bring her over to the sitter until you can get cleaned up. Besides, you should probably go with Jaime Jo to the hospital and get yourself looked at as well."

"No, I'll be alright. Wouldn't want to give that animal the satisfaction of knowin' he laid me up. No, I'll just head on home. I believe a few aspirin and some ice'll work wonders."

Jo Bob raised an eyebrow, as he radioed for an ambulance. "You sure? You look pretty damaged to me."

"I said I'll be just fine, Sheriff. Why don't you just do your job and worry about catching the beast done this to me and my daughter."

Jo Bob felt that old twinge of guilt resurface again. "Sure. Sure. I'll get him. Meantime, I'll just drop the child over at the sitter's. Maybe she'd be better off there until Jaime Jo's out of the hospital anyway."

The preacher took exception to the sheriff's suggestion. "Oh, she ain't goin' back to her momma."

Jo Bob thought he hadn't heard right. "What do you mean she ain't goin' back to her momma?"

"Just look around you, Sheriff. Her momma lives in a car. My daughter chooses to live in a damn car. She's obviously lost her mind. And as if that wasn't bad enough in its own right, here we got that maniac of yours on the loose. Almost wiped out the entire Tremper family tonight. Be serious, Sheriff. It would be irresponsible of you to leave that child under her care. Not in her current state of mind. Now, when she comes to her senses and decides to come home, the child will be there, safe and sound, under my protection."

Jo Bob couldn't argue with the preacher's premise about Jaime Jo. It was probably for the best. Yet as bad as Jo Bob felt at failing to protect the Trempers, he was less than impressed by the preacher's success at handling the situation on his own.

Warren Tremper saw the implication in Jo Bob's silent reply. "Oh, don't you worry about me, Sheriff. I'll be ready for him next time. With or without your help."

"Well just don't do anything crazy," suggested Jo Bob as he heard the ambulance siren finally approaching.

The preacher spit blood. "A man's got to protect his family. Besides, crazy times call for crazy measures, Sheriff."

Jo Bob didn't like the sound of that, but knew there was nothing he could do about it at this point. So he took the child he wore like a medallion about his neck over to the Camaro and sat with her until the ambulance could arrive.

As the siren grew louder, he looked over at Jaime Jo still in la-la land, but breathing comfortably, and thought of Tommy Harris. Jo Bob knew he'd only grow into an old man waiting on that boy to come in on his own. The boy could hold out indefinitely living off the land. Jo Bob knew he'd have to go hunt him down, gather up a posse and some dogs and head up into the mountains after him. And Jo Bob didn't like the idea one bit. It wasn't going to be no turkey shoot. He knew that it was Tommy's country up there, where he held a strong home-field advantage. Jo Bob wasn't a complete fool. He knew odds were they'd be walking into a trap. But what other choice was there? He had to try. This whole business had gotten out of hand. Jo Bob knew if he couldn't end it, someone else would. Only it wouldn't be on Jo Bob's terms. And if that's how it went down, he saw things ending badly. There'd already been one murder in Pleasant Valley. Jo Bob didn't want another. Not on his watch.

Chapter 26

Tommy Harris had grown accustomed to sleeping during the day. The nights were reserved for standing guard over Jaime Jo. Yet when he woke up that afternoon with blood on his hands, he knew something was different. He tried to remember the events of the previous night. What had he done? Had he been hunting? Must have bagged some big game, as no bird could have accounted for that much blood. Must have landed and gutted a wild boar. He'd have his work cut out for him preparing the meat. But when he looked about for where he'd hung the carcass, he found no reward for a successful night's hunting.

Then, staring at his sore knuckles, it started to come back to him. It was big game, all right. But not the four-legged type. And he'd failed to make the kill.

Things were always a little hazy when he came out of one of his trances, but he could usually piece enough visions together to get the general idea of what he'd done. He could weed out the crazy bits about Vietnam and enemy troops, and distill it down to the basic facts. He'd been watching over Jaime Jo when her father'd attacked her. It happened so fast, Tommy was almost too late. But he believed she was still alive when he pulled the preacher off her. No, he wasn't too late to save Jaime Jo. But he was too late too finish off her father. He'd been interrupted by a sudden air raid. No, not an air raid. It was the sheriff. Buckner broke up the party. If not for Buckner, that preacher'd be preachin' in hell right now.

But Tommy knew he wasn't being entirely honest with himself. He couldn't really blame Buckner for Tommy's failure to complete the mission. It was Tommy's fault. Tommy knew he could take that preacher out any time he wanted to. Tommy was a trained killer. He had any number of weapons at his disposal. One scoped sniper shot to the head. A homemade explosive just waiting for the man to start his car. One sweep of a hunting knife across the throat. A baseball bat to the head. A shovel. Shit, he didn't need any of that. His bare hands would do just fine. And he knew how to stalk his prey in silence such that the enemy never knew what hit him. But where was the fun in that? Where was the honor? No, Tommy wanted the man to know exactly what hit him.

The preacher'd had the advantage those years ago when Tommy was just a misguided teenager in love. But that was then. Things had changed. His military training, and then Vietnam, had fixed all that. Tommy'd evolved, or devolved, into a lethal weapon. And he'd held onto only two facets of his former self. His love for Jaime Jo Tremper, and his grudge against her daddy. And that's where all those new skills, courtesy of the U.S. Army, would come in handy.

Yet, he hadn't completed what should have been a straightforward mission. For some reason, he'd chosen to run and hide in the mountains. Why? Was it simply out of habit, on Jaime Jo's orders not to go after her father out of some twisted love for a parent, some perverted religious version of justice that let her believe it was all her fault, that she was to blame and not her father?

Then there was the doubt in his mind about himself and Jaime Jo, that maybe she'd moved on while he was overseas, or maybe his hideous facial scars were too much for her to stomach. Or maybe they'd both been broken beyond repair and a loving relationship between two damaged individuals was no longer possible, their love shattered into pieces so small they defied mending. Whatever magic they'd had had vanished. Their chance had come and gone.

There were any number of possibilities, and Tommy was never the type to get it all sorted out. Besides, none of that was even relevant anymore. None of it mattered now. Not what Jaime Jo wanted, or even if she loved him. Tommy knew it was only a matter of time before the man killed his own daughter. And it was all on Tommy's shoulders to put a stop to it. Killing the man would be so easy. And yet he hadn't done it. Not yet, anyway. And there was a reason for that, one that even Tommy never thought of.

Tommy Harris was no murderer. He was a soldier. He'd killed only when necessary. He'd never taken any pleasure in it. Not even when he was out of his head, fighting battles that raged only in his mind. No, killing had always been plan B. There was still another way. There always had been.

Even as teenagers, when all the trouble started, Tommy'd planned to take Jaime Jo and run away. Just up and go, leaving all their troubles behind. It didn't work out then. But that was a long time ago. Things were different now. No one would stop him this time. Just let them try. And for those that got in the way, there was always plan B.

As soon as she was out of the hospital, he'd take her away like he should have done years ago. Had they done so then, they could have avoided a world of sorrow. Pleasant Valley would have had to find something else to gossip about. The infamous legend of Jaime Jo Tremper and the Harris boy would have been just another story of young lovebirds flying the coop. No one needed know the sordid details. As it was, the town was the last to know. Way before anyone else even knew Jaime Jo was being abused, before anyone could blame Tommy Harris, he and Jaime Jo knew.

Tommy didn't even have to see the bruises. He saw it in her eyes that very first time her father'd beaten her. All he had to do was look into her eyes to see her shattered soul. But there was no talking to her. Tommy'd tried to encourage her to report what her father was doing to her. And when she refused, he was ready to do it himself. He did everything he could to convince her that it wasn't her fault. But her father and her God told her otherwise. So she stopped him. And he let her.

She tried to be good, and avoid Tommy Harris. And at first she did. But her father didn't believe her, and she soon realized the beatings would continue whether she saw Tommy or not. So she began seeing him again, and soon he was all she had. If they weren't exactly serious before, they soon were. They lived for each other. She held onto Tommy Harris as if he were her lifeline, the only thing keeping her alive, as if he were the air she breathed. And Tommy held her like a precious thing that needed him, succumbing to every man's inherent weakness. A man needs to be needed, or he's lost.

So things got out of hand as the beatings continued. And when the whole town began to notice the abuse, the preacher convinced them all that Tommy was to blame. Tommy wanted to tell, to set the record straight, when he felt the accusatory looks from people, even his own father and Billy. But Jaime Jo had her secret. And Tommy would keep it for her, no matter what. He thought of killing her father even back then. And he'd have done it if not for Jaime Jo and her God. No, there was another way. They'd run away together. In the middle of the night. Just up and leave that shit-hole of a town and never look back. That was the plan.

But her father caught her sneaking out in the middle of the night, her things stowed in her school backpack. She'd never been to the hospital in her life. Not until that night. And she was never the same after that. Her will had been broken, and they never tried to run again.

So when they finally escorted Tommy to the bus depot to pack him off to Vietnam, he put up no resistance. He wasn't afraid. Instead, he was relieved, relieved in the hope that this might finally bring some peace to his beloved Jaime Jo. He climbed the steps to the bus like a death row inmate with no hope of pardon from the governor. But he wasn't concerned for himself. Like a steer to slaughter, he let them send him away. No one, not even Tommy, cared if he ever came back.

But he did come back. And when he did, he quickly saw that almost nothing had changed. Except one thing. Tommy had changed. He realized that now. No one told Tommy Harris what to do anymore. Not even Jaime Jo Tremper. He would do what needed to be done. Whether she still loved him or not, as soon as she was up to it, he'd collect Jaime Jo and leave this shit-hole behind. And God save the poor motherfucker that tried to stand in his way. No, Tommy Harris was no murderer, never was. But he was a warrior now, a warrior with a mission. And no amount of collateral damage would deter him from completing that mission.

* * * *

Jo Bob had a bad feeling that morning as he looked about him at the rag tag posse he'd thrown together. He couldn't bring his deputy Jimmy in on this one. Not to hunt down his own kid. So this is what he was left with. He knew they stood a snowball's chance in hell of bringing in Tommy Harris. But the boys were game and a Hail Mary for the end zone always had to be respected.

Jo Bob feared it was about time to bring in some outside help, to place a call in to Greensboro to send some professional reinforcements, real law enforcement to remedy the situation. But Jo Bob hated admitting to those self-righteous big city boys that he needed their help. They never lost an opportunity to suggest to Jo Bob that he wasn't the real deal, that he was just some washed-up high school ball player babysitting some hick town of no consequence. No, that was going to be an awfully bitter pill to swallow when that day came.

Then again, looking at the team of misfits assembled about him, he could already start to taste it. Buford Higgins had rounded up most of the football team he'd played alongside back in high school. It had only been two years since they'd graduated and they weren't in the greatest shape even then, having lost more games than they'd won. But the difference two years could make was shocking, how lifting beers instead of weights for two years could bring about such a transformation. Looking about him, he thought these could have been the poster boys for every high school health class on the dangers of a sedentary lifestyle.

No, Jo Bob didn't hold out much hope. But Buford saw things differently. Tommy Harris may have gotten the better of him one on one. But now he had the team together again, the same good old boys used to gang up on the likes of losers like Tommy Harris back in the day. There weren't any football games for them anymore. But getting the boys together again for a little Harris ass-whuppin' was the closest they'd ever get to reliving those glory days. Buford Higgins fully expected to be back in time for lunch, Tommy Harris's scalp hanging from his belt.

* * * *

Only things sometimes have a way of not working out according to plan. The posse didn't find Tommy Harris that first day. Everyone but Jo Bob was surprised by the fact. But they didn't let it get to them. After all, that was no reason to ruin a good hunting trip. They'd get him tomorrow. Meanwhile, as Jo Bob took the first shift at night watch, the boys sat around the campfire yucking it up about the good old days and drinking beer. Despite the anticipated capture of Tommy the first day, they'd brought along quite a supply of beer. Still, they felt obliged to finish it that first night as no one wanted to carry it around for another day crawling all over that damn mountain.

Jo Bob didn't mind taking the first shift, but he'd be damned if he was going to stay up all night babysitting these boys. Still, even after he'd assigned them each two hours night watch apiece, Jo Bob slept with one eye open as long as he could. But eventually even that one closed as visions of Charlotte Sawchuck replaced those of some drunken redneck boys farting around the campfire.

When he woke up in the morning, he was glad to see they weren't still sitting around the fire reminiscing. They would need a good night's rest if they were going to spend another day fugitive hunting. But Jo Bob's first impression that all was well turned out to be a brief one. He saw their sleeping bags, but no one was in them. He didn't expect these boys to be early risers, and he prayed to God they didn't go off half-cocked, planning to take things into their own hands.

Jo Bob got up amid a crackle of bones as his aging joints attempted to realign. He felt like some kind of Boy Scout troop leader off to find a bunch of lost boys. It didn't take him long. In fact, he spied them as soon as he stood up. At first he thought they'd taken up positions in front of trees spaced along the perimeter of the campsite. But after he rubbed the sleep out of his eyes just to be sure, he realized they were tied to those trees. Each and every one of them, gagged and tied to a tree. Oh, and they were naked.

Jo Bob had to give credit where credit was due. That Tommy Harris had skills. At least no one had gotten hurt. Tommy could have killed them all while they slept. But he didn't. Those were Jo Bob's thoughts as he sat alongside the campfire and poured himself a second cup of coffee. He didn't let the moans for help from the still bound boys disturb him. They'd have plenty of time to make excuses once he removed their gags and pointed their sorry asses down the mountain toward home.

But right now, Jo Bob was busy contemplating his next move. Nothing came to him right away. He couldn't go traipsing after Tommy on his own. He knew better than that. Well, the least he could do before bringing in the pros was to check up on his deputy to see if there'd been any progress on the Sawchuck murder. No point in having the big boys from Greensboro show up to find both a psycho *and* a murderer on the loose. Jo Bob never for a minute believed the two were one in the same.

So after he'd finished his coffee, he dowsed the fire, placed a pocket knife in Buford Higgins's bound hands, confident the boy'd be able to free himself and his teammates, and headed down the mountain into town for breakfast at Frank's before checking in on his deputy. Maybe Jimmy Harris was having better luck.

Chapter 27

It would be two full days before Jaime Jo awoke from her coma. As was often the case, she couldn't really remember the events that led her to wake up in the hospital, but the details didn't really matter one time to the next. Experience taught her that the theme was always the same, something about Tommy, her father, sin, guilt, God, and, what was that last thing? Oh yeah, getting pounded into unconsciousness.

Then, as always, her first thoughts went to Scarlet. Jaime Jo waited to ask the nurse when they planned on releasing her from the hospital so she could pick her baby up from the sitter. One fractured arm in a cast from her initial attempts to fend off her father's attack, she wasn't surprised to hear this time was worse than most, and they planned to keep her under observation while she mended for a few days. She could tell that much whenever she turned her head and saw stars. But there was something in the nurse's eyes at the mention of picking up Scarlet that left Jaime Jo uneasy.

"What's wrong? My little girl's OK, isn't she?"

"Oh, your baby's just peachy. Such a cute little thing. I've been assured she's just snug as a bug, being well cared for," answered the nurse, checking Jaime Jo's IV and fluffing her pillow.

Jaime Jo suspected there was more, something the nurse wasn't saying.

"You're sure now? Cause I can't wait to see her. She's the only reason I allow you people to keep patching me up. If not for her, I'd just assume finish the job myself."

"Oh, you hush now. Don't talk crazy like that. Your little girl's just fine, waitin' on her momma."

Jaime Jo tried to smile, but it hurt too much. "Well, good then," she began, relieved, "because she's all I've got."

The nurse smiled back, but her eyes didn't. Her eyes were withholding vital information.

And Jaime Jo could see it. "What is it? What's happened to Scarlet?"

The nurse tried to cover. "Nothing. She's perfect, like I already told you."

Jaime Jo pressed on. "What is it then?"

The nurse hesitated, checking her watch to see if her shift was over, hoping to avoid the whole topic. But then she saw the look in Jaime Jo's eyes, and seeing the emotional pain behind the physical, she knew she had to say it.

"They say you was livin' in a car? Could that be true?"

Jaime Jo didn't see where this was going. "Yeah. So? What's that got to do with anything?"

"Well, maybe it's not my place and all, but, do you think that's best for the child?"

Jaime Jo felt the hair on the back of her neck stand up. Then she lashed out at the nurse.

"You're right about one thing. It *isn't* your place. And what's best for my child is to be with *me*, whether that means living in a car or under a rock." She could hear her pulse beeping on the monitor over the bed. There was no hiding the increase in tempo.

The nurse took a defensive step backward. "All's I'm sayin' is I could see how some might think that wasn't no way to raise a child."

Jaime Jo sat straight up, pulling her IV line taut. "How dare you? What gives you the right to judge me? Maybe after you walk in my shoes, then you can—"

"Now hold on there," the nurse interrupted. "It ain't for me to say. Don't shoot the messenger."

"Messenger? There's a message? What message?"

"Don't get all excited," the nurse implored. "Look now. You've gone and pulled out your monitor," she scolded, secretly relieved not to hear the rapid-fire beeping of her patient's heart.

Jaime Jo gave the nurse the stiff arm when she tried to approach the bed to reattach the monitor.

"Freeze," she warned, grabbing the nurse firmly by the wrist. She looked the nurse in the eye. "This is my child you're talking about. And you'll tell me exactly what's going on this instant."

The nurse tried to pull her arm back but found the grip on her wrist surprisingly strong for a frail young girl just been in a coma for two days. So when she began to feel pins and needles from the loss of circulation, she figured she'd better come clean.

"Look, don't blame me. They said I wasn't to upset you, in your condition and all. But they're sayin' it's bad enough you're livin' in a car. But now, what with that maniac after you, there's no tellin' what might happen. It ain't safe for a little girl to be livin' in no car. They're sayin' you ain't fit to care for her no more. They've taken her from you. The sheriff's placed her under protective custody with your daddy where she's to stay until you move back home with them."

The nurse felt the blood flow returning to her hand as her patient's grip began to ease.

Jaime Jo felt faint. The nurse's words hit her with no less force than a baseball bat to the side of the head, one particular form of assault Jaime Jo was well acquainted with. Any further pronouncements from the nurse faded from Jaime Jo's consciousness. She felt her arm fall away from the nurse's as the room went dark.

* * * *

Later that very day, Jaime Jo Tremper found herself back out at the quarry in Tommy Harris's car. She didn't remember yanking out her IV and getting dressed. She didn't remember signing out of the hospital against medical advice. She didn't remember the cab ride out to the quarry. And she didn't remember why she'd gone there. Did she expect to find her child sound asleep in the back seat of the Camaro where she'd left her?

Maybe it was the blows to the head. Maybe it was the medication from the hospital. She didn't know. She didn't care. She just sat there, hands gripping the steering wheel, staring straight ahead. The furnishings of the quarry had somehow changed in her eyes. There used to be a story behind each and every abandoned car and broken beer bottle that littered that giant hole in the ground. For the immortal young that frequented the quarry, it was a place to ditch school, a place where young couples could let passion reign, a place to talk of fame and fortune and world conquest.

But no more. Not for Jaime Jo. For her, the quarry no longer served as that place of refuge it had come to represent for every young person doomed to grow up in Pleasant Valley, no longer a place where it was safe to dream, to find first love and imagine a future full of all things great and impossible. Instead, it had reverted to its original form, a gouged out hole in the ground, a grave where dreams lie dead and buried.

It seemed to Jaime Jo as if the passage of time alone had rendered her no longer qualified to be there, as if some invisible door were slammed shut in the face of all those that reached a certain age or life experience. Seemingly without any advance notice, she'd been prematurely evicted from teenage Neverland, exiled to the world of the grown-ups, a cold and dark place void of hope.

Every few hours she'd notice the sun had moved a little further in its path across the sky, signaling the passage of time. What thoughts filled that time, she couldn't say. But she always came back to little Scarlet, in the hands of the preacher... motherless... defenseless.

Jaime Jo didn't think her father planned to harm the child, at least not at first. This was just his way of getting to Jaime Jo, his way of getting her back. But say she went back. Then what? Did she really believe that would fix all that was broken, that things would ever have any semblance of normalcy in that household? No, she didn't believe that for a second. All those bridges were burned to ash long ago. The man had beaten her for years, murdered her only friend in the world. That would have been enough on its own. Yet there was more. There was the other thing, the thing Jaime Jo'd buried so deep in her subconscious that it would never see the light of day, the part she couldn't bring herself to acknowledge, the part she couldn't discuss with anyone, not Billy, not Tommy, not God, not even herself. Could something so completely denied be at the same time so unforgivable?

She used to believe Tommy was the catalyst responsible for setting off that lethal chemical reaction between her father and herself, as if removing Tommy from the equation would render the mixture inert. But she didn't see it that way anymore. She knew it was only a matter of time. Sitting behind the wheel of the Camaro, staring out the windshield, she'd looked into her future, cheated and peaked ahead at the last page of the book. She could see how the story would end with or without Tommy Harris. It was linear and predictable, to the point of cliché. It was only a matter of time until her father killed her.

But that wasn't what mattered anymore. Jaime Jo Tremper hadn't cared if she'd lived or died for some time now. Like in her dreams, she just knew the life after would be a better one. It had to be. But that wasn't the point. She was still trapped in this one, still tethered to this Earth by the child, by her Scarlet. She couldn't leave her, not in his hands. Yet that was the vision she saw each time her trance lifted and she wondered where her mind had wandered. She saw that once she'd left this world, like her own mother did all those years ago, little Scarlet would be next.

And so it went through the night. The shadows grew longer as the sun set over the rim of the quarry, ultimately replaced by starlight. Jaime Jo remained behind the wheel of the Camaro, staring straight ahead, waiting for some kind of sign, praying for guidance. She didn't sleep. At least her eyes were open, her face aglow in the blue light emanating from the AM radio she didn't remember turning on.

There was only one word to be heard on AM radio through the dead of night in rural North Carolina. And that was the word of God.

Talk radio was alive with his presence. One station after another, all religion, all the time, filled the airwaves with the word of the Lord, humming like high-voltage lines.

And the Lord had an answer for everything. Whether through straightforward sermon, or in answer to those desperate for his love who phoned in looking for salvation, there was scripture for every situation. Through the night, as the tinny voice of God hailed forth from the cheap dashboard speaker, Jaime Jo's face seemed to absorb the blue light of the radio until it grew warm and began to reflect that light back at the world in an idiot smile. Like so many who'd found salvation on the radio that night, Jaime Jo Tremper placed her life in his hands and was saved.

It wasn't a conscious thought she had or decision she made. Yet by morning, before the sun even hinted its return to the horizon over the quarry, she'd seen the light. That gentle guiding hand of the Lord had touched her, tenderly, yet powerfully.

Jaime Jo smiled in his eyes as she fired up the Camaro and headed home to take her father's life.

Chapter 28

Deputy Jimmy Harris needed a drink, somethin' fierce. But what else was new? No time for that now. He'd made the rounds of every sad old flop house wannabee in a hundred mile radius trying to sniff out any leads on Pleasant Valley's little crime of passion. He remembered most of those places from when he'd been a recent high school graduate. What else was there to do with a pocketful of paycheck and hormones? But that was a long time ago. That was before he fell in love and got hitched. When a Harris boy falls in love, it's for good. After his wife passed, he fell in love again, only this time it was with the bottle. And by then, he didn't feel the need to go back to those places no more.

But his travels were for naught, not a single lead to be had. He was feeling kind of low about having to meet up with Jo Bob having nothing to show for his efforts. In fact, he was on the verge of stopping in at Chezzy's and blowing off Jo Bob altogether when he got the call.

He would have liked to have taken credit for breaking the case, but it never occurred to him to poke around some two-dimensional porn shop like The Junction. Not much of a market for that kind of stuff when Jimmy was young. So it was to be Jimmy's first visit to The Junction when he pulled into the parking lot just as Jo Bob, responding to his call, pulled in along side him.

"Didn't think this was your kind of thing, Jimmy," teased Jo Bob, slamming the door of his cruiser behind him.

Jimmy looked genuinely offended. "What are you talkin' about? I've never been in this place before. But I get this call out of the blue from a guy named Lou. Says he owns the place. Heard I was workin' on the Sawchuck case and thought he might be of some help."

Jo Bob slapped his buddy on the back. "Well let's go have a word with this Lou guy." Then, wagging his finger at Jimmy, "But I don't want to see you lookin' at any of that smut in there. I don't want your innocent mind corrupted."

Jimmy spat on the weed-infested parking lot in response before they made their way through the front door. His eyes had barely adjusted to the flickering fluorescent lighting before he was distracted by the rows and rows of half-naked women adorning the walls of the place. He never imagined such a place existed. And he wouldn't have known who Lou was even if he'd noticed the pasty faced middle-aged weirdo behind the counter.

"Hey, Lou," shouted Jo Bob. "Long time no see."

"Hey, Jo Bob. Got your new Juggs mag here for you. Guess you were too busy to pick it up like usual last week, what with all that's been going on."

Jimmy eyed Jo Bob suspiciously. Apparently Jo Bob and Lou were no strangers to each other.

"Oh come on, Jimmy," objected Jo Bob. "I never claimed to be no saint. Besides, Charlotte's got me all backed up down there," he added with a nod to the friend below his belt.

Then, turning back to the man behind the counter, "So, Lou, what have you got? Jimmy says you've got a lead for us on the Sawchuck thing."

Lou's eyes nervously darted about the place, confirming it was otherwise empty at this early morning hour.

"Well, you know I don't like meddling into other people's affairs or passing judgment, Jo Bob. You can imagine how that wouldn't be good for business. I can't have people being afraid to show their faces around here."

Jo Bob glanced over at his deputy. "Yeah, I can see how some might be embarrassed to admit they're not perfect in the eyes of the Lord."

"And I wouldn't have said anything still, until I heard about the Sawchuck boy. He was a good kid. He didn't deserve what happened."

"So how did you know Billy?" Jo Bob asked suspiciously, wondering what Lou had to do with Billy Sawchuck.

"Come on, Sheriff. Where else is a faggot to go around these parts to find a little excitement?"

"I wouldn't exactly know, Lou. I'm afraid you're going to have to tell me."

Lou sighed. "Well, Billy been coming around as soon as he was old enough to drive himself out here. He always knew he was queer. He just didn't know what that meant exactly. And where do people go to find information, to gain some knowledge about a thing?"

Jo Bob looked over at Jimmy, giving him a shot at answering the quiz. Jimmy just shrugged his shoulders, going over to get a closer look at some of the magazines.

Lou continued. "The library. They go to the library. Well, this here's a library of sorts. And this is where Billy did his research, to figure out what he was all about. You didn't expect him to hear it from his momma. This here's got nothin' to do with birds and bees."

Jo Bob had to chuckle at the thought of Charlotte teaching her son how to please a man.

"Well, there ain't a whole lot of sissy boys around these parts, but Billy soon found when a hard up young man gets enough liquor in him, well, anything could happen."

Jo Bob's eyes widened. He turned to his buddy Jimmy.

"Hey Jimmy. Is that so? You mean I shouldn't turn my back on you no more over at Chezzy's?"

Jimmy just rolled his eyes and went back to his magazine. "You wish. Besides, you ain't my type."

"What do you mean, I'm not your type? Am too."

"No you ain't," Jimmy replied.

"Well, what's wrong with me? Do I smell?" he kidded, lifting his arm for a sniff.

"Shit yeah, you smell. But that ain't it."

"Well, what then?"

"You're too fat."

"I can start workin' out."

"And you're too old."

"Oh, well there's nothin' I can do about that. You're just playin' hard to get now."

"And stupid." Finally Jimmy put the magazine away. "Could we just get back to business, Josephine?"

Jo Bob blew a kiss to Jimmy and turned back to the counter.

"All right, Lou. Let's cut to the chase. What have you got?"

"Well, Billy was in here a couple of weeks ago. Got lucky with some hard-up hayseed from over in the next county," he said, nodding to the back room.

Jimmy went over out of curiosity and peeked through the beaded curtain to the back room, spotting the video booths. He'd never considered himself a prude by any means, but this was just weird, he thought.

"What did this hayseed look like?" inquired Jo Bob. "Case of buyer's remorse?"

"No, he ain't your man," answered Lou. "They did their business, and the boy hightailed it out of here to go forget what he done. But Billy didn't come out right away. He likes to hang back and pull himself together."

Jo Bob decided there was such a thing as too much information, and didn't know where to look as certain unwanted images filled his head.

Lou continued. "Next thing I know, Billy comes runnin' out white as a sheet, like he been shot from a cannon. He was runnin' scared as if Beelzebub himself were on his heels. Didn't say goodbye or nothin'. He'd have gone right through that glass door if it had been locked. I didn't know what was goin' on. Didn't know whether to reach for a fire extinguisher or the 45 I keep tucked up under the register. Two heartbeats later, this other guy comes runnin' out too, only this guy ain't scared. He's mad. Crazy mad. I seen it in his eyes."

Jo Bob's interest was piqued. Even Jimmy was able to tear himself away from the magazines to come over and listen. "So tell me about this other guy."

"The guy gives me the willies. I mean I seen all kinds, but sometimes you know when a guy's just not right. You can see it in his eyes. Like they was already dead and rotted inside. He don't come around too often, but when he does, he's only interested in my nastiest stuff."

"What kind of stuff is that?" asked Jo Bob, looking around the place.

Lou came out from behind the counter and led the men over to S & M corner, as he referred to it.

"Anything involves beatin' up women. All these mags are dog-eared from this guy. Never buys nothin', though. Eventually heads out back for the videos, gets his rocks off, and slinks on out o' here."

Jo Bob and Jimmy leafed through the S&M magazines, cringing at the scenes depicted inside.

"This is some sick shit, Lou. You tellin' me people get off on this stuff?"

"I don't judge," Lou replied. "You know, glass houses and all. Whatever floats your boat. Long as it's consensual."

Jimmy felt his stomach turn thinking about his Tommy.

"So what can you tell me about this guy?" asked Jo Bob. "What did he look like?"

"He was an older guy, mid forties."

Jo Bob snorted defensively at the suggestion that forty something was old. But Jimmy perked up as he first realized it wasn't Tommy that Lou'd been describing. He threw the magazine back on the shelf in disgust, angry at himself for ever believing Tommy capable of such things. Jimmy gave Jo Bob an I told you so look, making sure he'd heard what Lou said.

Jo Bob was happy to concede they weren't talking about Tommy Harris. "What else? Height? Hair?"

Lou thought about it. "Average height, I guess. But his hair was red. And he had a pointy nose." Lou had to laugh. "Kind of reminded me of a woodpecker."

Jo Bob and Jimmy looked at each other knowingly.

Jo Bob got to the point. "So you think this guy had it in for Billy Sawchuck?

"Oh, he's your guy all right. I poked my nose out the front door and saw his car peel out down the road right after him."

Jo Bob realized they were onto something. "You seen what kind of car he was driving?"

"Better than that," answered Lou. "I wrote down his plate number," he added, rifling through the register to get it for the sheriff. "You know, at first I didn't think too much about it. Figured Billy just hit on the wrong cowboy. But as soon as I heard what happened, you know, him bein' murdered and all, well, I knew this was the guy. Here it is." He handed Jo Bob the scrap of paper he'd jotted the plate number on.

Jo Bob was practically salivating over this break in the Sawchuck case. Then, thinking of both Billy Sawchuck and Jaime Jo Tremper, he asked, "So Lou, you say you don't judge what goes on between people as long as it's consensual."

"That's right."

"But what if it ain't consensual, Lou? What then? What if it ain't?"

Lou thought it must be a trick question. But he gave the obvious answer. "Well, that's what you're for, Sheriff."

Jo Bob smiled. "Good answer, Lou. Good answer."

Walking with purpose toward their cars in the parking lot outside The Junction, Jo Bob muttered, "Now I know what Otis meant when he said God killed Billy Sawchuck. Only an imbecile like Otis Williams could see God in that preacher. But that wasn't God up on that bridge. That was the devil himself, just a wolf in sheep's clothing."

"You know, Jimmy," he continued, "even as kids we all knew there was something off with Warren Tremper. Remember back in high school, when we'd find him stuck head first in a trash bin by a bunch of bullies? Well, you know what I'm thinkin'? I'm thinkin' sometimes the bullies are right. Sometimes, for the sake of the herd, you got to weed out the weak and the sick. We should have left his ass there with the trash."

Jimmy couldn't argue the point. But he wasn't thinking of the Sawchuck boy anymore. "And what about the man's daughter? What about Jaime Jo?" Not quite yet able to digest all they'd discovered about their preacher at The Junction that morning, about his filthy perversions, Jimmy turned to Jo Bob looking for assurance that he wasn't just kidding himself. "You reckon he's the one been beating her all these years? It weren't Tommy after all?"

Concentrating on the Sawchuck murder, Jo Bob had to admit he'd missed the fact that Billy wasn't the preacher's only victim. So when he absorbed the significance of Jimmy's words, the revelation stopped him in his tracks. He abruptly turned to his friend.

"I'm sorry, buddy, sorry I doubted your boy."

Jimmy Harris appreciated the gesture, but he had to admit even he was beginning to believe the stories. "Shoot, Jo Bob, the whole town had him tried and convicted. Can't hold it against you."

Jo Bob turned to face his friend. "That's horseshit, and you know it. Of course you can. Maybe they tried and convicted him. But I carried out his sentence. I sent your kid over to fucking Vietnam for God's sake, a death sentence, but for the grace of God. We been friends our whole lives, and look how I've behaved."

Jimmy Harris saw his friend was sincere. "It's OK, Jo Bob."

"Oh no it ain't," countered Jo Bob. "I'm ashamed of myself, Jimmy. You deserve better than that. That's two I owe you now. And Jo Bob Buckner pays his debts."

Jimmy Harris turned to walk toward his car so his friend couldn't see the tears welling up in his eyes, tears over words from his best friend in the world.

Jo Bob shouted to him as he crammed his gut behind the wheel of the cruiser. "Hey Jimmy, I'll bet my left nut that psycho's got a 38 hidden up his ass."

Chapter 29

Jaime Jo didn't need a plan. She'd placed her life in the Lord's hands and become a soul unburdened. She no longer had to figure life's puzzles out on her own. All she had to do was follow his lead, wherever that might take her. And the first place his divine guidance sent her that morning was to church. Only, it wasn't to pray, not this time. This time, the Lord had a different sort of plan in mind for Jaime Jo Tremper. And she'd be needing that gun.

The sun was still low in its daily arc as she entered the Lord's house. A kaleidoscope of colors greeted her as the morning sun shone through the stained glass window at the east end of the church. She felt the Lord gently guide her to the pulpit and bend her knee so she might retrieve the cold steel tool of destruction hidden there beneath the floorboard.

Yet when she pried the board up and looked into the gun's hiding place, she discovered the Lord had second thoughts and there'd already been a change of plan.

"Looking for this?" she heard him ask from the very same pew at the back of the church where she'd heard his confession and observed him hide the gun days earlier. She knew her father's voice even before she looked up to see him smiling in victory, fondling the 38 she'd sought in his hand.

He was surprised but pleased to see her. "I knew I was in danger and had better be prepared to defend myself," he began, feeling the weight of the gun in his hand. "After our little dance over at the quarry, I knew it was only a matter of time. I knew that idiot sheriff would never catch Tommy Harris. So it was your boyfriend I was expecting to come kill me. But not my own daughter. No, that's the last thing I'd expected." He rose from the pew. "It's the wolf we're warned to fear. One doesn't expect to be blind-sided by the lamb. But isn't this is a pleasant surprise?" He turned and locked the front door to the church.

Jaime Jo didn't know exactly what was running through her father's mind. Never did. His thoughts and compulsions were things foreign to her, things void of logic. But it didn't really matter, did it? There was going to be physical punishment involved. The particular details, the means and method, were only secondary. She looked up at the gun and thought maybe this would be the end of it. Maybe eternal rest was what God had in mind for her when he brought her to church that day. Jaime Jo remained on her knees at the altar in silence, resigned to whatever fate He had in store for her.

"I never would have thought you capable of murder," he began quietly. "Didn't think you had it in you," he continued as he slowly made his way down the aisle, advancing toward her. "But that's why you're here, isn't it? You intended to murder your own father with this gun," he accused, holding the weapon up for her to see. "Apparently I was mistaken. I knew you were a sinner, no different than any other woman. But this? Murder? No, you're different all right. You're the worst I've seen. Even worse than your mother."

His approach down the aisle toward the pulpit seemed to take forever.

"Oh, she was bad, your mother. Like you, she never repented. And she'd taken a lot more punishment than you. A whole lot more. She knew she deserved it. I always did my best to relay God's disappointment in her shortcomings. And there were many. Yet she never turned on me. She knew her place. All those years, she never raised a hand against me."

Jaime Jo didn't know how to process these revelations. It never occurred to her that he used to beat her mother too. She felt a selfish sort of vanity in believing that it was only herself that had suffered.

But now she knew her father'd become so well practiced at what he did only by honing his skills on another before turning his attention to her. She simultaneously felt both guilt and forgiveness for the woman that she'd blamed for abandoning her as a little girl. No wonder she'd taken her own life, something Jaime Jo'd considered many times herself. Who could blame the woman, the woman that had left Jaime Jo to take her place, in more ways than one?

He stood over her by then, still talking of her mother as if he were relaying fond family memories.

"That's right. She was a sinner just like you. But your mother was a fine woman. She accepted her punishment with poise and grace, right to the very end."

His voice grew quiet, as if to impart some special meaning to that part of the story. "I remember that night over at the bridge. She was nothing like your friend Billy. He tried to run like a coward. But you can't run from the Lord. Even after I caught up with him, he still wouldn't concede to fate, that his time was up, and the Lord's will would be done. No, he fought back, surprisingly tough for a homosexual. That's where this came in handy," he smiled, waving the gun in her face.

Jaime Jo'd already heard this particular confession, but there was more this time. The family story wasn't over.

"She should have known better, your mother. She should have known I'd never let her go. When she up and told me she was taking you and leaving me for good, I knew she'd lost her mind. So I tried to beat some sense into her that night out on the bridge. But I think even your mother knew it would be the last time. She knew when she'd crossed the line, when I was all out of forgiveness. And she realized there was only one way off that bridge for her. She struggled a bit at the railing, probably thinking about you, about never seeing you again. But I didn't need a gun with your mother, not like with the Sawchuck boy. I like to think she had too much class for that. But I know that's not really the case. It was much simpler than that. Ella was weak. Your mother practically let me push her off that bridge. Almost as if she wanted me to. Seemed as if she knew. She knew the devil was in her. So she wanted to go. Everyone thought she took her own life when they found her washed up on the rocks below. And I like to think they were right about that. She wanted to do it. But she was too weak, too weak even to take her own life, while I had the strength of the Lord within me. So she needed my help, and there's nothing so gratifying as doing the Lord's work. Nothing ever felt so right as throwing your mother from that bridge."

Jaime Jo felt faint. She hadn't seen it coming, not that particular revelation. Her whole life, Jaime Jo'd blamed her mother for running off to be with God and leaving her behind with the monster now looming above her. But now she knew it wasn't that way. Her mother'd tried to save her, to take her away from him. Her mother hadn't taken her own life after all. It was him, the thing with horns that claimed to be her daddy. He'd killed her.

And now her father's words hit harder than his fists ever had. She was going to pass out. She hadn't taken a single blow yet, but she knew what was coming. She'd wake up in the hospital, if she ever woke up at all.

But her father wasn't done with his sermon yet. "You know why it felt so right? Because of you Jaime Jo," he said softly, reaching down to stroke her cheek. "Because I still had you. And with your mother gone, I could raise you without her interference, properly, to be a righteous woman under the watchful eyes of the Lord. Pure as untouched snow."

He paused, and something went dark behind his eyes. "But then that Tommy Harris showed up. And my Jaime Jo changed. All that was innocent and chaste was sullied and driven from you by that boy. You became just another woman, impure, and touched by the devil himself."

He seemed on the verge of tears. "I tried. I tried to keep him away. I tried to drive the devil from my little girl. But I failed. And soon my Jaime Jo was gone." Then, looking with contempt at the woman cowering at the foot of the altar, "He left you in her place. Satan thought I wouldn't notice. But I did. Any man would know the sinful body of a woman, a vessel full of the devil. That's the whole point, isn't it? To drive us to distraction, to corrupt us with the desire to drink from that vessel, and all to make us do his bidding."

He suddenly stopped talking and stared at her, noticing the fit of her clothes, the smoothness of her skin against the palm of his hand, the scent of her hair. He seemed to lose his train of thought, as though the devil in her were speaking to him, softly, sweetly, stirring something hidden and buried deep within him, something he'd spent his whole life trying to control. Yet it remained, always there, seething just below the skin, every so often breaking free and erupting to the surface with furious abandon.

Warren Tremper felt himself fading away, engulfed in the shadow of the beast. He'd felt that feeling before, Satan taking control. This wasn't the first time. And he knew it was futile to resist. Soon, for a moment in time, he wouldn't be himself anymore, he would vacate the body he was born to. And what acts the devil would commit in his absence, using that very body the preacher left behind, only Satan knew. Satan and God, that is. But it was futile to worry about God now. It was too late for that. Warren Tremper was already gone. He'd return to his body when Satan was through with it.

Jaime Jo watched her father walk over and place the gun on a pew safely out of reach. When he turned and she saw that familiar look in his eyes, she began to cry. She briefly thought to make a run for the door, but knew she'd never make it. In a brief moment of panic, before his fist silenced her with a busted lip, she made one last plea for help. But not to her father. Not even to God. Her soul cried out instinctively for the one being she knew would move heaven and Earth for her. She screamed his name with every last ounce of strength she could muster.

"Tommy!!!"

And that was it. That was all she had left. She didn't call out again. There was no point. She knew what was coming. And she knew she was powerless to stop it. Instead she would just hide, somewhere else, somewhere deep inside herself.

And she did. Jaime Jo went to a place of comfort and safety, a place no one could find her, a place where everything would be OK. She'd even stopped crying as her face went blank and Jaime Jo Tremper vanished amid the shroud of evil that swallowed her.

Warren Tremper wasn't completely gone, though. The voyeur in him never really left at times like these. Like all those times back in high school, hidden in the girl's locker room, or unnoticed by the distracted lovers out at the quarry, or more recently, in the dark back room of The Junction, transfixed by the flickering light of the video booth, Warren had always preferred to watch. And watch he did, as Satan, in preacher's guise, walked toward the sacrificial offering at the foot of the altar, unzipping his trousers and bringing forth his obscenely erect phallus.

And yet, at the last second, something made Satan hesitate, distracting him from his animalistic yearning to copulate, something unforeseen and glorious. As if from heaven itself, a magnificent shower of light burst forth in a rainbow of colors from the stained glass Jesus behind the altar. Flashes of colored light came raining down upon him, and Satan shuddered with the realization that God had come a-callin'.

Chapter 30

Tommy Harris remained always one step ahead of the sheriff and his deputy. He'd left the posse tied up in the mountains and gone to check on his Jaime Jo at the hospital, only to find she'd already checked herself out. He thought maybe she'd gone back out to the quarry, but there, found both her and the Camaro missing. That's when he knew he'd better head for the Tremper place. Whether that's where she'd gone or not, he didn't know. But he did know one thing. If she was in danger, it surely involved her father.

He was on foot, but that gave him time to settle some things in his mind. He was taking Jaime Jo away from there. They were finally leaving. He didn't know where they'd go, but that didn't matter. As long as they went. And if that sick bastard father of hers tried to stop them, Tommy would be more than happy to send him home to whatever greater power he claimed to serve, whether that be resting peacefully in heaven above or burning in hell below. It didn't make any difference to Tommy Harris, so long as the man was rid from this Earth.

He'd been trained to run for miles on end. So it didn't take him long to find the Camaro next door to the house, parked outside the church. He didn't know what he'd find inside. But it didn't matter. A good soldier is always prepared.

First he tried the front door, but found it locked. He'd just made his way around to the back of the church looking for a window to peer through when he heard her scream. It was Jaime Jo. She only screamed his name once, but that was all Tommy Harris ever needed. He instantly hurled himself through the stained glass window, landing in a shower of glass and light.

At first, Tommy wasn't sure who or what was attacking his Jaime Jo. It seemed a wild and fiendish thing, inhuman. But in the seconds it took for the creature to lock eyes with him, Tommy watched it morph into the familiar villain he'd been battling since that day he first walked Jaime Jo home and it confronted him on her front porch. Whatever that other thing was, it had fled like a coward rather than challenge a worthy adversary, instantly abandoning its filthy deed, and leaving only the preacher behind to face Tommy. A wise choice on its part. Tommy Harris was not happy.

That's when Warren Tremper, frustrated by the untimely interruption, suddenly wished he hadn't placed his gun so far away, for Tommy Harris had the preacher locked in the sites of his rifle long before the man had a chance to dive for the nearby pew to retrieve it.

Tommy calmly addressed the preacher, momentarily ignoring the impatient trigger finger itching to finally close the matter once and for all. "You'd better zip that thing back up where it belongs, mister. It may be small, but I can pick off a squirrel's pecker from a hundred yards, and I'm not seein' a whole lot of difference from where I'm standin'."

The preacher did as he was told, as his mind raced for a way out.

Tommy was in control now, and knew what had to be done. The initial plan was one of evacuation and retreat. But the situation on the ground had changed. The scene that greeted Tommy upon his unexpected arrival only served to confirm what he'd known all along. Sometimes retreat just wasn't good enough. Sometimes the cost of letting the enemy survive to fight another day is simply too great, and the call to vanquish becomes paramount. Tommy's new orders were clear.

For a moment, he feared one of his flashbacks might surface, as they tended to do in times of confrontation. But then he realized that didn't matter anymore. Not this time. The mission remained the same. He could just as easily kill a Vietnamese gook as he could Warren Tremper, or Satan for that matter. There was no difference. The kill was all that mattered.

Precisely for that reason, Tommy remained focused where he stood, in the First Baptist Church of Pleasant Valley. He didn't have to trek halfway around the world to Southeast Asia to vanquish this demon. He never took his eyes off the enemy as he spoke to Jaime Jo, who'd returned to the here and now at the first sound of Tommy's voice.

"Go fetch Scarlet and get in the car while I kill your daddy."

His instructions were so cold and matter of fact. There was a time when Jaime Jo would have hesitated, even objected. Something about guilt, and deserving all that befell her. But not this time. She herself had come to church on the very same mission as her Tommy, to kill the beast with horns. But where she had failed, Tommy would not. And that was OK with her. She turned to carry out his orders.

"Where do you think you're going?" from the creature that used to be her father. "You would allow this, condone the plans of a homicidal maniac?"

She tried to ignore him, continuing toward the exit.

Warren Tremper knew his life was in her hands. Any hope he had was headed for the door. "You come back here, young lady!"

The sound of a parent scolding a petulant child would seem woefully inadequate, given the circumstances. And yet, years of abuse would not go unrewarded. She mechanically stopped and turned.

Tommy saw it from the corner of his eye, and would not have the mission placed at risk. "Jaime Jo, do as I say. Go get in the car."

Jaime Jo Tremper had taken orders her whole life, but only from those she feared. She never feared Tommy Harris. She loved him. And she would not endanger the mission. But she would hear out her tormentor this one last time, allow him his final words. Maybe she could hope to glean the tiniest bit of remorse from him before he went to his maker. Maybe he would ask for forgiveness, if not from her, than from the Lord. Maybe it was absolution he sought.

Maybe not.

"That's right. You heard me," her father continued. "You get your ass over here and call off your psycho."

Jaime Jo calmly approached, until she stood alongside Tommy.

"You have something to say to me?"

Her father went from frightened to furious. "Don't you sass me. I said call him off," nodding at the gunman at her side.

"I can't do that," she answered.

Her father's mouth opened, but, at first, no words came out, as if he were having a stroke. Then, finally they came. But they weren't the words of apology she'd sought.

"You would have him do this. That makes you as bad as him. You'll both burn in hell. Unrepentful sinners to the end. First fornication, now murder. Have you no shame?"

He was speaking English. Yet the words no longer made any sense to Jaime Jo. She would respond. She was merely deciding where to begin.

"You would dare call me a murderer? You killed Billy Sawchuck. That boy wouldn't hurt a fly. And you killed him."

Her father sought to justify the taking of Billy's life. "He was a sodomite. He—"

But Jaime Jo wasn't listening. It was her turn to talk and she wasn't finished. She cut him off, her voice rising in force.

"And my momma. You killed my momma. All these years you let me think that she left me, that she *chose* to leave me. But she didn't choose. *You* did. You chose for her. You pushed her off that bridge. And you would call me a murderer?"

The preacher would not be swayed.

"She had the devil in her. Like all women. A fornicator. Like you."

Jaime Jo wouldn't deny it.

"I guess I am. But that was never my choice, was it? Tell me. Who do you blame for that?"

The preacher pointed an accusing finger at her face.

"I blame you, walking around like some brazen siren. I can almost forgive your crazy soldier here. After all, how's a man to fight such constant temptation? Yet he must share the blame for letting down his guard, for letting the devil in, for his part in what he done to you."

Jaime Jo appeared genuinely confused.

"For what he done to me? What has Tommy Harris ever done to me?" She looked at the boy standing at her side. "He's done nothing but love me."

The preacher had her. He'd won the argument, triumphantly delivering the winning blow with a snicker.

"And that little bastard over at the house is proof enough of that. My own granddaughter, Scarlet, is all the evidence we need, a product of the devil's own seed."

For the first time since crashing through the stained glass window, Tommy momentarily took his eyes from the preacher so he and Jaime Jo could share a look of disbelief.

Jaime Jo had to confirm what she now suspected, as unbelievable as it seemed. She turned back to her father.

"What are you saying? Are you saying Tommy had something to do with Scarlet?"

Her father found her question ridiculous.

"Unless you're telling me there were others, that he wasn't the only one you've lain with. Who else? Who else would it be? Who else could her father be?"

Tommy actually began to lower his rifle in bewilderment. He turned to Jaime Jo.

"He's not kidding, Jaime Jo. I think he's for real. He doesn't know."

Jaime Jo wouldn't have it. She didn't believe denial could be so absolute. She threw the accusation back at her father to hear it confirmed.

"You think Tommy is Scarlet's daddy?"

"Of course he is," her father replied, not wanting to believe there were others. It was bad enough being soiled by the Harris boy. But to imagine there were others was more than he could stomach.

Jaime Jo and Tommy looked at each other, almost deflated by what they now knew to be the case, that it was even worse than they'd thought. Her father had done more than fool the whole town into believing Tommy was the one abusing her all this time, that Tommy was the one left her with child when they'd finally shipped him overseas for her own protection. That her father had managed to deceive a whole town was bad enough, but that he'd succeeded in deceiving himself was truly remarkable. Warren Tremper had fooled himself into believing his own lie.

Jaime Jo couldn't believe she actually had to tell him the truth she knew lay hidden within him.

"Daddy, Tommy and I, we... we never..." She still had trouble saying the words in front of her father. She spoke like a little girl accused of stealing from a cookie jar. "Tommy and I never did nothin'."

Her father looked back at her blankly. He didn't understand.

But Jaime Jo wanted to be sure he understood. She would say the words.

"Tommy Harris and I never had no sex."

Warren Tremper's anger flared. She was lying to him. He didn't believe there were others.

"If not him, then who? And don't lie to me. Not in God's church. Who else was there?"

"There weren't any others," she shot back. She was yelling and beginning to cry at the same time. "I was a good girl, Daddy. I would never do nothin' like that and you know it. How could you say that to me? You know better than that. And I want to hear you say so. Say the words." She glanced up at Jesus hanging from the wall. "Say it! Say it so God can hear you! You know who it was!"

Warren Tremper was briefly taken aback by the insinuation that he knew who it was. He'd never seen her with no other boys, other than that Sawchuck kid. But he didn't count. Then he finally saw what she was saying. And it struck him as sadly comical. He broke out in laughter. He had to marvel at the lengths to which Satan would go to hide one's sins.

Shaking his head in disbelief, "So what does that make you, my child? The Blessed Virgin? Is that what you would have me believe?

That that little girl back at the house is a product of immaculate conception? That little Scarlet represents the second coming?"

Jaime Jo put her hand to her mouth! He really didn't know!

Tommy'd had enough. He raised his rifle, prepared to end the nightmare.

But Jaime Jo grabbed the barrel of the gun, moving it aside. She wasn't through yet. She'd stopped crying. She looked the devil in the eye. She was calm. Cold. And angry. She remembered when he'd first started beating her, as if that was the worst thing in the world that could happen. But it turned out she was wrong about that. All wrong. She had no idea what could be worse, what other degrading type of punishment a man was capable of inflicting on a woman, a little girl. But she soon found out.

Because from the beatings, things only went downhill, and soon there were secrets Jaime Jo couldn't tell even her beloved Tommy, things she couldn't say out loud. Yet it turned out she never had to say them. Because soon she was pregnant for all the world to see, and Tommy, the only one that mattered, knew all he needed to know. Jaime Jo never had to actually say the words before. But she would say them now! She would say them to the man who dared stand right in front of her pretending it never happened!

She felt the words rise in her throat, like some bilious vomit that wouldn't be stomached any longer. They would come forth in involuntary spasms, spewing from her mouth and splattering the walls of the church, God's church, with their odious stench.

"It was you, Daddy! It was you who did me, and you damn well know it!"

The walls of the church reverberated with her words, as the truth, bound and gagged all those years, finally broke free at last.

In the ensuing silence, the preacher stood mute, unable to process the words. Because he didn't know. It wasn't possible. Not with his own daughter. It couldn't be. It didn't even merit a denial.

"You've lost your mind, girl. I know it's not your fault. Only the devil himself could put words like that in a child's mouth. But I'll not have it. Not in my church. You'll take those words back, and you'll do it now!"

Jaime Jo'd said the words, the words she'd buried deep within herself all those years. She'd unearthed them and finally brought them out kicking and screaming into the light of day. She'd thought hearing them might free her. And yet, it didn't matter. It brought no satisfaction, no peace of mind. The words would even be denied in front of the only three people in the world who knew them to be true. She felt cheated. She'd tried, but was sorely disappointed in the outcome. It had taken everything she'd had to say those words. And she hadn't said them only to have them denied. She would have her say. But not with words. The time for words was over.

Jaime Jo yanked the rifle from Tommy's hands with such sudden fury that Tommy was shocked by the ease with which he'd been disarmed. He glanced over at her face and knew by the look in her eyes that she intended to put an end to the discussion right then and there. She would snuff out this blight on God's Earth. He would never harm another soul from that day forward. Not ever.

At first Tommy was proud of his Jaime Jo, proud that her will hadn't been broken by that sick motherfucker, proud that she would have her say, even if it was only with a bullet. Tommy would shed no tears for the man.

And yet, something about it just wouldn't sit right with him. Tommy was the killer. He knew all about killing from Vietnam. But Jaime Jo? She didn't know anything about killing. She didn't know the unintended consequences, the remorse, the nightmares, the guilt. No, Jaime Jo had nothing in her whole life to feel guilty about. And Tommy Harris wouldn't allow her to start now.

Besides, they were leaving. They were finally leaving, together. Why let the man win in the end by having them hunted the rest of their lives for murder? As much as Tommy wanted more than anyone to kill Warren Tremper, he knew that taking the high road was the better path.

"Don't!" he shouted. "Jaime Jo, don't do it!"

She wavered at his voice, but did not lower the weapon.

"He ain't worth it, Jaime Jo."

She looked at him from the corner of her eyes, thinking Tommy Harris would be the last one in the world to save her father.

"Don't let him win," he continued. "You're no murderer. That's his to own, not yours. If you do this, they'll come after us. We'll always be looking over our shoulders. Don't do it. Let's just go."

Jaime Jo wasn't ready to concede.

"And let him free? Let him get away with everything he did? To my momma? To Billy? To you?" And then, with tears beginning to fall, "To me?"

Tommy wanted to take her in his arms. He wanted to dry her tears, then kill the thing that had damaged and scarred them both. But he just knew that wasn't the answer. He knew the Camaro waited just outside to carry them away to a new life together, free of guilt, with no remorse.

"He's not getting away with anything, Jaime Jo. He'll never be free. God knows what he done. And somewhere deep down inside, he knows it too. Let's not let him off easy. Death's too good for him. There's worse things than death. Let's leave him in God's hands. God will surely punish him. He'll have to live with himself, with all the things he done, like a cancer, eating at him from the inside, for the rest of his days. It's not our place to enact God's vengeance. Let's leave that between them, between your father and his maker."

Jaime Jo heard Tommy's words. She heard the wisdom in them and was proud of her Tommy. She slowly lowered the rifle, allowing Tommy to take it back from her.

"Let's go," he calmly urged her. "Just let him be."

Without another glance in her father's direction, Jaime Jo turned with a clear conscience and walked, unfettered, toward the door. Tommy backed out behind her, keeping the preacher in sight.

Warren Tremper heard all the speeches. And frankly, they left him bewildered. He wasn't capable of acknowledging the accusation leveled at him, not the part about him and Jaime Jo. That was too sick to even consider. Yet he could see the handwriting on the wall. His beloved Jaime Jo was leaving, taking his granddaughter with her. He would be left all alone, alone with his church and his god, a place he somehow wasn't sure would have him anymore. He couldn't admit it, but Tommy was right. Somewhere deep down inside he knew he carried a tremendous debt, a debt to God, a debt he knew he'd be paying the rest of his life.

As he watched them heading for the door, his mind raced for a way to stop it, a way to fix everything, to make it all right. But when he looked down at the stained glass remains of Jesus at his feet, he knew it was shattered beyond repair.

His eyes were then drawn toward the 38 still lying over on the front pew. It called to him. It said he didn't have to let her go. There was still time to stop her. He looked back toward the exit where Jaime Jo had just left his life forever, and saw Tommy Harris standing in the doorway, calmly staring at him, smiling, daring him to go for it.

Chapter 31

Jo Bob Buckner thought it best he and Jimmy first check on the Tremper girl over at the hospital just to make sure she was safe. So naturally, he could wanted to kick himself when they found she'd already left and gone to fetch her baby back from her daddy. Jo Bob knew he was to blame for whatever the outcome. After all, he was the one who'd placed the child in the man's custody. He and Jimmy rode together in the cruiser toward the Tremper place hoping to avert a calamity.

"You think he'll kill her?" Jimmy asked.

"If she don't kill him," Jo Bob replied.

Jimmy was taken aback by the comment.

"You think little Jaime Jo could kill a man, let alone her own daddy?"

Jo Bob didn't doubt it.

"Come on now, Jimmy. You remember that crazy she-bear with the cub we cornered huntin' that one time? We both emptied all the ammo we had in her but she just kept comin'. Well our Jaime Jo's gone to collect her cub and I think she just might have shifted into momma bear mode."

"And what about Tommy?" Jimmy asked.

Jo Bob couldn't deny that Tommy was the more likely choice.

"I'm afraid that's the real problem. If Jaime Jo's headed over to the preacher's place, you gotta' believe that's where your boy's gonna' turn up. After all, that little girl of hers is his too. And as bad as a momma bear can get, that ain't nothin' compared to a lion protectin' his pride."

Jimmy looked Jo Bob in the eye.

"That man don't stand a chance against my Tommy."

"Well let's just hope we get there before your boy finishes what he started over at the quarry. So far, seems your Tommy ain't really done nothin' wrong. He certainly ain't no murderer. Let's just hope we can stop him from becoming one."

Jo Bob flipped on his siren and stomped on the accelerator.

"Let's just pray we can get there 'fore someone else in this damn town gets killed."

But it wasn't to be. They wouldn't get there in time. Jo Bob and Jimmy hadn't quite reached their destination that morning when Jo Bob got a call over his CB radio from Wendy Stratton, the emergency dispatcher.

"Better get on over to the church, Jo Bob. Old man Kwartler from next-door just called reporting some kind of shooting. The man actually thinks someone's been killed. Can you imagine somethin' as crazy as that? Over at the church, for Pete's sake. You better run over there and check on the man's hearing aid or somethin'. It's just way too early in the morning to be dealin' with this kind of nonsense. I haven't even had my coffee yet."

Jo Bob and Jimmy exchanged a knowing look of defeat.

* * * *

They drove right past the Kwartlers serenely rocking on their front porch and pulled up to the church. The Camaro was gone, leaving behind only a deep pair of parallel ruts as it peeled out of the drive headed for parts unknown. Jo Bob pulled out his gun, just in case, as he and Jimmy entered the church to see what was what.

Jo Bob knew old man Kwartler wasn't the type to make things up. And sure enough, they found what was left of the preacher at the foot of the altar lying in a pool of blood. Squatting beside the body, Jo Bob had to marvel at Tommy's marksmanship. He couldn't have been that close, as the preacher'd been armed himself, still clutching the 38 revolver. Yet Tommy'd managed to nail him right between the eyes.

"Ya gotta' hand it to him. That boy of yours is some crack shot," commented Jo Bob, noting how it was still uncomfortable looking the preacher in the eyes, even in death. Still had that spooky look and all.

Jimmy wasn't so sure Jo Bob's compliment was a good thing. Hearing the law pronounce your child a murderer didn't seem like cause for celebration.

"What makes you so sure it wasn't your she-bear killed the man?"

Jo Bob turned on Jimmy with an annoyed look on his face.

"You can't be serious, Jimmy. You really think that little girl made a shot like this? No, this is the work of a marksman." When Jo Bob realized what he was saying, he wished he could take it back. Then, as if to change the subject, "Least we got Billy Sawchuck's killer. That 38 Preacher's got in his hand is bound to be the murder weapon. At least my Charlotte can have some little peace of mind knowin' her boy's killer's paid for what he done." Jo Bob stood up with a grunt, his knees crackling. "Guess we don't need Doc Henderson to determine cause of death on this one. My guess is that bullet between the eyes did the job, all right."

Jimmy couldn't disagree. "I think that'd be a safe bet, Jo Bob." He couldn't deny the facts. That perverted creep never stood a chance against his Tommy, a trained killer. Yet Jimmy tried to see it in a positive light. The man on the floor was better off dead. After all, that little chat with Lou over at The Junction made it clear as day that Warren Tremper had been beating his own daughter for years. Then he killed that poor Sawchuck kid. And the man called himself a preacher. What kind of man of God was that? Well he was a man of God now. And as far as Jimmy Harris was concerned, God was welcome to his sorry ass. That preacher deserved what he got. Justice had prevailed. Jimmy's boy had done everyone a favor. The boy was a bonafide hero. Shit, the whole damn town ought to get on their knees and thank Tommy Harris.

But Jimmy knew that wasn't how it would be. After all, Tommy wasn't the law. It wasn't even self-defense. Tommy came to the church on a mission. This was a goddamned premeditated execution. There wasn't going to be no tickertape parade down Main Street for no murderin' piece of trash like Tommy Harris.

He looked away from the body to find Jo Bob staring right through him. Jimmy could have kicked himself for even thinking those thoughts, convinced that Jo Bob had read his mind.

Jo Bob broke the awkward silence between them.

"Well, I guess we'd better go next door to the Kwartlers' and get a statement from our witnesses."

* * * *

Jeb Kwartler's rocking chair didn't even break rhythm as he watched the sheriff and his deputy approach his porch. This was going to be fun, he thought. Jeb Kwartler did not suffer fools gladly and he didn't have too much faith in Pleasant Valley's law enforcement team. These two clowns made the keystone cops look like pros, one a washed up high school jock who couldn't keep his dick in his pants, and the other a pathetic rummy couldn't swim his way out of a bottle of bourbon. Those two were gonna need a ouija board if they expected to solve this crime on their own.

"Hey, Jeb," began Jo Bob, leading the way up onto the porch.

"That's Mr. Kwartler to you, Son," answered Jeb, frowning at the shirttail hanging out the back of the sheriff's pants. If the man couldn't wear the uniform properly, maybe his momma shoulda' dressed him.

Jo Bob proceeded, never sure why the old man never took a liking to him.

"Little early in the day for a shootin', ain't it?"

"Oh, I'm sorry. Would you boys prefer to come back when it's a little more convenient for you, Sheriff?" asked Jeb, launching a black squirt of chew over the porch railing. "I can have the butler prepare some finger sandwiches."

Jo Bob tried not to let the man get his goat.

"No, no, uh, Mr. Kwartler. No time like the present, I always say."

"Well good for you, Sheriff. Good for you."

Jo Bob looked about uncomfortably, noticing how the old man always made him feel like he'd been sent to the principal's office.

"Look, Sheriff. I'm a very busy man, as you can see," Jeb prodded, gently rocking his chair. "And at my age, it don't pay to procrastinate. Already overdue for my nap. So you got somethin' to ask me or not?"

Jo Bob thought he'd rather pull porcupine quills out of his ass than deal with this old fart. So he might as well get to the point.

"Why don't you just tell me what happened, Je—, uh, Mr. Kwartler."

"Tell you what happened? What are ya' blind? You did go over to the church, didn't you? I'm sure you seen it. There was a shootin'. That's what happened."

Jo Bob couldn't help rolling his eyes, and briefly thought there might just be a shootin' right there on the Kwartler's front porch if this old man didn't stop fuckin' with him. He looked over to Alice Kwartler for some help, but she just kept her nose in the embroidery she was working on. Back to Jeb.

"Oh, I seen there was a shootin' all right."

Jeb turned to his wife. "Well, I'll be, Alice. Nothin' gets by old Sherlock here."

"Why don't you just tell me what you seen?" suggested Jo Bob, beginning to fear his head might explode. "Was Tommy Harris out here this morning?"

"Hey, that's right. I forgot about that. You still haven't caught up with that boy yet. He sure has given you a run for your money," Jeb jabbed, sending another stream of tobacco juice off the porch, some remnants of which ran down the corner of a crooked smile.

"Well, was he here or not?"

"Oh yeah, your boy was here all right."

"At the time of the shootin'?"

"That's right. Took off with the Tremper girl and her kid right afterward."

Jo Bob observed Jimmy Harris turn his back on the conversation and take a seat on the porch steps. Jo Bob felt bad for his buddy as he watched Jimmy place his head in his hands.

Seeing the poor man suffer, Alice Kwartler was losing patience with whatever game her husband was playing. "Can I get you some tea, Jimmy?"

"No thank you, ma'am," Jimmy answered without turning around, his eyes fixed on the church, the scene of his son's downfall.

"Preacher's dead, ain't he?" inquired Jeb, resuming his own line of questioning.

"Oh, he's dead all right."

"Shot, was he?"

"Right between the eyes."

"So I guess now you'll be wantin' to bring in Jimmy's boy for murder," assumed Jeb.

Alice Kwartler froze, dropping her embroidery in her lap. "Jeb Kwartler, what mischief are you up to?"

"You hush now, Alice," he replied, wishing that woman of his would let him have some fun for once.

Jo Bob looked over at the back of Jimmy's head and knew he'd come to a crossroads. A big one. He remembered how all those years ago he'd come to, in a drunken stupor, to find his best friend Jimmy Harris pulling him out from behind the wheel of that mangled car. When the police showed up and found that poor dead girl in the back seat, they looked to pin her death on a drunken Jo Bob, and rightly so, but a sober Jimmy Harris stepped forward and said he'd been driving, not Jo Bob. Jo Bob good as murdered that girl and would most likely be in prison to this day but for his good friend Jimmy Harris. Jo Bob never had to ask his friend to do it. And Jimmy never thought twice about doing it. Now here sat Jimmy Harris, his son facing the same fate, or worse, as Jo Bob did back then. Only seemed fair to Jo Bob he should do right by his friend.

Jo Bob didn't answer Jeb Kwartler right away, but looked toward the church for divine intervention, for some inspiration on crafting his lie. He pictured the scene of the crime, seeing the preacher sprawled at the altar, a gun in his hand and a bullet in his head. Then it came to him. Jo Bob surprised even himself at how quickly it all took shape in his mind. Seemed lying was something Jo Bob was good at, not nearly as hard as he thought it would be. After all, the old couple on the porch may have heard a gunshot, but they weren't inside the church at the time. They didn't actually see nothin'. And dead men tell no tales.

Jo Bob took one last look at the back of Jimmy's head bowed in despair, took a deep breath, and turned to answer the old man's question. "Now why would I be goin' after Tommy Harris?"

Jeb Kwartler raised one suspicious eyebrow, took a quick glance over at his wife, and turned back to Jo Bob.

"Oh, I don't know, Sheriff, how about for killin' a man? You know, first degree murder? Or ain't that still a crime around these parts no more?"

"Murder? What are you talkin' about? Weren't no murder committed here," answered Jo Bob.

Jeb stopped his rocker. "No murder, huh? Did I hear you right, Sheriff? I suspect that dead man over at the church might see things differently. After all, he didn't just fall on that bullet resting between his eyes."

Alice Kwartler stopped rocking as well now, eyeing her husband suspiciously, beginning to wonder if this game wasn't getting out of hand.

Meanwhile, Jimmy Harris had finally turned to look at Jo Bob, unsure if he heard right.

But Jo Bob was locked in a staring contest with old man Kwartler. Jo Bob was a stubborn man. And once he made up his mind about a thing, no amount of sense would change it.

"I told you, weren't no murder. This here's a simple case of suicide."

Three pairs of eyes went wide at Jo Bob's pronouncement, while Jeb Kwartler, falling over backward in his rocking chair, nearly choked on his Red Man chew.

His wife scrambled over to assist him, but he pushed her helping hands away in annoyance. "What's that you say?"

"You heard me. Suicide."

Jimmy Harris stood up. "But Jo Bob, you said yourself—"

Jo Bob turned on his friend, hands raised. "Now Jimmy, I know you been deputized and all, but this here's serious police business now, and real crime solving ain't no amateur sport. Sometimes it takes a trained eye to put all the pieces together."

Jimmy tried to interrupt him again, but Jo Bob wouldn't have it.

"Jimmy, I been doin' this type of work a lot longer than you, and I ain't stupid. I know a damned suicide when I see one."

Jimmy opened his mouth to object one more time before it finally hit him. He looked Jo Bob in the eyes and finally saw what the man was about. By that time, Jo Bob's private wink was completely unnecessary.

Jeb Kwartler, however, wasn't ready to give up.

"OK, Sherlock, since you got it all figured out, why don't you tell me why the hell Preacher would have taken his own life?"

Jo Bob could tell when he was in the groove. He didn't even hesitate.

"Well, Jimmy and I have indisputable evidence that Preacher's the one killed the Sawchuck boy. Bein' a man of God and all, seems only natural he'd be overwhelmed with guilt."

Jeb Kwartler lived next door to the man a good long time. And you don't live next door to someone all those years without seein' and hearin' a few things. Oh, he knew the preacher had plenty more than the Sawchuck boy to feel guilty about, but he also saw right through what the sheriff was up to and he didn't like it one bit.

"Now you look here, Sheriff. I wasn't born yesterday. What do you think you're tryin' to pull?"

Alice started to interrupt. "Now Jeb, don't get yourself all worked up."

Her husband turned on her, the blood rushing up his neck. "Don't get worked up? The man's just coverin' for his friend's kid and you know it. These good ol' boys are enough to make you sick!"

Alice Kwartler'd had enough. "Now Jeb, you're only gonna' get your pressure up again. Why don't you just let the sheriff here do his job?"

"Do his job?! You know damn well he's makin' it up. He's full of sh—"

"Jebediah T. Kwartler! I won't stand for that kind of profanity! Sheriff, I apologize for my husband. I want to thank you for coming out as quickly as you did, but if you have no further questions for us, I'm going to bid you a good day before my husband has himself a conniption."

It seemed Jo Bob had pulled it off, played them old geezers like a virtuoso. So he thought it best to leave while he was ahead.

"I'll send Doc Henderson out to fetch the body," he shouted, taking Alice Kwartler's advice and dragging a dazed Jimmy Harris down the porch steps after him.

He thought he'd pulled a fast one, all right. Yet like a naughty little boy with a face full of evidence trying to tell his parents it wasn't him stole that box of chocolates, Jo Bob Buckner had no idea that the Kwartlers knew damn well exactly what had transpired over at the church earlier that morning.

* * * *

At least she waited till the police cruiser carrying Frick and Frack had rounded the bend out of site before Alice Kwartler broke out in a full on belly laugh. Wasn't often she had a good one at her husband's expense. In all her days, she couldn't recall ever seeing her husband so flummoxed. And it was a site to behold. Even after her laughter subsided a notch, she still had trouble getting the words out.

"I damn near thought your head was goin' to pop right off, Sweetie" she cackled, wiping tears of laughter from her eyes.

Jeb did not share in her joviality. He knew he looked the fool and simply refused to acknowledge there was anything humorous about the situation. So instead of laughing along with his wife, he started rocking his chair again, a scowl on his face.

Alice began to feel just a tiny bit sorry for him. "Aww, come on now honey. Admit it. You never in a million years thought Jo Bob Buckner would figure it out."

Jeb turned away, unwilling to look her in the eye. "But that's just it. He did nothin' of the kind. That fool hasn't a clue what really happened. He just made up a big old lie to cover for his drunken buddy. Now don't that sound familiar? You remember that young girl killed in the back of Buckner's car when he was just a teenager? The boy was drunk as a skunk. Guilty as hell. Whole town knew it, too. But then that pal Jimmy of his steps forward claiming to be the driver. Probably the last time that one was ever sober, too. Well, here we go again. Only the shoe's on the other foot. This time it's Jimmy the drunk had a bad day. And here his pal the sheriff comes to the rescue, spinning some cockamamie story out o' thin air. Simple case of payback, that's all."

Alice didn't see what there was to be so upset about. "But that preacher surely did kill himself, Jeb, and you darn well know it."

"Oh *I* know it, all right. But **Buckner** don't. He thinks he's lyin'. He wasn't here. He don't know what we know. Didn't even ask. We saw them two come out of that church. They was loadin' little Scarlet into the boy's car when we heard that gun go off back inside. Weren't no one else in there but Warren Tremper. Those two kids ran back in after they heard the shot. The girl came out cryin', but that boy, he was cool as a cucumber. Guess that military trainin' paid off. He kept it together. He knew it didn't look good for them. Everyone would assume *he'd* pulled that trigger. He didn't know we saw the whole thing. He didn't know they had an alibi. You saw the way he herded her and the little girl into his car hopin' to get out of town before the shit hit the fan. You and I saw the whole damn thing. But that fool sheriff didn't know none of that. Far as Jo Bob Buckner's concerned, that whole suicide story was a complete fabrication."

"Well, irregardless, turns out it was the truth anyhows," chimed in Alice.

"You're missin' the point, Alice. It's the principle of the thing."

"Now Jeb, you're just upset Jo Bob Buckner finally got somethin' right for a change."

Old Jeb wouldn't have it. "Shoot. Even a busted clock's gonna' be right twice a day."

"Well maybe, just this once, the end justifies the means," Alice offered.

"Now when did you become such a philosopher?"

"Oh, just let it rest, Jeb. How about some rhubarb pie?"

Jeb's wife of many years had a way of coolin' him down when he was overheatin', and he did have to admit he'd worked up quite an appetite, what with all the excitement and all. Besides, life was too short to be goin' around hungry.

"Don't mind if I do, young lady. I suppose that body'll keep 'till Doc Henderson shows up."

And so, in exchange for a slice of pie, old man Kwartler dropped the subject and got on with his life, what was left of it. No point in dwelling in the past. After all, what was one more lie in a town chock full of 'em?

Epilogue

That old bridge out of town continued rusting a little more every day, sure as the sun insisted on rising each morning over Pleasant Valley. Charlotte's Beauty Salon & Bridal Shoppe remained the center of that particular universe, and as always, not a thing went on about town wasn't overheard by those bridal gowns hanging in the back room. Course without Billy Sawchuck to keep order, it wasn't long before all the sizes and styles fell out of place and a layer of dust began to collect.

Charlotte Sawchuck would eventually allow Jo Bob Buckner back into her bed. She was never the same without her Billy, but taking care of Jo Bob seemed to help fill the void somehow. After all, he'd done just what she'd asked of him. He got the scum what killed her Billy. She even pondered privately whether that whole suicide story was just another one of Jo Bob's lies. She wondered if maybe Jo Bob had taken care of things himself, you know, an eye for an eye. Well if he did, she was all the more proud of her Jo Bob. He was a good man.

As for Jo Bob, things finally seemed to be going his way for a change. At last he was free to go back to fishing instead of hunting psychos. He'd solved two murders... well, one anyway. He kept forgetting the second was really a suicide, wink wink. And he'd finally repaid that debt to his friend Jimmy. Jimmy was long overdue for something good anyhow. Even if Tommy never came home, at least Jimmy could rest knowing his boy wasn't wanted for murder. Besides, he and that Tremper girl would finally have their chance. Tommy'd be in good hands with that one. And speaking of good hands, Jo Bob was back in the saddle himself, getting just about all he could handle over at Charlotte Sawchuck's place.

Wasn't long before Jo Bob met Jimmy over at Chezzy's to celebrate how things had turned out. Jo Bob was pleasantly surprised when Jimmy ordered a cola and informed him he didn't drink no more. But when Jimmy started talkin' about how he'd seen the light and how Pleasant Valley would be needin' a new preacher and all, Jo Bob damn near choked on his beer.

Otis Williams didn't need no preacher. Never did. The Lord himself came daily to visit Otis in his humble cardboard cathedral. Otis Williams claimed he'd seen God out at the bridge with Billy Sawchuck that night, and it was somethin' fearful. But Otis known better'n that. It don't take no revelation to know the Lord when you see him. And that thing on the bridge sho' enough weren't Him. The Lord is all things good, after all, and it was only by His grace that Otis managed to evade that car come barreling across the bridge that morning the preacher was found.

Tommy and Jaime Jo never looked back. That Camaro practically drove itself across that bridge heading out of town, as if it knew there was only one escape from Pleasant Valley. Oh, Jaime Jo'd had her little cry over her daddy's body that morning. It was complicated, after all. But once they hit the interstate, she knew everything was going to be all right. She had Scarlet, who began calling Tommy Harris, Daddy. And she had Tommy. And that's all that mattered. She'd leave the rest in God's hands.

After what her father'd done to her all those years, Jaime Jo might never feel completely comfortable in the arms of any man, least not that way. And Tommy, well, he might never be able to hear so much as a cork pop without reaching for a rifle. But these were just two simple folk never asked for much. They certainly never expected perfect. Jaime Jo Tremper and Tommy Harris were truly happy for the first time in their lives, flying out of town like two lovebirds, broken wings and all.

The town of Pleasant Valley had plenty of fodder for gossip and speculation for years to come over at Charlotte's place. Initially, most of the talk seemed to center around how that Harris boy up and abducted the Tremper girl after her poor daddy killed himself, if that's even really what happened over at the church that day. At least that's how the talk went. After all, what people say and what people know are often two entirely different things.

Word quickly got around about the preacher's peculiar predilections out at The Junction, so it became painfully obvious what had really been going on between him and the girl all those years. And so consensus was the man clearly deserved to die. Enough said.

But what actually happened inside the church that day grew blurry over the years, what with all the different theories floating about. One could define urban legends as big city lies that everyone talks about but no one really believes, while small town secrets, on the other hand, are lies everyone believes but no one ever talks about. In any event, both, by definition, are untrue. Everyone swore they knew the truth about that day, though there were several conflicting accounts in circulation. The sheriff claimed it was suicide, but the whole town knew better than that. Half believed it was really the Harris boy's doing, while the other half believed it was the girl, finally pushed over the edge. But at some point, the truth no longer matters, not even to the ones who make it up.

As to whatever became of Tommy Harris and Jaime Jo Tremper, some say they rode off into the sunset together and lived happily ever after, while others say Jaime Jo froze to death one winter living in Tommy's car after the police put him down for shooting people at random from some water tower. But most folks tend to come down somewhere in between those two extreme viewpoints. Because in *their* reality, shit happens, love prevails— at least for a while— and life goes on. As they saw it, Tommy and Jaime Jo would quietly blend into the woodwork of some other small town down the road, becoming one of them, paying their bills the best they could, joining the PTA, and keeping secrets, lots of dark, yet surprisingly ordinary, secrets.

ALSO BY DAVID ABIS

LOSER:
CONFESSIONS OF A HIGH SCHOOL SHOOTER

High school shootings are unheard of in 1977, but there's always a first time for everything. Audrey Spencer thought the world a safe place, until the summer before middle school when she's forced to move to a sketchy trailer park at the outskirts of a West Virginia coal town. There she befriends Zachary Ledbetter, simultaneously fascinating, dangerous, and anything but normal, that missing link between impetuous young boy and psychopath. Coming of age together, confronting abuse, abduction, and relentless bullying, even the line between love and stalking becomes blurred, until things literally blow up at prom when shots are fired. LOSER is a nail-biting novel of ill-fated teenage romance, born of obsession, rage, and survival, where only the unbreakable bonds of childhood can prevail over unspeakable acts.

CALAMITY IN SWEET SPOT:
A POLITICALLY UNCORRECT WHIRLWIND
REDNECK ROMANCE

All they needed was a natural disaster and they'd all be living on easy street. As mayor of Sweet Spot, Mississippi, a pathetic collection of dilapidated shacks and underachievers situated smack-dab on the very buckle of the tornado belt, Buck Jones believes it's his civic duty on behalf of his little town of antigovernment moonshiners, gun-toting preppers, and born again meth addicts, to score some of that sweet federal aid being thrown around so freely. Well, Buck Jones may be a man of vision, but the last thing he envisions is falling madly in lust with Jennifer Steele, that spitfire journalist from CNN who arrives when Buck's prayers are answered by a crew of naive Yankee reporters assigned to cover tornado victims in the rural South. Fireworks abound between the redneck flimflam man and the bleeding-heart city girl as the scheme to defraud the government threatens to blow up in their faces and the town's very existence is imperiled by a thoroughly peeved Mother Nature who finally sends Sweet Spot's chickens home to roost. In the end, it may be up to small town U.S.A. to save the day, but it's up to Buck to get the girl.

PURE CANE

Coming of age on a sugarcane plantation during the 1986 Philippine revolution, young Lisa Salonga, pampered niece of the wealthy Delgado family, lives only for hacienda socials amid the sweet scent of the cane harvest, that is until her idyllic childhood ends when she falls hard for a mere cane worker from the other side of the tracks who turns her carefree world upside down. Even though her relationship with Johnny appears doomed from the start by a class-conscious society, Lisa remains determined to unravel his mysterious past in America and the unspoken taboo surrounding his family ties to the plantation. Their fledgling romance only grows as Lisa and Johnny play pivotal roles in the church-led people's revolution overthrowing the corrupt Marcos regime, but soon, amid a growing communist insurgency, the lovers are caught in the crossfire and Lisa begins to wonder which side her Johnny is really on. It's only when a deadly typhoon threatens to destroy them all that she discovers just who her Johnny really is and what he represents for the future, both the plantation's and hers.

VILLAGE IDIOTS

Just a naive young medical student from Manhattan's Upper East Side, Benjamin Walker's cloistered world is thoroughly rocked by his very first patient on the psych ward. Angel McGovern, exotic dancer by trade, is a nymphomaniac genius with two and a half PhD's. An overwhelmed Ben is kidnapped by Angel and taken on a wild and crazy road trip to the tropics, accompanied by two other zany escaped inmates from the asylum. Makesh Guptah is a rocket scientist who believes aliens plan to destroy the Earth. Juan Martinez is a slow-witted giant who wouldn't hurt a fly, but is headed for the electric chair if found mentally competent. Will Juan beat the rap? Will Makesh save the planet? Will Angel ever scratch that itch? Will Ben make it home alive? VILLAGE IDIOTS, a sexy farce with heart, is kinky, crazy, and ultimately out of this world.

* * * *

If you enjoyed
THOUGH I WALK THROUGH THE VALLEY,
please like it on Facebook at
Sweet Spot Publishing

Made in the USA
Coppell, TX
31 January 2020

15219013R00144